NOTHING NO ONE

SCARLETT FINN

ISBN: 9781917248341

www.scarlettfinn.com

Also by Scarlett Finn

GO NOVELS
GO WITH IT
GO IT ALONE
GO ALL OUT
GO ALL IN
GO FULL CIRCLE

EXILE
HIDE & SEEK
KISS CHASE

WRECK & RUIN
RUIN ME
RUIN HIM

THE BRANDED SERIES
BRANDED
SCARRED
MARKED

FORBIDDEN PREQUEL DUET
ALL, ONLY,
ONLY YOURS

THE FORBIDDEN NOVELS
FORBIDDEN DESIRE
FORBIDDEN WANT
FORBIDDEN WISH
FORBIDDEN NEED
FORBIDDEN BOND

BOMBSHELLS & BILLIONAIRES (ROXIVERSE)
NOTHING TO HIDE
NOTHING TO LOSE
NOTHING IN BETWEEN: ONE
NOTHING TO DECLARE
NOTHING TO US
NOTHING IN BETWEEN: TWO
NOTHING TO SAY
NOTHING TO GAIN
NOTHING IN BETWEEN: THREE
NOTHING TO YOU
NOTHING TO THIS PREQUEL: ONE WILD NIGHT
NOTHING TO THIS
NOTHING IN BETWEEN: FOUR
NOTHING TO DO
NOTHING TO NO ONE
NOTHING TO FEAR
NOTHING TO DENY
NOTHING TO BEAT
NOTHING TO THE WEDDING
NOTHING TO TELL
NOTHING TO IT
NOTHING TO SEE
NOTHING TO WIN
NOTHING TO OFFER
NOTHING TO PROVE

LOVE AGAINST THE ODDS STANDALONE COLLECTION
SWEET SEAS
HEIR'S AFFAIR
RESCUED
MAESTRO'S MUSE
GETTING TRICKY
THIRTEEN
REMEMBER WHEN...
RELUCTANT SUSPICION
XY FACTOR

KINDRED SERIES
RAVEN
SWALLOW
CUCKOO
SWIFT
FALCON
FINCH

MISTAKE DUET
MISTAKE ME NOT
SLEIGHT MISTAKE

LOST & FOUND
LOST
FOUND

THE EXPLICIT SERIES
EXPLICIT INSTRUCTION
EXPLICIT DETAIL
EXPLICIT MEMORY

TO DIE FOR...
TO DIE FOR TRUTH
TO DIE FOR HONOR
TO DIE FOR VIRTUE
TO DIE FOR DUTY
TO DIE FOR LOVE

RISQUÉ & HARROW INTERTWINED
TAKE A RISK
FIGHTING FATE
RISK IT ALL
FIGHTING BACK
GAME OF RISK

ONE

THE SPEECH WAS GOOD. What of it she'd heard anyway. Bambi Bennett was not a Hollywood darling. Not even close. She wasn't in with the cool kids or on the A-list. There wasn't a list for lackeys only backstage to service those with famous faces.

From their tables front of house, her role was to escort the shiny people, celebrities, backstage. Some were presenting awards, some just doing intros, others gave speeches.

The Lighting Darkness Awards were bestowed on regular civilians generous enough to give back to their communities, whether that was time, money, or fundraising. Having a big heart was the only condition. Being in LA, it just so happened that the event was sponsored by most of the big studios. Charity was great PR and a tax write-off... too cynical?

LA was pretty... sort of. Not like Wishbone, Washington, her tiny hometown. Small town life wasn't so bad... when she was eight. Took her another seventeen years to get out of there, but didn't results matter more than the process?

Spreading her wings, building a new life, started somewhere. For her? Lighting Darkness was it. Well, the Brooker Agency, her employer, sent her wherever she was needed. That night, it happened to be there.

After the celebs did their bit on stage, she and three other chaperones worked in rotation to escort them wherever they were going next. Chaperones weren't allowed on stage. No, only glamorous models in glittering dresses were allowed to stand under the lights.

Working for Brooker paid the bills. Lighting Darkness? The charity was aspirational. She hadn't quite got the knack of the LA way yet. No one cut anyone else a break. Her wary colleagues weren't the most welcoming bunch. Odd maybe in their line of work, but this was LA. LA. LA. The city's name was often taken in vain, to cover a multitude of sins.

Her boss, Renata, came rushing over, earpiece still firmly in place. The woman had been running around ragged all night, snapping at everyone.

"Bambi, when Mr. Lowe comes off stage, he wants to exit."

"Exit?"

So far everyone went one of three places: back to their table, the private green room, or to a reserved hotel room. No more needed to be asked about that. Someone else was setting up the rooms as requested. Not her department. Nope, sirree. That honor was granted to more senior employees. Given the conversations she'd overheard, they were welcome to it.

"The building, Bambi, the building," Renata said. "He has to go out the back. The rear exit… you know, the one we use for discreet departures?"

Wide-eyed, she said nothing, waiting for her boss to catch on to her naïveté. Stood to reason there would be swift, secret departures, but she couldn't learn the process by osmosis. This was the only time she'd ever been in a Grand Hotel.

"Where exactly is that?" Bambi asked. "The rear exit?"

"Basement two, east to the end, third left. Through the storeroom and out."

Repeating the instructions in her head, her mouth moved in time with the words. "Okay, I can—"

"It's a regular red door," her impatient boss said. "Roman knows where it is."

Good, some reprieve. If Roman Lowe knew where it was, she could just sort of be there. Maybe he wouldn't notice leading.

"Okay."

Renata didn't look too impressed. "Don't forget his gift bag," she said, lunging to grab one of the male bags from the side table to thrust it into Bambi's hands. "And smile, for God's sake, Bambi. You won't get far in this town if you don't start working what you've got."

Her boss flipped around and flounced away. Work what exactly? What did she have? As a woman, she knew how to flirt and seduce. She did okay. Men weren't a complete mystery. But in California, "*working what you've got*" was something on a whole new level… that usually involved a surgeon.

Just seconds later, applause rose in the ballroom. Those in the shadows jumped to attention. A sleek, sexy model strutted past the stage curtain, her arm hooked around that of Roman Lowe's.

On a deep breath, Bambi went to join them. "Mr. Lowe, if you'd like to follow me," she said, the same as she had to every other person she'd escorted that evening.

Except this time the model stopped short, forcing Lowe to as well. Adjusting her hold on his arm, the model pulled him down to whisper in his ear before pressing her glossed lips to his cheek.

Oh, uh, awkward much. Intruding on a clearly private moment, she lowered her chin. Privacy was an illusion. There were twenty or thirty other people around, getting on with their jobs. Unfortunately, at that moment, hers was to stand there, waiting, pretending she couldn't see the intimate exchange.

The model eventually relented the kiss and her hold, presumably to go introduce herself to the next assigned shiny person.

Bambi straightened up and widened her smile. "Mr. Lowe?"

Though he didn't focus on her, he did start moving her way. Good. A man on a mission knew where he was going. She whirled around to hurry after him as he strode past her and the corridor with the dressing rooms to go down the few stairs to the elevator lobby. Not a fancy one, or meant to be public-facing, it was an employee elevator, in the blah innards of the hotel. So much went on behind the scenes. Oblivious guests only saw the frosting, not the cake beneath. True in many walks of life.

The elevator came as soon as he pressed the button.

They stepped inside. Being nearest the options, she pressed B2. That meant basement two, right? This was the first time she'd gone down as opposed to up.

As the elevator moved, she felt it. It? What? No idea. A dense, heavy weight in the air swirled with a sense of expectation that didn't anticipate words. Something new. Brand new. A mass in the pit of her stomach, thick and wanting, alive and yearning. Something was going on beneath her skin.

When the elevator came to a lumbering halt, she was none the wiser. The doors took a second to open. When they did, the aura burst, and she almost punched the air.

Okay. One step closer to completing her task. A sign opposite indicated which way was east and which was west.

Confident, like she'd known the whole time, she strode out. About halfway down the long corridor, she had a crisis. Left or right… two turns or three? Maybe it was four. What did Renata say?

Slowing down, she got more in line with Lowe. Walking behind him would be too obvious, she was supposed to be his escort. Oh, God, was this going to be bad? She really didn't want to get reamed out. What would failing mean for her new job?

If he was leaving and knew the way, why did he even need her? Maybe he was the entourage type, some people needed those, no matter how small. It wasn't an affliction confined to celebrities either. If it was protection he wanted, he'd picked wrong. She sure wouldn't be good as a security agent. Especially next to the capable actor. Roman Lowe was an action star in an upcoming spy thriller TV show. According to his pamphlet anyway.

Even through the tux she could tell he was ripped. His muscles were obvious in the breadth of his shoulders. His height, somewhere around six four, didn't diminish his physique, it only made him more imposing.

At the end of the corridor, she was forced to make a choice. Right. He'd correct her if she went the wrong way, wouldn't he? His silence, and that he stayed at her side, spurred her on.

Right and right again.

The lights dimmed and she slowed. Why did that happen? Suddenly, isolation got cold. They were far, far away from the crowds and guests. The corridor was bare, the pale-yellow walls and gray floor were almost sickly in their pallor. They hadn't seen another soul since stepping off the elevator.

"Is there a problem?" Roman asked, reminding her it probably wasn't a good idea to stand there squinting at nothing.

"No," she said. The lights faded up again, and bam, the red door near the end of the corridor ignited her triumph. "Right up here."

The weather outside was awful. Could that cause a power issue? The weatherman forecast thunderstorms. Last minute, Renata panicked some guests may not show, and they'd scrambled to erect a canopy over the red carpet. With the wind the way it was, the thing was probably two states over by now.

She needed to get back upstairs asap. Renata might need her. And, yeah, okay, so it wouldn't be such a bad thing to get away from the labyrinth of corridors in the spooky bowels of the hotel.

On opening the red door, she expected to be outside. They weren't. Hadn't Renata said something about a storeroom? Yes, storeroom and out.

Out.

Roman didn't enter her mind until she heard the red door close. In that same second, the lights went out. They didn't fade. Didn't dim. In an instant, they were consumed in black ink.

She froze.

All she could hear was her own breathing. Nothing else. In. Out. Short. Faster. Calm. This was bad. So bad. She didn't hear Roman's breathing or know he was approaching until he touched her shoulder. At least she assumed it was him.

"Are you okay?"

Startled by the deep, masculine voice at her side, her hand rose on instinct. Not that she noticed until it spread on soft fabric. His tux. Her palm was pressed to his abdomen. Touching a stranger was beyond inappropriate, but all her concentration was on breathing, she couldn't think about being polite.

"Say something."

That voice again. Her lips managed to move, actually making sounds was beyond her throat's capability. His fingers curled, gripping her shoulder tighter. The signals to his muscles seemed connected to her too. Hers did the same, scrunching the fabric still beneath her palm.

A flash of light. Quick and red, it disappeared then came back, bathing the room in a dull scarlet glow.

"Say something," he said again, his free hand directed her jaw up until their eyes met.

"What happened?"

His shoulders dropped, releasing some of their tension. When his hand descended from her shoulder, he interlinked their fingers, removing hers from his jacket.

"You're okay," he said. "Are you okay? Do you suffer from anxiety? Panic attacks? Asthma? Do you need medication?"

Roman Lowe was thorough. What a great start to their association that her behavior should scream "drug me" to reach the bar of normality.

Focusing her thoughts wasn't easy. Especially with that… was that his cologne she could smell?

"Uh, no, I… I'm just freaked… Maybe I do."

"You're doing great."

Adjusting to the new hue, she scanned the room. Maybe ten by fifteen feet. Open door to the right, near a bunch of stacked mattresses. A huge, folded table stood by the wall next to them with some boxes in front.

That was as far as her observation went before Lowe went to the closed door they'd been heading for, the one that should get them outside. He tried the handle, but the door didn't open.

"It's locked?" she asked, watching him stride

back across the room to the door they'd entered by.

That one was unlocked; they'd just come through it. No reason it shouldn't—the door didn't budge when he rattled the handle.

No. No. No! Alarm shot through her.

"Both are locked," he muttered, scanning the room.

The open door, the one in the corner.

"What's in there?" she asked because his angle gave him a better view.

"Bathroom."

Oh. A bathroom. Great. So they would get out of there… how exactly?

A storage room. Would this be her tomb? How often did anyone check it? Boxes. More boxes. Decorations. No sign of another way out. Small vents at the top of the far wall were only four inches tall.

Lowe, rescuer extraordinaire! Yes! She'd never been so elated to see someone holding a cellphone.

"Oh, thank God," she said, rushing a few steps toward him.

"Don't get too excited," he said, raising the phone higher. "No signal down here."

Fuzz! Being two floors beneath ground level came with limitations, apparently.

Her brow creased. "If we're underground, how were you supposed to exit?"

"There's a service ramp to the private parking area on the first basement level." Still going around the room with his phone, he wasn't giving up though did glance her way. "You didn't know that?"

Being his escort, he could be forgiven his surprise. His signal searching kept him occupied, so she chose a little redirect.

"I'm sure, whatever this is…" she said. "It's just a temporary glitch."

He exhaled and dropped his arm, abandoning his search. "The power's out in the whole building."

Surprised, she blinked. "How do you know that?"

He pointed upward. "Listen."

TWO

PIQUING HER EARS, her eyes rolled around as she tried to pick out whatever she was supposed to hear. "I don't hear anything."

"Exactly. Their power management systems are down here. We should hear them or feel the vibration." She felt something, though hadn't pinpointed what the weird gut quivering was yet. She'd put it down to their predicament, except she'd felt it in the elevator too. "If it's the storms, the cellular network could be affected too."

He put his phone back in his pocket.

"Oh," she said.

Being in a restricted space with such a famous, and attractive, man hadn't been on her night's itinerary.

"I'm sorry," he said, looking up at the ceiling. "If this is a hotel or city-wide problem, we could be here for a while." In the face of his honest contrition, her laughter was completely inappropriate. She smiled but was quick to lift her hand to her throat, somehow damming it. "Are you laughing?"

"No," she said, clearing her throat and shaking her head. "No!"

"What's funny?"

"Nothing, I just..." No point denying her amusement. "You're Roman Lowe..." That wasn't much of an explanation. "Action star, right? I sort of expect you to pull out some gadget or start scaling the walls... maybe shoot your way out." When he didn't smile, she panicked. Had she offended him? This was real life, not a TV show. It wasn't the time for dumb jokes either. "I'm sorry, Mr. Lowe, that wasn't funny, I... I didn't mean to say that..."

The dazzling power of his unexpected smile immobilized her. The gleam was impressive given the lack of light and the ten feet between them.

"Don't think I'm insured to perform stunts at charity events."

Valid point. A guy like him was valuable... What fate would befall her if something happened to him?

"Well, I guess if I was going to get trapped with anyone, a superstar is a great choice. Someone will come looking for you, won't they?"

The smile faded as he slid his hands in his pockets.

"Won't someone come looking for you?" he asked. "Should I know your face?"

"Oh no, I'm not famous like you."

Keeping up with the latest happenings must be difficult for actors and crews given they worked such long hours.

"I work for Brooker, part of the event management group."

"That organized tonight?"

She nodded. "I haven't worked for them for long... and if the power in the building is down, they'll have other things to worry about."

"Then I guess we better get comfortable," he said, nodding at her side. "What's in the bag?"

The gift bag in her hand, right, yes.

Jumping to it, she hurried to him, arm extended. "It's for you."

"Me, huh?" From the bag, he produced a bottle of Scotch. "Thank God for small mercies."

After tossing the box aside, he opened the bottle and held it toward her, being polite.

"You want me to…? Oh no, I'm working… and my employer paid for that."

Someone did, and it wasn't her. Not getting sloshed while she was on the clock was one of those unwritten rules that—actually, it probably was written somewhere on the paperwork she'd signed when joining the agency. Shame, a little liquid courage would go a long way.

"You can't make me drink alone," he said, urging it toward her. "What's your name?"

"Bambi," she said, curving her hand around the bottle. Before raising it to her lips, she pointed it at him, making eye contact for the first time. "And it's been my name for the last twenty-five years, so believe me, I've heard all the jokes."

Another smile. The lip of the bottle met her mouth, but she couldn't drink with their eyes locked. Fixating on someone most people only ever saw on screen was odd. The power had a tractoring force, like it would if he was in some major blockbuster. Only this time, he was staring back.

Gravity begged her closer, while weak restraint told her it wasn't a great idea. What would she do if she went over there? Embarrass herself, no doubt.

Whatever was churning in her gut didn't feel like intimidation. She wasn't starstruck. Whatever was in him, looking back at her, seemed curious. What an ego, why would he care about someone like her?

When it was impossible to delay anymore, she tipped the bottle and winced at the taste of the liquor. Swallowing was a fleeting victory as she coughed at its potency.

Lowe breathed out a laugh. "Not much of a drinker?" he asked, taking his turn.

"Not something this rich." She wiped her mouth. "I've never had Scotch before. I'm more of a sweet wine girl. I don't drink hard liquor…" Shaking her head, she laughed and wrapped her arms around herself to squeeze her own shoulders. "One mouthful and I'm rambling already."

Lowe wasn't nervous about drinking. In the time she'd been talking, he'd had another three mouthfuls.

"You're not freaking anymore, Little Fawn." He gave the bottle to her again. "It's good for something."

"Liquor will do that, I guess."

Leaving her there pondering whether to drink more, Lowe went to the stacked mattresses and picked one up. Just like that, he plucked it up and carried it across the room. Stepping aside, he let it fall flat on the floor and used his foot to push it flush to the wall.

"Do you want to sit?" he asked, taking off his jacket to lay it at the head of the bed.

"On a bed?"

He loosened his tie and undid a couple of shirt buttons. "I don't see any chairs."

No, she didn't see any either and he was Roman Lowe, it wasn't like she had to worry about her virtue. Crawling onto the bed, she kicked off her shoes, conditioned not to put them on a mattress.

"If anyone should be sitting on the jacket, it should be you," she said, picking it up to offer it back as he sat on the opposite edge.

"Why?"

"You're the superstar, Hollywood guy."

He took the jacket and leaned closer. "What would the paps say if I was anything less than a gentleman?"

That put a smile on her face. Once he'd laid it out flat again, she scooched higher to sit, resting against the concrete behind them. He didn't retreat and stayed at her side, shoulder against the wall.

"This must be a nightmare for you," she said, sipping from the bottle. "Sitting doing nothing, nothing going on."

"Nothing going on, sure." He accepted the bottle when she handed it over. "But I'm used to it. There's a lot of hurry up and wait on set."

Making TV shows probably wasn't as glamorous as people thought. Since she had one of the world's number ones with her, she could find out.

"I bet you have plenty of people to keep you entertained during the wait part."

"People?" he asked.

"Women."

LA, Hollywood, the whole entertainment industry seemed rife with flirtation and innuendo. At work, sex came up fifty times a day. Everyone wanted to know who was with who, who had a chance with who, and who they had to do to get what they wanted. The top was within the reach of everyone and no one.

His nasal inhale took a long time to come back out. "Not a lot of time for women on set."

Honestly? She didn't know much about Roman Lowe and didn't own a television. Movies were fun. She loved the experience of buying popcorn and sitting in a comfy chair waiting for the lights to go down.

But she couldn't tell Roman she'd only seen clips of his work, shown by Renata in meetings about the event, along with a bunch of others. Insulting the man would be insensitive. They'd be stuck there for God knew how long, she didn't want it to get awkward.

"I'd love to know what it's like," she said, twisting to face him.

Lowe lingered over sampling more liquor. The sullen sort of displeasure in his eyes was new. So far, he'd only seemed to look at her in a positive light. Maybe asking about his work gave him the wrong idea about her interests.

The bottle left his lips. "Every set is different."

"I'm not an actress," she said, tugging her dress down her thighs. "I have no interest in being on the screen, big or small."

"Then LA was a strange choice."

"It wasn't really a choice," she said. "I had to leave home... my hometown, so I got on the internet and applied for jobs all over."

"And you got a hit in LA?"

She nodded. "I traveled to a few interviews in different states, but the LA job... I couldn't really say no... and the pay was good, so..."

He smiled. "It's good until you realize it's expensive to live around here."

She laughed. "Tell me about it. You hear about the big city, but nothing prepares you for it."

"How long you been here?"

"Almost three months."

"Where are you from, Fawn?" he asked. "Originally."

All the questions, she didn't expect such a talented superstar to be interested in a nobody like her.

"Wishbone, Washington," she said, noting his quirk of amusement. "Yep, that's me, Bambi from Wishbone."

He offered the bottle to her, but she shook her head.

"Come on, you won't get in trouble, I promise. Got to keep the talent happy, right?" Maybe, but there were limits to what she'd do. Probably not a policy many in town subscribed to. Lowe put the liquor bottle in her hand. "So, Bambi from Wishbone, are you running from something or looking for something?"

Her eyes stayed on his as she drank. She gave him back the bottle and breathed through the burn.

"Running," she admitted. Though Lowe's lips were occupied by the bottle, his brows rose. Guess he hadn't expected her to be so open. "I was with a guy for a few years, I broke up with him and… he didn't want to let go."

Twisting away, he put the bottle on the floor behind him. "I can understand why."

When he tried to touch her face, she shook her head. "You can't understand Kevin, least I hope you can't."

Her feeble joke didn't amuse him.

Instead, he frowned. "Did he hurt you?"

"He tried to," she said. "But I've taken control. I'm proud of the life I'm building… well I was. God knows what will happen after tonight."

"Tonight wasn't your fault, and you said it yourself, Brooker have other things to worry about. You won't lose your job, I'll make sure of it."

Grinning, she stroked his arm. "I bet you know all sorts of people."

And could pull all kinds of strings.

"You like fame?" he asked. Noting her confusion, his head tilted. "Yeah, you said you don't want to be in the movies, doesn't mean you're not turned on by notoriety."

Something in the way his attention drifted caught her interest. There was something there, in his countenance and expression, something concerning.

He'd touched her when the lights first went out. So touching was allowed, right? She shifted onto her knees to slide a hand onto his jaw, bringing his gaze back for her examination.

Looking into him, a rush of worry consumed her. What was that? What was in him that dimmed his light? Overwhelmed by distress and pity, she crawled closer to stroke his other cheek, still holding his jaw.

"What is it?" she murmured, wishing she could see beyond his façade. "What's wrong?"

THREE

HIS LIPS PARTED but no words passed them for a few moments.

"I'm tired," he said, maybe not ready to trust her too much. "I didn't want to be here tonight. I have work to do, and I don't like to be distracted by bullshit like this... Not the charity, that's worthy. The cause is the only reason I came. It's important to people I care about. But the drinking, the shoulder rubbing, gladhanding, the name dropping, I can't stand it."

Her interaction with him thus far proved the image was far from the reality. Okay, so she knew little to bupkis about the entertainment industry. She'd only got to LA a couple of weeks before starting her job with Brooker and wasn't exactly boning up on the intricacies of Hollywood politics. And no one could judge, how could she have known something like this would happen?

One thing was clear. What little she knew about Roman Lowe was completely wrong. A better way to put it? Brooker's information packets were completely wrong. According to those, he'd been a teen sensation, as famous for his partying and womanizing as he was for the movies he starred in. At some point, there was a fall from grace, and the studios stopped casting him.

More recent updates suggested Roman Lowe had gotten his act together and secured a TV role in *Undercover…* something.

Could people ever change? Depended on the issue. If the partying trashed his career, maybe he'd matured beyond all that. Hopefully anyway. She had a low tolerance for shallow, immature people, didn't everyone?

Lowe was proving himself neither and seemed sharp, even in spite of the alcohol.

Sitting there, gazing into him, her whole being sank into a hypnotic state. Men didn't intoxicate her, hadn't before this night. Lowe's brown eyes drew her in, brought her nearer, tempted her curiosity.

The warmth of his fingers slid upward on her cheek, over her ear, through her hair, around to the back of her head and guided her forward, joining their mouths. Potent like the liquor, the slick need of his tongue begged her response; she was helpless to refuse.

In the last three years, only Kevin had kissed her. With him, it had never been like this. Kevin controlled her with physical affection, used attentiveness as a tool to manipulate her. Accepting Lowe's kiss severed the last thread connecting her to that past. She didn't belong to Kevin anymore, Lowe washed away that claim to replace it with another: his own.

Gratitude rushed through her veins, boiling the fuel of arousal. She could unzip her dress, slide her hands over the globes of his impressive shoulders into his hair—

Gasping away, she touched her lips. Whoa, she'd been so ready to give herself to this man she'd only just met.

"I'm sorry," he said. "Shit, I shouldn't have—"

"It's okay." Bambi grabbed his thigh before he could withdraw from their shared seat. "I... thank you."

He frowned. "Thank me?"

"I came to LA to get away from what I was... And to show my ex he didn't have the power to control me anymore. You just... he was the last man I kissed, the only man for a long time." She smiled. "He doesn't have any part of me now."

Curling his fingers, they drifted across her cheek. "Do you want more liquor?"

She laughed. "Definitely."

As he retrieved the bottle, she absorbed her salacious reaction to the guy. Buying herself some time to regroup, she enjoyed another drink then offered the bottle back.

"Do you have family, Fawn?"

"A whole bunch," she said, fingering the heavy fabric of the jacket beneath her. "I have siblings. There are cousins all over. A couple of aunts and uncles in Wishbone. It's not a huge place."

He toyed with the hem of her dress that had somehow ended up on his thigh. Was he as interested in what was beneath her clothes as she was in what was under his tux?

Geez, what was wrong with her? Damn, they hadn't drunk that much, yet she was all in already. Time to dial it back, except... she didn't want to. Insane though it was, nothing ever felt so right.

Being wanton wasn't her usual style, though alcohol did up her flirtatious confidence and lower inhibitions. Not like she was alone in that. Who hadn't warped boundaries with liquor in their veins?

That couldn't be it, not the only thing at work. In the past, before Lowe, she'd never felt such a strong need to be near another person. It must be the x-factor. That intangible quality stars needed to become famous and successful. If she was in the position of casting director, he could have the cow, the farm, and any other damn thing he wanted. Natural charisma would get him any part without an audition.

"How did they feel about you moving here?"

Right, home, they were talking about her home. "Most people from Wishbone stay in Wishbone… in my family anyway. They had their reservations."

"I can understand that," he said, making contact with her skin beneath the edge of her skirt. "It was a big move… did it feel good?"

His touch felt good. Did it suddenly get hotter? "Jury's still out."

His heat seemed to match hers. The sly knowing in his gaze was filled with just the right amount of confidence.

"I'm glad you took the leap… Otherwise, God knows who I'd be stuck in here with."

Being locked in was a new experience. If someone asked how it would be, she'd assume traumatizing. So far, it was the exact opposite.

She reached across him for the bottle. Just as her fingers curled around the smooth glass, his did the same around her chin until she was staring into him. A shiver went through her when the strength of his finger compelled her chin higher. She wanted him to kiss her again… now.

"Are you cold, Fawn?" When he leaned in to ease away from the cool wall, his mouth came closer. She stopped breathing, fearing the taste of his breath would thrust her into orgasm there on the spot. "You can put the jacket on if you'd prefer."

More clothes? No.

Opening her hands on his chest, she took the

liberty of insinuating herself closer. "You're a real gentleman."

Something she hadn't encountered for a while.

His short laugh was almost a scoff. "Are you flirting with me?"

"You've already kissed me." The adrenaline of want paired with the infusion of alcohol inspiring her confidence. "We're past flirting, beau."

When he ran his hands up her sides and down over her breasts, she pushed into the caress. If she was allowed to stroke his chest, he should be allowed to touch hers. Fair was fair; didn't hurt his attention melted her insides.

Taking the hint, he put her out of her misery and kissed her without an ounce of hesitation. He opened his mouth, scooped a hand through her hair, and hauled her tight to him like she'd belonged to him forever.

The need was beyond physical. Just like in the elevator, that sensation, whatever it was, beckoned. Begged her to settle herself in him, to give in to him. Intuition betrayed surrender.

Whipping off his loose tie, she fought to feel him as his hands explored her. Natural instinct didn't dawdle, he snatched her over to straddle his lap. Her fingers worked on unbuttoning his shirt as his, under her skirt, squeezed her ass, pulling her flush against the bulge in his slacks. She rocked herself against his erection until a desperate rush of blood sped through her heart, intensifying the buzz of alcohol coursing through her.

Suddenly, he gripped her arms, separating their mouths. "Wait, baby. Shit, hold on."

Wait? No. No waiting. She wanted him. Wanted to keep going, to explore some more, to feel as invincible as he stimulated her to be. Her body was drawn to his and although he still had hold of her arms, she swayed in, taking another short kiss before their foreheads met.

Panting into the narrow ether that existed between their mouths, she slowly returned to reality. They were strangers. Complete opposites too. They couldn't have anything in common. Just because they were attracted to each other… or maybe they weren't really attracted to each other at all. Maybe they were only responding to the confined, stressful situation.

"We shouldn't be sitting on beds together," she whispered.

"Not until after at least three or four dates."

Her lips curved. They could have freaked out. Well, she could've freaked out, he was probably much better at dealing with romance stuff. More experienced anyway.

Rather than panic and run, she stuck close, relaxed, and accepted his teasing comfort.

"We did have a drink together, that's got to count as one," she said, loosening to sit back. His hands slid from her upper arms to her wrists. "Though liquor's probably where the problem started."

"We should've done dinner first." He threaded their fingers together. "Don't think there's anything around here to eat."

"There are gummy bears and marshmallows in your gift bag," she said, to which he reacted with amusement. "Kids from the community center made the suggestion."

"I guess that's a start."

Climbing off him, she went to grab the bag from by the door and brought it back. Kneeling on the edge of the bed, she didn't venture far and made a point of pushing it across to him without getting close.

"Okay," he said on a laugh, obviously getting the point of her playful, exaggerated distance. He dug out the candy packets and held up one then the other. "Which do we start with? Shame we don't have a flame to toast the marshmallows."

"Nobody carries a lighter anymore. Start with the gummy bears. They're more nutritious, right?"

"Nutritious?" he asked, putting the marshmallows back to open the gummy bears.

"They're fruit flavor."

He tipped the bears into his palm and held it toward her, side-nodding. "I promise no more kissing. Come over here. Ladies' choice."

Scooching a little closer, still on her knees, she selected a couple.

"Are you allowed to eat these?" she asked, collecting the red ones to set them on the corner of his jacket.

"Why wouldn't I be allowed to eat them?"

"You're buff, beau. You must have a strict diet and exercise regime." She held up a green one. "What's your favorite color?"

"Blue."

Bambi laughed. "I don't have any blue ones. Do they come in blue? I have red…" She set another red one on his jacket. "Orange…" When she offered it to his lips, he accepted it. Next she picked up a white one and set it aside, away from the red ones. "I don't like the white ones… Yellow." Bambi showed him one of those and another in the other hand. "And green…" With one between each thumb and forefinger she raised them up and down. "Which do you prefer?"

"What's wrong with the red ones?"

Pleased, she pushed her shoulders back. "They're my favorite, we eat those last."

"You eat your favorite last?"

She nodded, wondering why his lips thinned. "Why is that funny?"

"It isn't." The words came out in a rush as he grabbed the side of her head. "It's adorable."

"Oh," she said, popping another between his lips. "I'm not only adorable."

"No?" He nodded when she held up the white one. "I'll eat whatever you don't like."

Bambi fed him the white one and accepted the yellow one from him. "You think because I'm a small-town girl that I'm naive and innocent. Is that what you like? Is that why you kissed me?"

"I kissed you because it's been such a long goddamn time since I looked at a woman and saw something…"

"What something?" she asked, taking the rest of the candy from his hand to dump it on the jacket in another pile.

FOUR

"PEOPLE MAKE ASSUMPTIONS," he said. "You didn't look like you were making assumptions."

"Assumptions like the woman upstairs?"

"What woman?"

Lying down, she tucked an arm under her head and adjusted each of the gummy bear piles so she could rest on his jacket.

"The woman, the model, who brought you off stage. What were you whispering about?" He didn't respond. "Sex… you were making arrangements to sleep with her." When he didn't say anything, she tipped her head to peek at him. "I told you I'm not just adorable."

"You're a sexpot too?"

"In my head sometimes anyway," she said, stretching her legs to point her toes. "I know what a woman in heat looks like… She wanted you."

"Did you see me talk to her?"

No, now that he mentioned it…. "I looked away, I didn't want to intrude."

"Well, you didn't. I don't have any interest in

women like that."

Oh, now, that was something. "What's a woman like that? Are you assuming she's loose because she propositioned you? If a man asked a woman for sex, you'd think he was amazing."

"Want to have sex with me?"

The question was so abrupt that she stopped organizing her bears to blink up at him. "Right now?"

He laughed. "Babe, I don't judge anyone for being direct. Games piss me off. I meant I'm not interested in what looks good. I won't lie, yeah, she invited me to her bed."

That was just confusing. "And because she's pretty, you don't want to be intimate with her?"

"Looks aren't nothing. How could she know she wanted to sleep with me when we hadn't exchanged two words?"

Rolling onto her back, she tossed a bear into her mouth, chewing as she talked. "I thought there might be something between us in the elevator." She shrugged. "You have an energy about you… I'd be upset if you judged me for experiencing it, please don't judge her…" She pulled the pins from her hair one at a time. "You must be used to it. It can't be new."

Once all the pins were out, she straightened her arm to lay them on the bed. Something warm touched her knee. It ascended in a tingle that put a smile on her face. His fingertips. Getting higher. Higher. She clamped her thighs together, stopping his tickling in its tracks.

Tucking her chin down, she crooked a brow in question. "What happened to three or four dates?"

"We had a drink, that's one. We're eating, so that's our second."

She sat up without freeing his hand, though he didn't seem to mind being so close when she rose to the optimum position to be checked out.

"You have access to some of the most beautiful women in the world, don't you? Women who'll *come* for you on call." His lips stayed shut. "Women who'd do anything to please you… I'm not one of those women, Mr. Lowe."

She flopped onto her back without loosening her legs.

"You don't prefer direct?"

"There's only one man I'd be on sexual call for: one committed to me. A man committed to our relationship."

"Fidelity's a prerequisite?"

When she relaxed her legs, he dropped an elbow to the mattress, holding his head on his palm, only the gummy bears between them.

"You think that's how to take the small town out of the girl?" she asked. "Promiscuity?"

He picked out the rest of the red ones to add them to her pile, eating the white ones as he went along. "You've got to do what makes you happy."

"What if I don't know what that is?" she asked. "Is that too deep for a third date?"

A smile quirked his lips and he rolled away to retrieve something. When he flipped back to face her, he showed her the marshmallows. "Third is the dessert date."

"You have a routine? A tried and tested route to seduction?" she asked. "I bet you've done this a thousand times."

"Found myself locked in an isolated corner of a hotel with a beautiful woman? This is my first time."

"It's drama though, isn't it? I bet your whole life is like a movie… Wild parties, jetting all over the world. Beautiful women on yachts in the Mediterranean, the Bahamas, the South Pacific… You must have lived some life."

"Don't count me out yet, Fawn. I plan to keep going another few years."

"On your show," she said. "Is that how you plan your future? Contract to contract? How many seasons are you tied in for?"

Damn, if only she could remember the show's full name.

"Leads of *Undercover Ops*? Four."

Phew, he'd clued her in without need for the question. "You have another four years… Do you love it?"

"Working on the show?" He shrugged. "It's work."

"I would think you'd have to love it."

"Do you love what you do?"

"Not yet," she said, shifting to get more comfortable. "I've only been doing it a few weeks. I haven't signed a four-year contract either. If I don't grow to love it, I can always move on. It's not like what you do. You have a whole cast and crew depending on you… and legions of fans you can't disappoint."

"What I do has its moments."

"You've been doing it a long time."

He opened the marshmallows and plucked one out for her. "You ever had a one-night stand?"

She laughed. "What is this? Deflection Derby? Yes, I've had a one-night stand. No, I don't plan to have one tonight."

"Just trying to figure you out."

"That's why people date, isn't it? To figure each other out. But it goes both ways."

He popped the mallow between her lips and scrutinized her as she lingered over chewing.

"I'm tired of talking about me," he said, grazing his thumb over her lower lip. "I don't want to talk about me. Tonight's about you, Fawn. Have you got kids?"

"No. Do you?"

Knowing so little about Lowe worked in her favor. She'd learn about him the old-fashioned way.

"Not yet."

That answer led to a natural next question. "Do you want them?"

Laying a forearm on the mattress, he descended toward her. "One day."

Her smile grew. "This is a little intense for a third date… shouldn't dessert come after a movie or something."

"You wanna break up the conversation," he asked, brushing a fingertip across her brow. His digits seemed drawn to her. "Or want something to make out to?"

"I thought you said no more kissing." The smirk that lit his eye came closer; kissing was exactly what was on his mind. Just before he got to the end zone, she drew back. "You're squashing our bears."

He retreated, giving her room to gather the pile of multicolored gummy bears into her palm.

"Care for the bears, huh?"

"I care your jacket's worth more than I make in a year."

She wriggled closer, pushing him onto his back with a forearm, resting it on him, holding the handful of bears above his mouth.

"I care that you care," he said, his arm creeping around her shoulders. "There aren't many left."

"Only these and the red ones."

Taking hold of her wrist, he guided it down and opened his mouth to consume all the bears in one shot. Oh, wow… His lips lingered on her palm, parting hers in anticipation of… something. Mmm. Just watching him eat churned her hormones, quickened her heart.

"I've never been jealous of gummy bears

before.”

His head bobbed as he swallowed them down. “Anything else you want to put in my mouth…”

Sitting up before she was tempted to do just that, the red bears were a better, safer, point of focus.

“Did you always want to be an actor?”

“No,” he said, linking his fingers behind his head.

“How did you get into it? You started young, didn’t you?”

“I bet I’ve got something downloaded on my phone,” he said, shifting to fold the jacket over to retrieve the device from his pocket.

“Something?”

“A movie. You wanted to watch a movie.”

“Don’t you like to watch movies?”

“I’m trying to see what I’ve got,” he said, scrolling, swiping. “Something date worthy.”

“No chick flicks,” she said, reaching over him. “Can I have some more liquor, please?”

He got the bottle and handed it over while still looking on his phone. “Only if you promise not to take advantage of me.”

She left the mattress to wander across the room. “I’m not that easy, Mr. Lowe.”

He glanced from the screen. “Where are you going, Fawn?”

“I want to know what’s in the boxes,” she said, tiptoeing toward them. “There could be a steak dinner in there for all we know.”

Doubtful, but she was still curious. She swigged from the bottle and slid open the flap of the one on top.

“What’s in them?” he asked when she peered inside without enlightening him.

Pulling one out, she showed him. “Wine glasses.”

“That’s an anticlimax.”

“Glasses could mean wine.”

"Whisky and wine? You said no more kissing, right?" he asked with a smile.

She maintained her search. Each one held a surprise. "I thought you were looking for a movie." Opening another box, she grabbed out the package on top. "Blankets!" Snagging a couple, she removed the plastic and opened them over him on the bed. "Will they get mad at us for opening them?"

"Not if you come lie down with me."

Scurrying underneath, she lay on her side with him behind her. "Cozy." Thick, luscious, these were good quality fabrics. "We could get up to anything under here."

"You said it, baby. No take backs now." He switched his focus to his phone. "Unfortunately, no horror."

"Why would I want to watch horror while locked in a scary red room?"

"Some people are into that."

"How about something with a little action?"

"And maybe we'll get a little of that ourselves?" he asked, selecting something and leaning over her to prop the phone up in front of her. He kissed the side of her neck and gathered her closer. "You drive, baby."

With him, she'd ventured into brazen. By her standards anyway. If he gave her the keys, she might just be tempted to use them.

FIVE

MOST OF THE MOVIE was a blur. Basically all of it. Could she even remember the title? Who cared? Oh, God, who cared?

On swaying away, he'd given her space to lie on her back. From there, hands and mouths went with instinct and the movie was forgotten. Something about being concealed under the blankets, even with him on top of her, carried a tease and a certainty.

Exploring the connection, learning his body, she didn't object when he unzipped her dress, or when his mouth traced to her breasts. Though his own arousal was obvious in its insistence, he diverted her persistence every time her hands got too close.

"Let me touch you," she panted in the humidity clouding their cavern beneath the blankets. "Please, beau." In response, his fingers crossed the threshold of her panties. "Mm."

Didn't matter what he did, those thick, sure fingers aroused her just with their proximity. Sliding one digit down her clit, he joined it with a second, massaging her slow.

"You're wet." The bass of those words reeked of approval. "Good girl."

Raising her hips, she moved as he toyed with her, changing pressure, angle, pace, pushing her higher, closer to venting the pressure of want building within her.

He circled her opening with a fingertip, tested her response, dipping one inside to the first knuckle, the second, then another finger.

"Yes," she pleaded, eyes closed, head nodding. "Oh, yes."

She couldn't breathe, her throat scratched, withholding its desire to release the scream buried beneath her heart.

"You're tight," he murmured, but didn't hesitate to drive two fingers into her. The slick connection flicked a switch and she cried out. "Fuck."

The hissed word barely made it to her ears that echoed with the pound of their warring heartbeats. His body moved, sort of tipped to the side and she grabbed his neck, fighting to bring his mouth to hers. When he resisted, her drowsy eyelids parted just a sliver. Arousal didn't cover what surged up inside her when his fingers slipped between his lips to taste her.

"Mmm," she moaned, writhing beneath him, desperate to pull him closer.

"Delicious," he groaned.

"Baby…"

"No," he said and kissed her quick. "I want more."

The whisper of her on his lips distracted her as he slid down low, kissing her breasts, her stomach, threading her legs out of her panties.

Was this a good idea? How could she be doing this? There with the—his tender kiss on her clit elevated her wondering to an overpowering bliss. And she went back to who cared?

"Ah," she gasped, drawing her knees high. "I want you…" Though he felt good, this was selfish, he should take, not just give. Cupping his head, she tried to pull him higher again. "Please, I want you inside me…" Nothing, he just kept on trailing his tongue through her folds. "Mmm, Roman…"

Floating on endorphins, she could only smile when he rose. The blanket fell from his shoulders, haloing the intimate red light around him.

"Fawn…" the whisper of his voice matched the delicate press of his fingertips on her thighs. "I have to tell you something—"

A whine pierced the air, and a thud followed. Darkness. Shit. Why had darkness returned?

She sat up to be caught in his arms. "What's happening?"

The lights came on, bright, jarring, jolting. And, fuzz, there he was, on his knees, the gorgeous sculpture that was his body, looming over her submission. Her spread legs relaxed around him, but, God, in that light.

Mood shattered, she shoved away and clambered to her feet, grabbing for her dress to cover herself. The zipper pinched her skin. On a yelp, she freed it and fought to position her shoulder straps again.

Her bra appeared in his hand in front of her. "Fawn, relax. It's just the power coming back on."

Yes, she could see that. Snatching the bra, that she should've put on before zipping her dress, a thunk at the door slammed her into keen mode. Rushing backwards, toward it, behind it, she watched and ignored it at the same time.

What was coming? Were they about to be caught?

The door opened and she leaped back again, losing herself in the rush of entering people. In the half dozen or so bodies that crowded the door, all voices, all focus, went to the man who'd just enjoyed her body.

Embracing the melee, she somehow got herself back upstairs to where she'd started. Like none of it ever happened. No chance of being lost or isolated with the number of people rushing around.

Renata burst from the mess. "Bambi, did the last of the vehicles leave?"

"I, uh—"

"Gather the leftover gift bags and get them to the stock truck. We'll have to send them out with some, something extra, whatever, we'll worry about that later. Then stick with Perry, she's delegating."

Delegating?

Her boss hurried off and she spun around to get to work. Maybe it should be upsetting no one noticed her missing, instead it was a relief. The fallout of the power cut would keep management busy. Thank goodness Renata was more interested in spouting orders than assigning blame. Good. She'd do her work and get home, fast. Really fast. And she'd never think of this night ever again.

SIX

AT HOME, she'd collapsed in bed, exhausted, chastising herself any time Roman popped into her head.

If Brooker was blamed for events of the night, there could be major fall out. No one could do that, could they? Blame Brooker? Its people didn't orchestrate the power cut, that was like an act of God or something. Totally outside their control.

And no one knew about her… their… Did it class as a hookup when they hadn't completed the transaction? Sad as it was, she would've done it. She'd have given herself to him right there on the floor. What a hussy.

Was she that sex deprived? Dating hadn't been high on her priority list. Maybe that should change. Until him, sexual frustration wasn't on her radar, now the two words went together like peaches and cream. Shit, did she have to go there?

The phone woke her up. No amount of stuffing the pillow over her head would shut it up. Damn thing.

As soon as it stopped, it started again. Over and

over.

Growling through gritted teeth, she tossed the pillow behind her when she leaped out of bed and stomped across the room.

The phone stopped ringing, damn, just missed it. Pounding on her front door brought her around; the phone started again, then her cell buzzed in the bedroom.

"What the hell is going on?" she said, frozen by decision paralysis.

Had she won the lottery or something? More likely the building was about to explode. Wouldn't it just be her luck to be smack bang in the middle of a terror plot? Maybe LA wasn't so great after all.

Focus. Which should she answer first? The cell? The door?

"Miss Bennett!"

Hollering in the hallway wouldn't be appreciated by her neighbors. Priorities clicked into place and she rushed to open it.

Three men stood on the threshold. Strangers. Serious, but not in uniform. Good. Getting arrested would be a crappy start to any day.

"Who are—"

"Miss Bennett, my name is Magnus Anders," he said. "Would you come with me, please?"

Wearing an oversized button-down nightshirt, last night's smudged makeup and her hair all over the place, she had to look like she'd just rolled out of bed because, well, she had.

"You… who are you?"

"Magnus Anders," he said again and shifted back a step. "I'm Roman Lowe's representative."

Oh… Big, huge oh.

Throat clear, she could handle this. "Oh." With that out there, the hair on the back of her neck prickled.

"Uh… look, I won't cause any trouble. If there's an issue with the technical problems last night, my superior—"

"Forgive me, but do you have a computer?"

"A… a what?"

"A computer," he said. "A laptop?"

Phones still droned in the background, though he didn't react to their insistence.

"Yes, why—"

"Search last night's event on Huddle Hunt," he said.

"Huddle—"

"It's a search engine."

"I know what it is."

She was from Washington, not Mars.

"Search," he said and stepped back, straightening his cuffs. "We'll wait."

Wait? While she searched…

Pushing the door closer to its frame without closing it, she breathed for a second. What the hell was going on? Had she woken up or was this a dream? Maybe she was hungover. Yeah, she was still recovering from the previous night's intoxication. That was it. Brain fog explained. As to the cause, the alcohol or the man, the jury was still out.

Ignoring the ringing, she quickly went to her laptop and booted it up. She opened the internet to type and grabbed the phone to shut the damn thing up.

"Hello?"

"Miss Bambi Bennett?"

"What?" Line after line of search results listed the scandal. Scandal! "Oh my God."

The voice came again, but she slammed the phone down fast. Ears ringing, her hand went to her mouth. The first thing that loaded was a still image of a video. Stacked mattresses, open bathroom door, this was her life! The spread blankets. Them beneath…

Her jaw sank.

Security footage of the storeroom. They were on tape! There were cameras? Darkness, the red light, the damn convergence of sucky fate and a bunch of unforeseeable incidents, and boom, their secret interlude was available to a vast audience, playing on a screen near you.

She didn't press the space bar to let the film roll, couldn't press it. The headlines beneath were horrific. One story after another supposed the truth, without citing their words were speculation.

The phone rang again, driving her to her feet. This wouldn't do, this… one thing at a time. Rushing across the room, she pulled the phone wire from the socket then dashed into the bedroom. This wasn't her wheelhouse. Hollywood scandal? Not even close. She needed help, direction. Roman would know what to do.

As she dressed, her stress level rose. They hadn't planned to see each other again. Would it be awkward? This internet interest was a huge responsibility. Anything she said to the press could cost Roman his career, right when he was trying to put his history of womanizing and partying behind him. Well done, Bambi, she'd screwed everything up, not just in her life, but his too.

The last thing she wanted was for him to lose his job or for his reputation to be impacted because of one impulsive decision. Because of her and goddamn gummy bears. Yeah, 'cause the bears were the guilty party.

Grabbing her biggest jacket and her purse, she went for the door and found Mr. Anders on the other side with the other two men.

"I'm sorry for this inconvenience, Miss Bennett," he said. "We will take good care of you… I'd advise you to put your hood up."

Her hood? Was the rain still falling? Gales—the reason slammed into her when the communal door opened. Dozens of reporters swarmed the street, cameras, aloft smartphones, flashing, waving, people called, shouted, her name was an erratic chorus on the crowd's unpredictable tide. Magnus kept a guiding arm around her while she held her hood over her face. The other two guys acted as security and did their best to keep a perimeter around her.

When she almost lost her footing, Magnus held her up to bundle them into the back of a car and then they were on the move.

She intended to sit up, but Magnus put a hand on her head and pushed it down. "Stay low a minute."

The flashes were still going. When his hand finally relaxed, giving her a chance to sit up, they were five blocks from her apartment.

"This is insane," she breathed out, watching the city go by.

"You'll get used to it, Miss Bennett," Magnus said, retrieving his phone from his inside pocket. "Roman's at the house. He'll be awake by the time we get there. This is his area of expertise. He'll help you understand how to deal with it."

"I don't want to deal with it."

Magnus was doing something on his phone and didn't react.

A second later, he raised the device to his ear. "Hey, it's me. You wake him up yet? What have we got?"

For the rest of the car trip, Magnus stayed on the phone. The clips of one-sided conversations didn't give her much clue what was going on. She got the gist they were fielding a lot of press requests, and that Roman wasn't up yet, so was oblivious to what was going on.

Lucky him.

A wrought iron gate opened as they turned off the street. They drove up a curved driveway to a two-story house, slightly taller wings flanked each side of the modest central building.

The car stopped and the door was opened by a driver, who waited for her to get out. Right, okay, 'cause why would she have gotten in the car if she didn't intend to get out when they arrived? Oh, butterflies, her throat dried. With more than usual effort, she climbed out and followed Magnus up the half dozen stone stairs to the covered entryway.

Inside, a double-height lobby with a grand central staircase awed her. "It's beautiful."

"Yeah," Magnus agreed, putting an arm around her to guide her into a huge living room.

And there was Roman, sitting in the middle of the couch.

"Oh, Roman," she said and rushed away from Magnus to go to him.

His lazy eyes widened above a grin. "Heya, gorgeous," he declared. His tone slowed her. "Wow, you're something."

"I… what?"

To her surprise, the heartthrob grabbed her wrist to pull her down onto the couch beside him. "I'm sorry about this, sweetheart."

Resting a hand on the front of her thigh, he slid it up beneath the hem of her skirt.

Something weird trickled through her. This wasn't like last night. This wasn't arousal or crazy surging hormones. Seizing his wrist, and using quite a bit of strength, she pushed his arm away. The other snaked around her, holding her close to him. His body felt different; he felt different. The air around him, everything was off. Why? What was it? Sickness weighed in the pit of her stomach.

"Roman, this is serious," Magnus said. "Very serious. We've worked hard to build your reputation. Now we're looking at tape of you drinking and fooling around with a stranger."

"I've seen it," he said and scooped her hair from her neck to bow and kiss her there. "You're a beauty, Bambi."

Sleazy. Something in his voice was sleazy. Opposite to last night. No. Pushing away from him, she put space between them, seeking his gaze. Maybe if she could look at him… his eyes were too busy checking out every inch of her.

The man in the hotel basement made her feel cherished, special. He'd been in no rush and let her lead, he sensed her needs. How could he be so different just a few hours later?

Being hypnotized by his allure, she'd assumed, was his star charisma doing its thing. If it was, it failed them both. The trauma of the morning erased every trace of that instinctive attraction.

Roman reached for her again, but she pushed his hand away. "How did they get that footage?"

"I don't know," Magnus said. "We're investigating. We'll get together with the lawyers to find out if we have any claim against the hotel or event organizers. Best we can guess, someone in security leaked the tape from the inside."

"But we can't deny it happened, can we, Sugar?" Roman asked and scooted closer.

She scooted away. Get the hint. This guy was creeping her out. How could she have been drawn in by him? The man had to be the world's best actor, beyond Oscar worthy. Either that or she was having some sort of psychotic break.

"We can't put a claim in against the organizers. I am the organizers. I work for them."

"You do?" Magnus asked.

She turned to Roman. "You didn't tell anyone that?"

He shrugged and slouched deeper into the couch to finger the hem of her dress. "Guess that detail slipped by me with everything else we were doing."

"You forgot?" she asked, pushing his hand out from beneath her skirt... again.

Sliding along to the arm of the couch, far from him, her face sank into her hands. She'd thought last night was a sign of inner strength. That she'd taken control of her own sexuality. Turned out she was a lousy judge of character, maybe she just had awful taste in men. Roman seemed mature and attentive, like the breath of fresh air her love life needed. She'd fuzzed it up again. How could she have fuzzed it up this bad?

"You smell amazing."

Lifting her head from her hands, she found Roman at her side again. Up close. Too close. That was rich when she'd been rolling around with him not so long ago.

"Roman, your rep can't take a scandalous one-night stand. Especially after the island. Your contract with the network states you won't get up to old antics. They can drop you in a heartbeat and if they do it's over," Magnus said and, judging by his expression, lingered on a thought. "You can't have a casual affair with a stranger, so what if she wasn't a stranger? What if she's the exact opposite of a stranger?"

"I don't understand what—"

"What if she's your fiancée?"

Roman laughed while she gaped. "His fiancée?"

His fingers curled around her knee. "Guess you're stuck with me, Sugarlips."

"No," she said. "No. No."

She stood.

Roman snagged her hand to pull her back down. "It'll be fun to be my girl for a while. We have a lot going on."

"No," she said. "I can't be your fiancée. No. No way."

Tugging her arm from his, she leaped up and swerved around Magnus who tried to get in her way.

Where was she going? No clue. One thing she knew was the way out. Sounded like a good start. She felt sick to her stomach that such a man had touched her. What the hell was wrong with her? Kevin was an abuser and Roman a letch, why couldn't she find herself a decent man?

Though the pair called after her, she ignored them to make a beeline across the foyer, front door in her sights.

"Fawn?" That voice stopped her in her tracks. "Is that you?"

SEVEN

SHE WHIRLED AROUND. A man on the stairs in dark jeans and a gray tee-shirt wore a face identical to the one she'd just left on the couch. Yet somehow, she couldn't explain why, it was completely different. He smiled and came running down the stairs toward her. When he got close enough to touch, she leaped back, holding out her hands.

Behind him to the right, Magnus rushed out of the living room with Roman in his wake or… maybe not Roman.

The guy in front of her checked them out, but his attention quickly came back to her.

"What the hell is going on?" she demanded.

"Ah, shit, Struan, trust you to be up early," Roman said. "Bet he's already done forty laps and 20K."

She focused on the man closest to her. The one who looked just like the guy she'd been intimate with last night.

"Bambi, baby," he said. "I can explain this. I am not Roman Lowe. My name is Struan, he's my twin."

"Oh my God," she said and stumbled backward. "He's your… but we…"

"Wait a second…" Magnus said. "Ah, fuck, you two pulled the bait and switch again!"

This Struan guy didn't explain, just kept his attention on her. "I wanted to tell you, but it's complicated. Roman was supposed to be there last night, but he… he was drinking and—"

"Yo, fuck, bro, don't tell her that shit!" Roman objected while Magnus chastised.

As they argued, Struan tried to get closer to her. No way, this was too… she backed up again.

"I'm sorry," he said, his eyes soft with contrition. Looking into him, she recognized the mesmerizing man from the storeroom. "I was going to call you today. You ran off last night. You disappeared so fast and—"

"I didn't want to get in the way and I… I thought the moment was sort of perfect on its own."

Dating a Hollywood star long-term hadn't occurred to her for a second. What they had was what it was and… except it wasn't.

He smiled though his head tilted in curiosity. "Then why are you here this morning? Didn't you come looking for me?"

"No, she didn't," Magnus said, appearing behind him. "You're supposed to be the sensible one, Struan. Your reckless behavior's caused your brother a lot of problems… enough it might end his career."

"End his…"

Yes, she was confused and pissed, but finding out they'd been recorded sideswiped her too. The guy deserved a minute to compute.

She laid a hand on his forearm. "There's a video," she whispered, stroking him, relishing the feel of those little dark hairs moving beneath her fingers. A buzz of electricity zapped her, him too, it was there in his eyes when they rose from her hand.

"A video of us together?"

"Or a video of us," Roman said, coming up at her other side.

When he tried to put his arm around her, she sidestepped, bumping into Struan.

"Can you please stop touching me?" she said, unsteadied by it all.

This was a lot to take in.

"Yeah," Struan said, wrapping an arm around her shoulders to hold her against him. "Hands off."

Shrugging off Struan's arm, she backed away from them both. "That goes for you too," she said. "You're no better… in fact, you're worse!"

It was easy to refuse Roman, the letch. Struan was a whole different ballgame. Their magnetism provided the perfect excuse to lean on him, which would be a huge mistake.

"Worse?" he asked. "Why am I worse?"

Roman laughed. "She doesn't want your hands on her, man. She thought she was getting me last night and didn't expect to hook up with the help."

Offended, her mouth opened. If he didn't have so many protectors around, she might've slapped the supposed star. Last night, her instant attraction to Struan had been visceral and real, regardless of his name, or his "position" in the family.

Roman's swagger fueled a need to take him down a peg. Swerving around him, she went to Struan and grabbed his face to pull him down for a kiss. The moment her mouth touched his, their ecstasy came back full force. Suddenly, there was no trouble, no craziness, nothing except their mouths. His arms realized what was happening before his mouth did. When he held her, she gave him control of her body. A second later, his tongue caught up with what was happening and merged with hers.

Before she lost her senses and asked for directions to his bedroom, she pulled back. Abstaining wasn't easy. Against him, in body contact, she didn't want to be mad. Hormones led, and, man, she wanted to follow.

"You're worse because this feels right. It's easy to run away from your sleazy brother. You're harder to resist."

The corner of his mouth reacted. Whatever the reality, that was a compliment. One she'd rather not give, but truth was truth.

Roman hissed. Good, let him be second best. Honestly? She was pleased he hadn't gone to the Lighting Darkness event. Imagining a second locked up with him was awful enough, never mind enduring the actual experience.

Magnus leaned in to pull her away from Struan. "Shame you'll never get to explore that," he said, lugging her toward the living room.

She reached for Struan and missed. Guy didn't help, just stood there dumbfounded until rage flared in his expression, signaling his returning acuity.

Magnus pushed her down on the couch. Struan and Roman weren't far behind.

"What the hell do you think you're doing, Mag?" Struan asked, sitting with her.

Cradling her face, he brushed her hair away to check she was okay, or offer more apology, she wasn't sure which. When he examined her wrist, what had been Magnus's point of contact, his offense rose again.

"Back off, she's your brother's fiancée."

"Excuse me," both she and Struan said at the same time.

Roman dropped onto the couch at her other side.

A confident, stern, man in charge, Magnus stood

in front of their trio. "Last night's events are on devices across the world right now, we can't ignore that. Roman has used all his passes and is hanging onto his career by the skin of his fucking teeth. This could ruin him. If the network thinks he's going back to his old ways, we're fucked."

"And I did nothing wrong," Roman said.

"Except getting wasted before the event," Struan said.

"If I didn't, brother, you wouldn't have got laid." A beat. "You're welcome."

He better not expect gratitude. He'd had his hand up her skirt, that was gratitude enough.

She laid a hand on each of their thighs. "I am sorry that this happened," Bambi said, pushing them both away. "I didn't mean to cause trouble for anyone's career."

"She didn't know who she was sleeping with," Roman said. "Who knew Struan could be spontaneous? Fuck, we sure he wasn't high? Really this is all his fault."

Struan reached behind her to shove his brother. "Shut the fuck up."

"Why don't you tell the truth?" she asked Magnus, attempting to catch each man's wrist to stop them wrestling with her in the middle. "Tell the media Roman wasn't the one at the event."

"We can't tell them they were conned. Roman was invited to the event, Struan went as him. This isn't the first time they've done this. The world can't know that. We can't have the family secrets getting out. Everyone will second-guess which Lowe brother they have at their event or on their set… And they'll ask why Roman didn't show."

Which would mean admitting Roman was drunk and Struan was saving his ass.

"And I'm sorry for that, but it's not my

problem."

"While the media are all over you it is. Whichever Lowe brother they think you're screwing, they have footage that won't go away. We can protect you if you stay. We can give you security and corral the media. Here, you'll have everything you need. Out there on your own, you're exposed, that could be dangerous. And you've got to think about your ass too. What will your employer think of you fraternizing with party guests while on duty? If they find out he's your fiancé and may be interested in making a donation to the cause… and perhaps making some appearances…"

She didn't like the sinister thread in his voice. "Are you blackmailing me?"

"No, he's not," Struan said, his voice deep and gravelly. "Because if he was, I'd be the first to make him pay for it."

"We need her help, Struan," Magnus said. "You know his past; we can't go through this again. What's the alternative?"

The men looked at each other. An air of guilt surrounded Struan. Okay, so she couldn't claim to know anything intimate about Roman's past or the family secrets, but there was something going on, something simmering not too deep beneath the surface.

"Okay, you guys figure it out. I wish you all the best."

This time when she got up, her tension was lower, though her heart was a little heavier. Turned out she might've found herself a good man, he just wasn't the one she'd thought.

In their few frames together, Struan was something special. Maybe she could have opened herself to him. Being so comfortable with a man that fast was novel. Rather than explore it, she had to walk away and would never know how it might've played out.

"Fawn!" Being closer to the door than last time made no difference, escape still eluded her. Goddamnit. Why couldn't she get there without someone interrupting? Licking her lips, she turned around just as he jogged up in front of her. "I'm sorry."

That threw her. "For?"

"Last night," he said. "I want to get that out first. I should've told you who I was. You thought I was Roman and I didn't correct you. I was attracted to you and I… there's no excuse, I'm sorry."

"Okay, thank you," she said. "I appreciate that. Have a good life."

He caught her before she could turn, crowding so close that her back hit the door. "This is on me. Roman's career is on the line because of that video, our video. And I'm not wild about you being out there alone with the paparazzi dogs hounding you. Stay."

"What?"

"Stay here for a few weeks until this blows over. I know I put you in this position and Roman too." Nothing about the years of bad behavior that put the other Lowe brother's coat on a rickety peg? "We're the ones who did what we did, he doesn't deserve to be punished for it."

It shouldn't have hurt, or shocked her, that he'd be so loyal to family. Actually putting it together though was difficult. He was suggesting…?

"You want me to play his fiancée?" she asked, concealing her hurt.

"I…" He swallowed. "No, I don't. But this isn't about what I want. The media have to think he's serious about you. Your career could suffer for this too, and I don't want that. So, please, let's just ride this out for a couple of weeks, maybe a month. I'll look after you. Nothing will happen that you're not comfortable with."

"I'm not comfortable with this."

"Okay, then help me out," he said, raising his arms in a loose shrug. "How do we fix this? Are you going to face the paps alone? They're vicious." She remembered. That morning, she might not have made it out alive if it hadn't been for Magnus and the security guys. "And Brooker will know about this now."

"You remember who I work for?"

His frown was confused. "Why wouldn't I remember? You told me last night." He had been listening. Oh, sigh. Knowing that didn't make the situation any easier. "Won't you let me look after you?"

"By telling the world I'll marry your brother?"

"He won't touch you, I promise."

Bobbing her head, she moistened her lips and put a hand on his chest to ease him back. "Okay, but it's sad."

"Why sad?"

Once again, truth was truth, bitter or not.

She breathed out a semi-sigh. "Because if the world thinks I belong to him… I can never belong to you."

"Mr. Lowe…" a guy called from somewhere behind him. "Chic is—"

"In a minute," Struan said without breaking eye contact with her.

"I'll need to go home and get my things."

"Is that agreement? You'll stay?" Their gazes answered. "Someone will fill your closet." He came in even closer. "You don't need to go anywhere. It's not safe for you out there."

"I have things I need to get." Oh, the line of his throat, thick, masculine—she closed her eyes, shaking loose the memories threatening to take over. "What was I saying?"

"Things," he said, touching her upper arm.

She bowed away. "We shouldn't do that?"

"Do what?"

"Touch." She scratched her lip. "I'm engaged to your brother."

He bowed to murmur. "I saw you first."

"This is not finders keepers."

"How about he who fingers…"

Trailing off that smile showed his dimple, taking a needle to her defenses.

"Don't," she said on an exhaled laugh.

"I'm your ally. You need an ally."

"Shouldn't my ally be my fake fiancé?"

"Didn't seem you were that interested in him."

"No. First impression? He's an arrogant letch."

Their fingertips met. "You don't have to be afraid here."

"Why not? Are you going to guard me?"

"If I have to." His fingers slipped between hers. "I'm sorry you got pulled into this."

"Are you?"

In unison, their hands lifted, fingers tangled as palm pressed to palm. If they'd never met, this wouldn't have happened. There would be no video. No career crisis. No hungry press desperate for every morsel. Was being free of the drama enough to make her wish away their night together…?

The front door burst open, startling them apart.

"Where is my muse?" the gorgeous, tan new entrant asked and fixated on her.

Damn, that muse might be her.

"Bambi, meet Chic," Struan said. "First time your new canvas is already a work of art."

Sighs and swoons, he probably shouldn't be saying things like that in front of people.

"Before I'm anyone's muse," she said, unsure how to react to the new man's scrutiny. "I need to make a call."

"A call?" Struan asked, then answered. "Wishbone?"

More proof. A good man not only interested in getting laid, he'd cared enough to listen. And she'd stuffed it up already. Wasn't life just one big laugh?

EIGHT

THE LAND OF MAKE BELIEVE encircled her. She'd woken in normality and, somehow, since then, had been elevated to princess status. Agreeing to the insane scheme turned out to be just the first stop on the crazy train. She'd been shown to a bedroom upstairs, her room, apparently, and given time to make her call. More insanity she didn't want to relive.

Her Wishbone conversation had been put to an abrupt halt when a bunch of people flooded her room. Stylists with clothes, hairdressers, makeup artists, beauticians, nail techs, and the waxing guy, he hadn't been fun.

Activity flurried around her. People appeared and disappeared without introduction or explanation. They gathered and discarded apparel as she was dressed up like Barbie, in this outfit and that. Most of the time, well, some of the time, she was allowed a glimpse in a mirror before one outfit was replaced with the next. Why was it so important to prepare her closet for every eventuality in one afternoon?

Obligation to surrender silenced her questions. Everyone was being so nice, how could she question their purpose?

Her hair was dyed and curled; false nails were buffed and polished. She was tweezed and tanned and waxed and shined in every intimate corner without regard for modesty, sometimes decency. Here and there, she caught a name, but couldn't figure out which body went with which moniker. Then just as quick, Chic, the man directing the performance, commanded everyone depart.

Carts and trollies and racks of clothes were wheeled out to be transported away in vans lined up in the driveway. From her room, the view was pretty damn amazing, probably not the best in the city but far better than any mortal, such as herself, should ever experience.

"How are you doing?" Struan's voice turned her on the spot.

When their eyes met, her smile was automatic. "You live a crazy life."

He snickered. "This isn't my life, not the one I choose. This is Roman's life."

Struan lived and worked with his twin brother, yet he didn't claim the same life? How did that work? Where did Struan's life begin? What was his?

"And you're just along for the ride? Everyone's so kind," she said, smoothing a hand down her hair, continuing the caress to her dress. "I don't know how anyone lives like this full-time."

"It's addictive. Mark my words on that. Usually, all it takes is a taste. Everyone wants to drown in it, terrified it might ever be taken away."

Like they would be taken from each other when this was over.

"You don't seem addicted."

His regard was curious, yet subdued, she couldn't figure it out.

"Not really," he said. "We've had more downs than ups these last few years. I keep thinking it'll straighten out, then some other drama, or some other crime—"

"Crime?" Alarm speared her. "Who's breaking the law?"

"I don't mean illegal." Slipping his hands into his pockets, he sauntered a few steps closer. The bed between them formed a physical barrier, like a manifestation of their new positions in the novel setup, close, yet far apart. "Though I can't deny the cops would be interested in some of the shit that's gone down. My brother's an addict. When you're that deep in, boundaries, morals, they don't mean anything. They come and go as the need grows."

Some of the glitter of the day had been tarnished by the man she'd met on the couch downstairs.

"I don't have anything to worry about, do I? Would you be honest with me?"

"Worry about? Roman's clean."

Or that was the line they were selling.

She was a stranger and wouldn't be allowed access to every intimate detail, of course not, but if she was going to spend time there, she had to be prepared. Had to know what her life would be.

"Downstairs he seemed…" How did she put it without insulting the men? "You're so different, you and him. In a way, I'm grateful for that because no lines will be confused, but I have to admit he made me uncomfortable at first." At first? That implied the discomfort was temporary, it wasn't. They hadn't spent enough time together to change that opinion. "For some reason, I trust you, more than I trust him. Stupid, I guess." Because she had no ownership of him, of either man. "I don't know much about your brother's addiction history, but I've seen what can happen when men are intoxicated."

"Most people can't tell us apart. Those who don't know us. Everyone thinks we're the same."

She couldn't claim to know him completely. One thing was certain though.

"You're not the same." Why would her opinion matter? "The man I met at last night's event would never put his hands on me against my will. And downstairs…"

"I'll talk to him," Struan said with an ounce of concern.

To be honest, though he was wary, he wasn't surprised or outraged. She'd bet it wasn't the first time a woman questioned his brother's amorous advances.

His concentration flitted to the closet, to the overabundance of luxury foisted on her. Was that enough? Was it payment for putting up with whatever went on in those walls? Was that the deal?

"I have my own things," she said, suddenly self-conscious. What must he think of her? She'd rocked up into this glamorous life and agreed to take up with his brother for a few lousy outfits and a new hairdo. Shallow? Cheap? She'd never considered herself either. Not until right then. "I appreciate everything that's been done." She touched her hair again. "I know people expect a man like Roman to be with a certain type of woman. The type of woman who wouldn't embarrass him with the way she looks or the things she says."

"You don't owe us anything. There's nothing wrong with the woman you are. Roman's more likely to embarrass you than the other way around. Believe me. I apologize for that now, and probably will every day until this is over for you." Her confidence slipped again. "You're welcome to all of this. It's the least we can do for what you're sacrificing."

"And what is that? What does being with your brother entail? Will it involve going out in public? Speaking to people? God, it better not involve cameras, of any kind."

"We'll talk about that downstairs, at dinner. I just wanted to…" What? Why did he go quiet? "You look incredible."

After that long pause, she doubted that was what he'd come to say. There was something else on his mind.

"Thank you."

Because what the hell else could she say? Questions might seem accusatory and she didn't want to do that to him.

He took another step. "Downstairs, earlier, you said—"

"Dinner!" someone called from beyond the room.

Struan faltered, exhaling as his chin hitched toward the shout. "I guess we should get downstairs."

"Should I change?" She fingered the fabric on her body. "This feels like a lot."

He smiled. "It's nothing to what you'll endure through this. Come on."

Dinner would be ready and waiting. The performance wasn't over yet, but she prayed this was her encore. Her nerves wouldn't take many more surprises. What had she gotten herself into?

NINE

DINNER SHOULDN'T BE daunting. Having Struan there to guide her into the huge dining space at the back of the house did take the edge off some of her trepidation.

The rear garden was lit up, the pool sparkled, the edge of the slate patio glowed. Another world? More like another planet.

"How was your day?" Magnus asked.

Struan guided her into a chair at the circular table and pushed it in under her.

"My day?" she asked of the man awaiting an answer. "Yes, uh, it was… interesting."

"I've got to have more say on the clothes if she's supposed to be my girlfriend."

Quite a talent Roman had for paying zero attention to anyone else while demanding his say with the crowd.

"What's wrong with her clothes? Chic has excellent taste."

"Yeah, but there's got to be a reason, right?"

"A reason?" Magnus asked.

"Why she got my attention. Not like she's got a name or a rep to back her up."

"Her lips," Struan said.

Wine. Good, there was—what did he say? Apparently, Roman wasn't the only one not paying attention to others.

"Her what?" Roman barked.

"Her lips," Struan said. "That plump cherry red pout. That's the first thing you noticed about her."

Usually "plump" wouldn't be considered complimentary, but, shit. Sucking her lower lip into her mouth, she dug her teeth into it.

"Good, yeah, it's like a script. Keep feeding me the lines, bro." Because Roman's head was somewhere else. "Talk to Priest today?"

They had their own priest? That couldn't be what he meant. A priest for an addict? Hollywood could be accused of worse.

"No," Struan said. "Even if I did, I wouldn't tell you. Leave her alone. She doesn't want you calling."

"We could take a stroll to…"

"New York?" Magnus asked. "Not a chance, you're on set this week. The calendar's full."

"They're not in New York yet."

"You knowing that highlights the problem." Struan distributed salad family style. "You didn't know what planet you were on last night, but you know where Sway was? Get over it, Ro."

"They?" she asked.

"Roman's ex," Struan said. "Sway Sheridan."

"Oh, God, Sway Sheridan, she's—" Gorgeous, glamorous, glittering. "Is she an addict?"

Real smooth. But, hey, she finally got Roman's attention.

"No one's a fucking addict," he snapped. "Don't

read the fucking press, they don't know shit." Offending him, well, that was one weapon against molestation. If he disliked her enough, he'd never get close. Bonus secret strategy? "And Sway's fucking perfect."

"And that right there is your problem, idolizing her doesn't change anything."

"You tell Priest to keep his hands to himself," Roman snarled through gritted teeth. "Touching my woman comes with a price."

"She's not your woman and can do whatever she wants."

"Just not Priest, anyone but Priest."

"You're the only guy on the planet who doesn't like him," Struan said. "Think maybe you're missing something?"

"I'm the only guy who sees through it, the bullshit act," Roman said, almost petulant in the way he stabbed at his food in his exaggerated slouch. "He's a dick, and I'll be right there to see it when the truth comes out."

Struan sighed and caught Magnus's eye. These men were no strangers to Roman's pout. She sucked her lips into her mouth again. Did she pout?

"Focus on keeping this truth under wraps," Magnus said. "You've got to sell this relationship, every minute, man."

"Her pout, I heard him," Roman said. "Rack isn't bad either." And she just sat there, being objectified. Great, offending him might keep him away, but it didn't repel his eyes. "Need to watch that video again, get myself familiar with everything that's mine."

"Nothing is yours," Struan was quick to warn him. "You touch her, or push her further than she wants to go, I'll walk out there and tell the damn world the truth myself."

That didn't surprise only her.

"Yeah, fucking right," Roman's initial surprise gave way to his usual arrogance. "You know your fucking place."

God, he was just vile. "Do you have to swear so much?" she asked. "It's unattractive and unnecessary."

In the corner of her eye, Magnus's jaw drop didn't go unnoticed.

"Who the fuck do you—"

"If we're supposed to be a couple, we have to be comfortable with each other."

"You some kind of priss or something?"

"There's a place to be naughty, and it's not at the dinner table with your family."

"Who the fuck is she?" Roman demanded of his uncle. "She can't talk to me this way."

"Yeah, she can," Struan said. "People in her world have to believe this too."

Her world? Hmm, right, yeah, she should probably call her mom back. Wishbone might be at the back of beyond, but they were connected to the rest of the world. Forgetting her phone at the apartment might be her saving grace. The thing had probably melted by now.

"Her world?" Roman scoffed. "Who gives a fuck about her world? Call Priest, ask him to stay here."

What the...? The guy claimed he wasn't an addict, but his personality sure said otherwise. Were they talking about Sway and Priest again? How did he swing back to that conversation without missing a beat?

"Why would he want to stay here?"

"Is he with Zairn?"

"I don't know," Struan said.

"Is he fucking her?"

"Let me guess, you called and she didn't pick up."

Roman ran a ragged hand through his hair.

"Yeah, only like forty fucking times. She needs to be here. To come here. If she's seen the video—"

"She's celebrating," Struan said. "Thanking the gods she's finally fucking free." His eyes cut to hers. "Sorry."

That he even thought to apologize was a massive step up from Roman's attitude.

"So Sway's your ex-girlfriend, and now she's with this priest? I thought priests were celibate."

"Not that kind of priest," Struan said, leaning a little closer. "It's a nickname."

Okay, that story would have to wait.

"We don't know where she is," Magnus said.

Quickly followed up by Struan. "It's not our business."

"Is she with Deacon?" Roman didn't let a little thing like reality deter him. "Is she fucking both of them?"

"Yeah," Struan said. "That's it, she's fucking everyone, Priest, Deacon, Zairn, even Logan. The Kintyre wedding this past weekend was a mass orgy. Know how many rich guys were in town? Bet she was screwing all of them. A lot of well-known faces to get down and dirty with."

Roman thrust to his feet. "We're going to the house."

"Have a great time," Struan said, the only one willing to challenge his brother, to meet obstinance with obstinance. "You think you can get into Knox Collier's house unseen? You think the guy doesn't have security? More headlines! Great, brother, Bambi's off the hook and your career sinks right down that drain it's circling."

The standing man's jaw moved as his lips thinned. Yeah, he was mad, but from what she could tell, he was doing this to himself.

"If she's your ex," she asked, "why is it your

business who she's hooking up with?"

Went to show that no amount of money or fame changed that baser form of men with his affliction. Narcissism, in its simplest form, poisoned the blood of people like this, those who believed they were better than others.

Was that the difference? Struan, Roman, from one man to the next, she tried to decipher what it was about them that made their difference in aura so stark.

"Stop looking at him like that," Roman barked, thrusting a finger her way. "You're my fucking girl."

"Okay," she said and pushed her chair away from the table. "I'm going to bed."

"It's not even nine thirty."

And maybe that made a difference in their world, not in hers. "I was raised not to humor the humorless. It's been a long day." She stood up. "I have work in the morning. Goodnight."

TEN

COFFEE. That had to be a staple in every person's home, didn't it? It was the great economic leveler. Yeah, okay, so the cost of java could vary, but at its core, it offered everyone the same relief.

And that was something she needed, hence her creeping down the stairs, seeking the kitchen. She'd caught a glimpse of it from the dining room the previous night. Now was a chance to explore. Not out of nosiness, no, she needed to find the caffeine.

Just entering was enough to blow the air from her lungs. The huge kitchen island on its own was possibly bigger than her whole kitchen back home. It didn't feel right to open and close cabinets, but there was no one around. She didn't need help, she could—what the hell kind of coffee machine was that? Oh, God, if she broke it—how much did something like that cost?

"Good morning." Whirling around to witness Struan close a door behind him, she intended to speak, but... The sweats, straining tee-shirt, the damp hair... Her mouth opened, but no words came out. "Have you eaten?"

Did it look like she'd eaten? The only thing that passed her lips was air. It dried her tongue and burned her throat with a desperation to whine in submission. Only as he came closer did she force words out.

"You shouldn't sneak up on people."

His quick smile flashed a dimple. "Did I sneak?"

"Yeah, well I didn't know you were going to creep in from—why are you up so early?"

"What time is it?" He stopped next to her, folding his arms, propping a hip on the counter. "It's after six."

Like that was a reasonable time for anyone to be awake and active.

"Is that your bedroom?" she asked, unable to break eye contact as she gestured with her chin. "Why does it lead off the kitchen? That's weird. No one ever told you that was weird?"

He laughed. "It's not my bedroom, the fitness suite is downstairs."

"Oh."

"You want a smoothie?"

"A smoothie?" Suspicion lit the question. He turned to open the fridge. "A green one?"

Another laugh and he glanced back. They were too close, so she boosted herself away from the counter to go stand on this side of the island a few feet away.

"You want it green, I'll make it green."

"I don't want green. LA is all superfoods, celery and kale, how do you live here?" As he gathered things from the fridge, her admiration may have just maybe slid down to his ass. Shit, the man was hot. "You probably enjoy it."

"Enjoy it?"

"With a physique like that..."

He came to dump various wares from the fridge

onto the counter.

"What's wrong with my physique?"

"Absolutely nothing." Licking her lower lip, she dragged it back and forth over her teeth as he spread out cardboard and Tupperware. "No, nothing at all… Which you know fine well."

"You objectifying me?" God, he was right. It was as wrong of her to do it as it was for any man to do it to a woman. Backing up a step, she started to turn. He caught her wrist. "Didn't say you should stop."

Something in the way their eyes danced lit a fire between them. Not even in her or him, them together, the fiery bubble of desire sealed them inside its smokey solitude.

"I should stick to coffee."

"This will be better, trust me."

By its stem, he offered a strawberry to her mouth. She caught the tip gently in her teeth and sealed her lips around it. Eyes dropping to the fruit, his throat bobbed in an obvious swallow. Something so simple. So seemingly insignificant, yet it ignited her brazenness. As he eased just a fraction away, she sucked the fruit deeper, returning him to her in a hurry.

He snatched the side of her head, fast and hard, like on instinct, jerking it upward as he came nearer, so much nearer that his arousal pressed against her.

"Yesterday," he growled, stooping lower, still pressuring her body with his. The edge of the counter dug harshly into her waist, but, man, any pain was worth it. "Yesterday, you said—"

"Hello!" A female voice chirped from an adjoining room. As Struan turned, the beauty came into sight. A tiny brunette stopped in the ingress above the half dozen broad stairs to the next… whatever was through there. "Am I interrupting?"

"Damn, Mieux Penrose, you didn't get enough

of us already?" Struan left her to meet the little woman, who stopped her descent on the second stair to accept his kiss on her cheek. "Thought you didn't work more than one job in a row with a client."

"Then it's a good thing I'm not here for Roman."

"You're here for…"

The woman leaned aside to smile at her. "Bambi Bennett?"

Her? "What? Me?"

"Mieux works with the Brooker Agency—"

"So do I," she said at the same time as Mieux's—

"So does she."

On a double take, he backed off. "Guess I'm just in the way." He returned to his previous place, not to her, to his fruit. "Want a smoothie, U?"

"You didn't feed me enough on the island?"

"You enjoyed it then."

Mieux laughed and raised a tablet and folder from her side. "Did I?"

"Yeah, why'd you come back for more if you didn't?" A pause lingered enough that Struan looked up at the woman approaching the other side of the island. "Rox Out?"

Mieux smiled. "I might've got a call."

"Woman's persuasive."

"Especially when she follows up with a ringer." Mieux unlocked the tablet before she and Struan made eye contact. "Priest."

In a silent, "ah," he went back to his smoothie prep. "Got dirt on you?"

"That's not the way he works."

"Oh yeah?" he asked, smirking. "Tell me more about how he works, Mieux."

"He's been your best friend for a long time. You don't need a lesson from me."

"And now you're here. Just in time." He opened

the blender. "Have you eaten?"

The man had an obsession with feeding people.

"If you're making the blueberry one, no, I haven't." Mieux looked to her. "If he pulls out the parsnips, run."

Another laugh from Struan. "Ignore her, we just spent a month in the Pacific, she's grouchy we had to come back."

"The Pacific…? Alone?"

What was that? Why did she ask that? More's the point, why did discomfort visit? Jealousy? No, she couldn't, wouldn't, go there.

"Working," Mieux said.

"You miss the waves, U? Sun, sea, sand."

"It was work."

"Only felt like that because you were stuck with Ro."

"You did a lot more wrangling than I did, which I'm grateful for."

They just talked, openly, about how difficult Roman was? Like it was no secret, or something to be challenged, they just accepted it.

"It's a bad habit," Struan said.

To give him a default pass? Yeah, sure seemed that way.

"Enough about him," Mieux said, setting her focus. "I've never been assistant to a colleague before, but I'm always willing to try new things and I can work with anyone."

"As proven by your work with Roman," Struan muttered.

"I doubt Bambi will be as demanding."

"Assistant?" she asked. "I don't need an assistant. That would just be—why would I need an assistant?"

"Think of me less of a personal assistant and

more of a logistics coordinator." Still none the wiser, she shook her head. "Your calendar's filling up, and we have requests to vet."

"Requests? What kind of requests?"

"Interviews, appearances, speaking opportunities…" Maybe it was her mouth falling open that set Mieux's smile. "Things change fast when you're in the headlines. I can advise which to accept and which to refuse, but ultimately, it's up to you."

"Let me see that," Struan asked, tossing something in his mouth then extending a hand to Mieux.

It wasn't possible to reach over the island, so the petite woman came around to put it in his hand.

"I don't want to talk to anyone. I don't have any—why would people care what—it doesn't matter that I—why do I suddenly matter?"

"Got a conflict of interest," Struan said, scrolling down.

"I know," Mieux said, dragging her folder around to open it. "And that's not the worst thing…" Screwing up her face, the woman was contrite as she pushed the folder her way. "I have something you need to sign."

"What is it?"

Mieux shot a pen over that she caught while trying to—Struan angled the document to read it.

"You've got to be kidding me."

Mieux shrugged. "Don't shoot the messenger."

"What is it?"

"An NDA," Mieux said. "I know you've signed one with Brooker, but this is different because it's—"

"Personal." The language seemed standard and she understood why it was necessary, but… "My boyfriend wants me to sign an NDA?"

It was difficult not to put "boyfriend" in air quotes or exaggerate the word. Admitting the relationship like it was true was icky. Because it was a lie, or because of the man? Best not to think too much about that.

"You'd be surprised how common it is in these situations."

With a shove, Struan skimmed the folder back to Mieux. "I don't want her to sign it."

"Well, she's not your girlfriend, Stru." In another pass, the folder came to stop with her again. "This is a formality."

"How can I sign this then do interviews about our relationship?"

"It's a balancing act." Mieux smiled. "Truth is fluid in these situations. People are less interested in the truth than they are the image." That didn't help. "You'll be coached. We'll get you the best."

Invisible weight crushed her chest. "This is a lot."

"Don't worry about it," Struan said. "I'll talk to him."

Mieux didn't have his confidence. "You know this won't be from Roman."

"Yeah, but he can stop it."

"Why would he?" she asked, raising her eyes to his concern.

From the conversation so far, it didn't sound like Mieux knew the truth of what was really happening. And Roman wasn't her biggest fan, wasn't any kind of fan. Struan might think he had sway with his brother. He didn't. Yeah, he was the only one to speak up against Roman, but his brother did what he wanted regardless.

"I can get you a lawyer," Mieux offered. "If you want someone to go over it on your behalf. It'll cost—"

"I'll pay for it."

"You don't get to pay for it, Stru. You're on the Lowe train, it's another conflict of interest."

"Priest'll pay for it."

The best friend she'd never seen. What kind of best friend avoided said friend at all times?

On a single nod, Mieux smiled. "That works."

"He's got to have a tab with Brooker already, or Breckenridge do, and—"

"He has his own account," Mieux said then faltered a little. "I mean, I—"

"With Brooker?"

"No. A private account."

"Oh, yeah?" Struan smirked again, clearly amused. "With little Mieux Penrose? The woman who takes on no regular clients?"

"Ha, yeah, ha, it's nothing sordid, he had some… personal business. I took care of it for him."

Her curiosity couldn't stretch into someone else's relationship when her own was a hot mess. A real hot mess and a fake relationship, man, she had talent in all the wrong places.

"It's a conflict of interest for Struan to pay for my lawyer?"

"Yeah, because he works with, and is related to, the other party in your NDA. It could be argued, if it came to it, that the lawyer they paid was biased."

"Yeah, I get that one. How does it relate to what you said before, a conflict of interest, about the interviews?"

"The show Roman's on, the one he signed on for, it's produced by WMC."

"I don't understand what that—"

"Whey Media Conglomerates," Struan answered.

"I know that but—"

"Our friends, and their proffered opportunities, the ones we'd ideally like you to choose, are associated with WMC's leading competitor: CollCom."

"Why would Roman sign up with his friends' competition?"

Both Struan and Mieux laughed. "They're not Roman's friends." Did he have any of those? "My friends, Tripp's friends."

"She could do the Stream Queen."

"Yeah," Struan said, returning to the tablet. "Might not officially be CollCom, but everyone knows, personally… He's marrying her best friend."

"Married already, depending who you ask."

"Stream Queen?" she asked.

"Lomond's Delight," Mieux explained. "Roxie Kyst."

"I… Wait, I…"

"She'll do us the favor?"

Mieux gestured at the tablet. "You see it yourself."

"They still in LA?"

"Last part of the documentary airs this week."

"Then it's back to New York?"

All of this talk, their back and forth, all of the… How was one person expected to absorb so much so fast?

"I need a cab," she said, retreating from the island.

"A cab?"

"I don't have a phone or any numbers, if someone could—"

"Your car's waiting in the driveway." Mieux gathered her things. "Standard Brooker treatment." Yeah, for other people. "And your phone is waiting in it."

And that shook some of the shock off. "My phone? How did you get—"

"Other things have been taken upstairs to your bedroom."

"You went into my apartment? You went through my things?"

"Not Mieux." Struan's hand landed on her shoulder. "That'll be Magnus. Can you give us a minute, U?"

"Sure. I'll wait in the car."

After the brunette left, Struan turned her to face him. "Don't sign anything today, okay? A lawyer friend owes me a favor."

"A friend?"

"Javier Perez, his name doesn't matter, anything you get, forward it to me and I'll put it in front of him. Even if it's not his area, he'll know someone."

"I can't forward anything to you, I don't have your number or email."

"Right." Digging his phone from his pocket, he unlocked it and handed it to her. "Put your number in there, your email, I'll send my details."

Except when he offered the phone, hesitation lingered. "I shouldn't—we shouldn't. I'm not your responsibility and—"

"I got you into this mess, didn't I?" They got into it together. In that basement. In the dark. Alone. "Trust me, Fawn, please."

That was what scared her. She did trust him. Misguided or not, she did. The instinct that pulled them together the night they met still magnetized them. While that was at work, trying to resist him was pointless.

Taking the phone, she did as asked and handed it back. "Maybe I'm an idiot, but I do. I do trust you, Struan."

Exploring him as he scrutinized her, their need held them together. She didn't want to walk away. In all of this, it was only with him she felt safe.

"The energy…" he said, showing his own vulnerability. "It only happens with you, Fawn."

She could argue. Tell him that he was attractive and plenty of women would desire… except she couldn't. His twin shared his face; looks meant nothing. She'd never felt anything in Roman's company, not like the power fizzing around this guy.

"I have to…" Gesture, she should gesture, but damn, she didn't want to walk away. "Will I see you later?"

"Guarantee it."

ELEVEN

"I KNOW THIS IS A LOT."

Mieux's voice stole her awareness from… somewhere. Who was she kidding? Only one thing played on her mind. One man.

"Yeah."

In the provided car, on their way to work, she needed something normal to invest herself in or this would consume her.

"Brooker will do what they can to keep you safe, keep you comfortable."

"Except Roman's paying for it, right?"

"Yes," Mieux said with enough confusion to draw her eye. "Why wouldn't you trust your boyfriend wants the best for you?"

Right, her boyfriend. That again.

"I'm not accustomed to this, any of this, it's… exhausting."

"I can imagine. If there's anything you need or concerns, don't worry about bringing them to me. It's my job to look after you."

"It's like stepping into a movie halfway through," she said, shifting to lose some of her slouch. "Listening to you and Struan… There's this whole world of… so many names, and people, and alliances. I don't belong in this."

"Being with Roman, there are only two names you need to know. Magnus Anders and Struan Lowe. They're Roman's closest confidantes. They'll never steer you wrong. They care about what he cares about."

Except Roman didn't give a crap about her.

"You have an unusual name. Do you spell it M-E-W?"

That was how it was said.

"It's French, M-I-E-U-X."

"Makes you stand out."

"Which isn't always a good thing." The assistant unlocked her tablet again. "Do you want to go through some of these interview and appearance requests? I don't have to send any hard yeses or nos right now, but it would be good for me to know your gut reactions to them."

"Why?"

"Because at some point, if you don't do it, someone else will tell me to approve or reject each of these requests. I can only argue your side if I know what it is."

"I can't come up with any argument for or against—"

"Let me worry about the argument, just share your thoughts."

"Honestly? I'd reject them all. Why would anyone want to speak to me?"

"The public are curious. Roman's been in the news on and off for years. It hasn't been the easiest road for him. Now he's got the show, he's with a new woman, his life is looking up. Don't be surprised if the world believes you're the reason for his salvation."

"Me?"

"As I'm sure you know, he was with Sway Sheridan for years, that was a tumultuous relationship, always some new story, some new scandal. They were mostly related to his addiction issues, but you know how the press sensationalizes everything." Did she know that? Not from the inside. "*Undercover Ops* is Roman's chance to get back on top." Had they known each other a long time or was Mieux spouting a script? "Like I said, you must know all this, stop me before I offend you."

Luckily, she wasn't easily offended… or was she? Roman managed it with little effort.

"Isn't it late in the year to start shooting?" she asked, nudging the conversation in a slightly different direction.

"Oh, preproduction started months ago, Roman wasn't even in the original pilot."

"He wasn't in the pilot? Why did they switch to—"

"Other guy got arrested." Oh, well, that was a good reason. "Less said about that…" Yeah, agreed. "The studio still wanted it." And Roman got the gig. Maybe not a smart idea to go from a guy in prison to a guy with addiction issues. Maybe it was a tale of redemption, who knew? "Didn't Roman tell you all this?"

Hmm, shit, yeah, she shouldn't be asking a stranger questions about the guy she was supposed to be marrying.

"We don't talk much about work."

"You were okay with the Sway stuff?"

"Sway?"

"You weren't on the island, were you and Roman together before—" Stopping, the woman exhaled and dropped her shoulders. "Sorry. Not my business. So we have the talk shows, online influencers are—"

"Really I don't want to…"

"Okay," Mieux said. "I'll handle it."

They stopped outside the Brooker building and the car door was opened almost immediately. What a turnaround. She'd seen people pull up and the suited doormen greet them before, she'd never been one of them, never even imagined she might be.

A security guy joined her and Mieux in the elevator. Was he there for her? Was this a…? No, she didn't need security. Why would she need security at her own workplace?

The security guy hit ten, ha, good. She reached for four, the floor she worked on, only to have Mieux intercept her hand.

"You don't work on four anymore."

She didn't? Wow, what a way to get a promotion.

On the tenth floor, she got out first, with Mieux at her back, and… yeah, the security guy was with them. Fuzz.

A boardroom in the far corner was already full of people. Mieux came to her side and nodded toward it. No way. She was going into a boardroom with—this was a bad idea. How did this become her life? And she was completely without a net, of any kind.

She stopped. "Can I, uh, use the restroom first?"

"Sure," Mieux said.

Her gaze went left to right. "I don't know where it is."

"Right." Mieux adjusted course and led her to a corridor and opened a door. "We'll wait out here."

Yeah, 'cause no one needed to hear her pee. She wasn't under arrest, though it kinda felt that way.

Checking all the stalls were empty, she went into the last one and grabbed her phone from her purse. Thank God Struan followed through because he was her first call, the only call.

"Fawn?"

"I can't do this."

"Do what?" His concern was instant. "What is it?"

"There is a boardroom full of people," she hissed under her breath, cupping her mouth near the microphone. "They are going to ask questions. I'm not qualified to do this. I was an idiot in the car with Mieux, asking stupid questions about *Undercover Ops*."

"Questions your boyfriend should've answered?" He exhaled. "Shit, baby, I'm sorry, we didn't prep you for this."

"I don't think there is prep for this. No one can prep for this. Now there's NDAs and people want interviews. Why were you on the island? The Pacific island?"

"With Mieux? Don't read into that, baby, it was work. A dumb competition thing meant to improve Ro's image. Course he screwed it up."

Like he screwed everything up. And instead of judging Struan for putting up with it, she ached to comfort him.

"Why wasn't I there?"

"People will want the story," he said, getting her meaning without missing a beat. "We should've come up with a narrative. I'll talk to Priest."

His best friend. "Why would—"

"Because things went down on the island, we'll need to prep Sway."

"People will ask her about us too, won't they?"

"She's been doing this a long time, she's a pro, but someone has to look out for her."

This guy cared about everyone. Roman cared about no one. Maybe there was a set amount of empathy imparted on a fetus and somehow Struan got Roman's dose too.

Though she didn't want to be pathetic, she asked, "Can you come here?"

A beat. "Me… or Roman?"

God, she didn't even know how to answer that. She wanted Struan's support, trusted him to have her back. If Roman showed up… Maybe he meant him as Roman. God, it was complicated.

"I'm sorry, never mind. Forget I said anything—"

"I'll come down there, baby, no questions asked. You just have to tell me who you want me to show as 'cause Roman is due on set. They're refilming the pilot. Roman wasn't in it, he wasn't the guy set to—"

"Mieux told me."

"Your stupid questions." Though he immediately grumbled. "I'm sorry we set this up and turned you loose. It isn't fair. I can tell Mieux—"

"I don't want more people lying for us."

And as frustrating or annoying as this situation might be, she had to remember that it was her actions that put them there. Her and Struan's. Even if she hadn't known who he was, she still shouldn't have been so forward, so willing to sink into him, so eager.

"I'm sorry I got us into this, baby."

This wasn't all his fault. "You think if the power hadn't come back on we'd still be down there?" she asked. "In the basement?" The point of the question was to ease the mood, though it didn't do that. Instead, it cranked the crackle to a sizzle; goosebumps rushed across her skin. "On that bed… you and me… alone…"

"I think if I could choose to be anywhere in the world right now, it would be back there with you. Anywhere alone with you."

His support lessened some of her burden. "I can be vague with them, nod along. Do what I'm told, but…"

"If you need me there, I'll be there."

How many questions would that raise? If he was Roman, okay, maybe, sure, her boyfriend would want a say, but he couldn't be in two places at once. Roman couldn't be on set, where he was supposed to be, and there at Brooker with her. Or he could, if they wanted the ruse revealed.

If either twin showed up for her, no one could be filming. They didn't need Roman seeming more unreliable. And he'd lord it over them if the situation went that way. More than that disgrace, she didn't want Roman at Brooker. If he showed up, she didn't trust him to care about her or help her out of awkward situations.

"If I screw this up—"

"You can't screw it up. It's karma. Whatever happens, it's not your fault."

"You sure?"

"Positive, Fawn. And if you want to walk on out of there—"

"This is my job, I can't do that. I still have to make rent." Whether she was living in her apartment or not. "I'll need somewhere to live when this is over."

When she went back to her life. Was she going to do that? What life? Would it even be possible, or would she always be known as Roman Lowe's ex? A jilted, dumped, humiliated fiancée? Somehow, she could tell this wouldn't end with everyone smelling sweet and innocent.

This was a fast education. A baptism of fire she'd rather douse. Struan's comment about this being Roman's life, not his, started to make sense. Somehow, she was on that same rollercoaster. This wasn't the life she chose, and couldn't make decisions for herself, none that would damage Roman.

Without looking both ways, she'd stepped out

into the street and been swept up by the Roman Lowe Express. No stops, no takebacks, just Roman at the wheel while the rest of them held on for dear life.

"You don't have to worry about money, Fawn, I'll cover whatever you need, but I wouldn't ask you to detonate your life. Just keep your phone close. If you need me, call. I'll pick up… Do you want me to call you back in a few minutes? Get you out the room?"

"No," she said and sighed. "I can do this. I'm sorry I—this is just all happening so quickly."

"Don't say more than you have to, don't ask anything you don't want to lead to other questions. You can text me, ask questions, call whenever you can. I'm with you on this, Fawn. I promise. I'm there with you."

"Thank you for letting me vent."

"Always, baby."

And the smile in those words reinforced her armor. Do this. She could do this.

On leaving the restroom, Mieux was at the opposite side of the hall with the security guy a little further down.

"Thank you," she said as they returned to their route.

"Good?"

Just a mild panic attack. "I'm good."

"Don't let it overwhelm you. If you want to step out or need a break, just give me the nod and we'll leave. You're in charge. Don't forget you're with the heartthrob, the one they want to impress, the one you can influence." Uh, no, not even slightly, but she couldn't confess that. Lowering her volume, Mieux leaned in when they stopped outside the boardroom. "They want your approval. Let them fawn over you. You don't owe these people anything." She smiled. "You get to share your bed with the hot, rich, famous guy tonight, every night. This is for him."

For Roman? No. If she cast Struan in that role…

"Thanks."

"It's what I'm here for."

When Mieux opened the door, everyone quieted. Renata was there, right in the middle of the room. The woman who'd owned her life just a few hours ago didn't seem so confident anymore.

"Bambi, we had no idea," Renata said. "If you'd said something…"

"She doesn't have to clue us in on her personal life. What's important is we know now."

Great. Except who the hell was that. Who were any of these people?

"I'm not looking for special treatment. I just want to do my job."

"Sure, yes." Renata beamed. "To make things easier, we wiggled roles around a little, so we'll be working on set."

"On set?"

Was that a good thing? What set? She couldn't mean Roman's set… could she?

"Perry and I will join you. And Mieux, of course, she'll make sure everything is just right for you."

Three months in LA and already someone was offering to peel her grapes. Impressive. If that had ever been her goal. It hadn't. So much for Struan calming her down. Her last dose of him was wearing off, she needed his coaching, needed him, again already.

TWELVE

SHE'D NEVER BEEN on a movie set, or a TV show set, or any kind of set. The hubbub of activity was wonderous to witness. Or it might be if her head wasn't already full.

Most of the people at the Brooker Agency meeting hadn't spoken a word. Which was fine because she hadn't either. Mieux was on the ball, taking notes, asking questions, and accepting commands as they were dished out by Renata and her supervisors. It was only a few seconds before the meeting ended that it struck her why there were so many purposeless people present: her.

They wanted a look at the small-town girl who'd come to Hollywood, hit the jackpot, and stolen the heart of one of the best-known, handsomest, faces in town. No one acknowledged that his face was so recognizable because of his scandalous exploits, not his acting talent. Maybe that was it, maybe it was exactly that. His face was recognizable for all the wrong reasons, yet she'd caught his eye and turned him around. Her, the opposite of wild, had tamed the untamable.

Funny, she'd moved away from home to experience new things and take risks. Men. Jobs. Opportunities. Adventures. Whatever came her way, she was supposed to embrace each chance, to be untameable herself, kinda. And there she was, tied down by a man, and a job, opportunities she didn't want, and escapades outside her control. Not that she wanted escapades with the man tethering her.

Struan. He'd be a different escapade. One she'd embrace.

After dispensing with the formalities at Brooker, they'd been driven to the set of *Undercover Ops* and escorted through security without a hitch. They were directed to chairs and told to wait, that someone would be along to speak to them. So they waited… and waited.

Outside in the fresh air and glorious sunshine, they only got peeks at what might be going on inside the huge soundstage. It didn't look like any filming was taking place. Though she hadn't seen Roman, and didn't know what any of the surrounding people did. How accurate were her uneducated assumptions? Not even a little.

She didn't care about seeing her supposed fiancé and wasn't looking for him. Given the choice, she'd avoid him at all costs. If he wanted her time, he'd have to get in line behind the Lowe at the front of that queue: Struan.

From that angle, she couldn't see fully inside the main soundstage, she could, however, see into the smaller building next to it. With its massive doors wide open, shadow concealed some of its secrets. But it didn't hide him. The Lowe she'd kissed, the Lowe who'd held her. The Lowe who'd looked out for her, supported her.

After the fact anyway.

He should've told her who he was in the hotel basement. She should be angrier that he hadn't. Why was she giving him a pass? Why did she accept what happened?

Because he did what he did for family. That's why. Revealing himself would've exposed his brother's secret. That left Struan two options. Embrace the moment and surrender, as she had, to the intangible force attracting them to each other. Or shut down, sit there cold and quiet and distant. Where would they be if he'd chosen that course? Not there, no, they'd be apart, strangers…Did she want a life free of Struan?

He hadn't noticed her spying on him doing his job, not as far as she could tell. He and a dozen other guys were talking and practicing fight sequences in slow motion. Though all big guys, well-built and strong, some seemed more confident than others. All looked to the mesmerizing man at the helm, the one she couldn't tear her eyes from. Even his abrupt actions seemed precise, choreographed. He was so careful, yet definite, in the way he worked each muscle. Was it art? Function? Both.

Why hadn't she asked about what he did day-to-day for his brother? There, busy, in some kind of leadership role, nothing was hidden, certainly not his existence. Hmm, curious, she'd tap that well later. Since the truth came out, they hadn't spent much time talking. With so much she didn't know, communication was important.

Elbow on the arm of the high wood and canvas chair, she relaxed her head against the heel of her hand, resting her curled fingers on the front of her chin. Damn, he was hot, which was nothing to do with the way he looked, okay, yeah, he was easy on the eyes too. That wasn't all though, he exuded it, that energy, the enticing force didn't let up for a second.

Struan Lowe. He'd kept her safe and calm when everything went wrong. He'd stepped in for her, looked out for her, apologized to her.

Struan Lowe, whose main concern when first seeing her on that new day was her wellbeing.

Renata and Perry were talking to each other, she could hear the murmur of their conversation but chose not to involve herself or pick out specifics. From the frequency of words passed between them, she guessed their excitement matched what anyone would feel on their first time in such a dynamic environment.

Although not at the most advantageous angle, her lips curled when Struan eventually noticed her. With any other man, she might be embarrassed about being caught drooling. Not with him. Her smile was rooted in his. His attention flicked over her to dart back, his reaction to her presence mirrored hers. Could she be just as enticing? Actually, his interest went a step further. In that second, his lips stopped moving and his body took over, instantly setting course for her.

Correcting her posture, her shoulders went back and hands dropped to her lap. Should she go meet him? Would it be too eager to jump off the chair and run to him? The hurrying over part would quickly be forgotten by onlookers when she threw herself against him.

Why was she so obsessed? They'd seen each other earlier, not that long ago. She shouldn't want to embrace the joy and thrust herself away from the chair to leap into his arms. That was crazy and not something she'd done with any other man… ever.

This wasn't the crescendo of any chick flick or holiday movie that saw the main characters finally coming together. Their story had barely begun. They didn't have a story. Weren't supposed to have a story. Did they have a story?

Confusion must have shown on her face because his eyes narrowed, though his pace didn't slow.

Roman never entered her thoughts unless someone brought him up. She and everyone else on the inside understood why. There wasn't even an inkling of interest, of acknowledgment. It wasn't just that she wanted to be near Struan, to be in his arms, talking to him, or just alone in that basement without power, once again.

Struan Lowe felt vital to her existence.

Her faux fiancé wasn't the only one to pale into insignificance. No man matched up. It hadn't occurred to her to look at any of the men in the vicinity. Even those in shorts or shirtless were invisible. Actors and crew members clearly used to the LA way with impressive physiques, perfect tans, and a sparkle in their eye were meaningless.

She wasn't a lioness on the Serengeti out desperate for any meal. She wasn't looking to sink her teeth into someone and never let go in hopes of holding on to the Hollywood dream. Hollywood meant nothing. The TV show meant nothing. WMC, CollCom, big company names were thrown around like she should be awed. She didn't care. The only thing that distracted her was the glimmer of jealousy that Mieux knew what Struan did with parsnips. Even if the result was hideous, she wanted a taste.

He got halfway to her when someone touched her shoulder. She turned and there was Mieux approaching with two men in her wake.

"Tommy and Teddy," Mieux said, pointing at one then the other. Yeah, she wouldn't remember that. "A couple of other guys work with them too. They're the film crew."

"For *Undercover Ops*?"

Everybody laughed like she'd missed something. Okay, so she'd missed something. Was it funny she'd missed something?

"Oh, no," said Teddy, maybe Tommy. "We're doing a *Making of…* special. We followed some of the preproduction and we'll film through the reshoot of the pilot with Roman. Right through every stage of prep, filming, press, everything. It's great exposure, especially these days, when you have to keep up an online presence and really hype what's coming, what's new."

"Okay," she said, neither impressed nor interested.

Maybe it wasn't subtle, but she twisted just a little while brushing her hair from her brow. Struan was rooted to the spot he'd stopped on when she got up. The space between his eyelids hadn't grown, but he didn't seem confused or concerned anymore. He was pissed off these two men got to her before he did, before he could.

She tried to smile while simultaneously attempting to conceal the truth of her fascination in turning back to the others.

Mieux, thank goodness, had her hand on the wheel. "You'll be working with them."

"I'll be working with them? Just me. Where will Renata and Perry be?"

"No! All of us will be working together," Renata said and looped an arm through hers as though they were besties.

When did that shift in their relationship happen? She'd missed the memo.

"Whatever your team needs, we'll provide. Leslie thought it was a good idea to keep a little separation between you and Roman, if you don't mind. Roman agreed with the idea."

"I know he did," she said like he'd already clued her in.

"You do?" Teddy asked, his eyes flicking to each of the faces around him. "We just got done with that conversation."

"We talked about it before."

Shooting for confidence may be a bad idea, but

she had to own it. On asking questions, she seemed peculiar and out of touch. When she didn't, she hit presumptuous and grabby. Would she ever get the balance right?

The physical link with her supervisor didn't last long, thank goodness. Renata and Perry were quick to follow the guys.

Mieux quickly took her place, using the connection to slow and put some space between them and the others. "Are you okay?"

"Yeah, I'm fine. We shouldn't miss what the others—"

"I'm here for you." Which had been said many times. "Do you want to find Roman?"

"No, he's working."

"Struan?" How did she not react to that? Eyes front. Keep walking. "My job involves discretion."

"I read Brooker's handbook too."

Was she getting snarky? None of this was Mieux's problem or fault.

"Not like this." Mieux pulled them to a halt. "I don't talk about my clients; I don't puff myself up. I pride myself on what I do. My job is the most important thing in my life; it's all I have."

Had someone said something or was this seemingly innocuous woman sharper than she let on?

Could be that, or she was taking a chance at grabbing some gossip. Something told her Mieux wouldn't be trusted by the people who trusted her if she was untrustworthy.

Huh?

"We should catch up with the others."

Though the *Making of...* crew were generous in their tour, too many eyes stalked her. She couldn't stand it. How could anyone stand it? Okay, so these people were just getting to know Roman. Maybe. She'd hit the headlines at exactly the point his *Undercover Ops* colleagues were most curious.

But shit, did people actually covet this kind of attention?

At the craft table, where crew and cast, lowly cast, socialized, they stalled.

Inside the soundstage everything moving and static had a place. Had a purpose. Needed to be there to bring the vision of—

"Bambi?" The man smiling at her made a point of blocking her from the others. "It's an honor to meet you."

Why? Because he believed her to be nailing the star of the show? Quite an honor.

"Are you Teddy or Freddy?"

"Tommy."

"Right. Sorry." And uh… "It's nice to meet you too."

"I hope you don't mind me asking, but is he like they say? That passionate?"

"You haven't met?"

Damn, was that another of her stupid questions?

"No, not yet, he stays on the back lot. The back, back lot. We don't have much time here, though I do hope we'll get some sound bites before we head out on location."

On location? She clamped her jaw tight. Location? Sure, they were going on location, she knew that. Just what location would that be?

Ah, ha, maybe she'd get a reprieve. She could stay behind while her boyfriend—wait, no. Damnit. She couldn't stay behind if Brooker were sticking with the production of these Making guys.

"A lot of fun to be had," she said on an awkward laugh.

What the hell did that mean? Maybe they

should've told everyone she didn't speak the language. Would be easier on all of them.

THIRTEEN

"BAMBI!"

God, she was popular. At least Mieux's voice was familiar. And welcome, she needed the interruption.

Tommy stepped aside to let her colleague—not calling her an assistant—and another guy get close.

"Randall Fichman," the new guy said, offering a hand. "Randy."

"Randy is the showrunner. This is his ship, bow to stern."

"Keel to crow's nest, only while things are running smooth. If things go the other way, it's some other guy's fault." Mieux joined in the fake laugh, saving her the trouble. Hopefully her smile sold her camaraderie. "Tick…" Randy gestured yet another new face over. Younger than the others, confident, though the exterior wasn't faultless. Finally someone who felt her pain. "Show Bambi round back. Put her in Roman's trailer."

"Oh no, I shouldn't—"

"He'll want to see you, and we've got time. Take

the chance now 'cause when things get underway, it could be a while 'til we take a break."

Randy walked off, Tommy darted after him, clamoring to get his airtime.

"Want me to come with you?"

"Oh no, I'm good," she said to Mieux. The fewer witnesses, the better. "I'll catch up with you…"

Somewhere. Thankfully, Tick had started moving, so she had to hurry to catch up. No time for follow up questions.

They wound around equipment and hopped over wires. She found herself stepping almost exactly where Tick did, for fear she might break something, like her neck.

When he pushed open the side door, light burst, startling her eyes. But it was welcome. Being outside, even in concrete and modernity, was better than the stifling indoors.

"This is his," Tick said, turning the handle to open the trailer door.

In there or not, she was left with little choice but to ascend the stairs and listen to the door close behind her.

Hmm. Now what was she supposed to do?

Recessed lighting. Blinds pulled down over every window. Roman wasn't there, that she could see, but she could smell him in the air. Yep, definitely his space. Exactly where she didn't want to be.

A TV, a fireplace, couches, a kitchen… wow, talk about full spec. Going to sit on the couch, she perched on the edge. Already living in the guy's house felt wrong, being there in another of his private spaces—

The door opened and she shot to her feet. Struan leaped inside and tossed something to the kitchen counter. Then he noticed her. If he'd been intending to leave immediately, that plan quickly evaporated.

"Hi," he said first, letting the door fall back into its frame.

Rather than the awkwardness she'd expected, a different kind of aura settled on them.

"Hi." Just looking at the man excited her. She needed to get a grip. "Where's Roman?"

"Makeup."

So it was just them… alone.

She slipped her hands into her back pockets. "You're busy."

"No, I… left some notes on the script for him."

No? That couldn't be further from the truth. Not the script thing, that was probably what he'd tossed to the counter. But she'd been watching him out there, for a while, he definitely had a full dance card. Though he didn't seem to be in any hurry to run off.

Time to start tapping. "What do you do here?"

"In the trailer?"

She laughed. "On set. I never asked what—you can't be playing Roman here too."

"I'm his stunt double, his body double."

It wasn't so wrong her eyes gave that body a once-over, was it?

"Your whole life revolves around him."

"I like what I do."

Good, he deserved some satisfaction.

"Body double," she said, "is that like… intimate scenes?"

He exhaled his own laugh. "Sometimes, but it's not like you think. Intimate scenes aren't that… intimate. It's about lighting and movement, little else."

"That supposed to make me feel better?" Her hands slid loose as she strolled toward him. "About you getting naked with gorgeous women?"

"I missed that." As she stopped, he leaned in. "When'd you get naked with me?" Her head tilted in question. "I hear 'gorgeous,' all I think is you."

So maybe she wasn't the only one obsessed.

"I'm sorry I didn't... I should've asked about your life."

"My job is low on the list of things you've got to worry about right now. What happened at Brooker?"

"Everyone wanted to gawp, just like here. It's probably why they hid me in here 'cause I know for sure Roman didn't ask for me."

"He's in makeup."

Which he'd already said. Their eyes met as her fingertips reached the fabric of his tee-shirt.

"Thank you."

"For what?"

"Supporting me," she said. "I wouldn't have got through this without you."

As her hands glided around him, he caught her shoulders. "You don't want to do that."

"I don't?"

Why was it like they shared a mind? This wasn't a rejection, instinct, and searing need betrayed that without words. This wasn't an indifferent, unaroused man.

"I have to confess—"

"Don't tell me," she whispered, choosing to skim her palms up as opposed to around. "Show me."

In the inevitable clash of their mouths, he dipped to catch her thighs as she threw her arms around his neck. Neither cared who was first, who instigated, who provoked, all came together in unison and consent.

Locking her arms tight, she pulled herself higher, forcing his head back as her spine hit the wall. Wall? What wall? This man was her wall, her stability, the clench that tightened around her veins holding her atoms together.

His powerful forearms supported her legs while

his fingers dug deep into her ass. This was what she wanted, her life's blood. The heat of his tongue pushing hers back, tempting her deeper, all she could think about was—she landed flat on her back, somewhere hard, soft… a bed.

"Stru," she whispered, losing her fingers in his hair, raising her hips, pushing against him.

A startling bang separated their mouths.

"We're on, Ro!" someone shouted from outside.

Fighting her shallow breathing, she might be looking Struan in the eye, but she wasn't giving him leeway to rise further. No, her arms were staying tight around him, for as long as they could.

"I have to go get him," he said, drawing in a long nasal inhale, mesmerized by her mouth. "Want me to apologize?"

"No."

Licking her lips, satisfaction burst around her heart when the need in his gaze flared.

"Good. Because I won't." And she could lay there all day under his adoration. "I saw you first."

Still clamped around him, her hips ascended, pushing, writhing, begging while making a promise.

"Am I your toy?" she asked, unable to refute being his.

"Oh, baby, if wishing made it so." A dimple. "Roman'll be shooting at least a couple of hours. Stay in here. Away from the gawpers. My trailer's two down, gray stripe on the door."

"Can I hang out there instead?"

"As soon as I come up with a good reason you'd be there rather than here." He kissed her again. "This is better."

"This?"

"You here," he said on another glimmer of a smile. "If you were in my trailer, I'd never leave it."

If they were in that place, she wouldn't have released him from their bed before leaving the house.

"I haven't decided if I'll let you go from here yet." Dragging her knees higher, she squeezed herself even closer. "It's only with you I feel whole."

On his next kiss, she relaxed. What an idiot. Why did she say that? Whatever was going on between them, it was too early to confess her own secret. Even after her arms and legs loosened, he stayed right there on top of her.

"Hold that thought," he murmured against her lips.

"I'm sorry, I shouldn't—"

"No apologies," he said, meeting her eye again. "We're going to figure this out, Fawn." After another kiss, he vaulted to his feet, and stayed there at the side of the bed, admiring her. "Now you're just lying in my brother's bed."

He extended an arm, offering a hand. The moment she took it, he pulled her onto her feet, then she was in his embrace. For a guy with a job to do, he wasn't rushing to do it. Not that she was complaining.

"Next time make it yours."

The pride of his satisfaction wrapped her in seduction. "Yes, ma'am." And if he kept looking at her like that, they might end up on the floor. "I'll send Mieux in to hang out. Watch a movie, there's food in the fridge."

"Does she know?" she asked. "Mieux?"

"Not explicitly, but she has a way of knowing everything. Don't underestimate her. She can be trusted a hundred percent."

That was good to know. Only what was she asking? That Mieux knew her and Roman's engagement was bullshit, or that her and Struan were…

"I'll come find you when I can."

She pulled him down for another kiss and laughed at his groan as they withdrew. Yeah, their lips shouldn't really be getting such a workout, but, come on, alone, in privacy, it wasn't like they could resist.

FOURTEEN

DINNER. With Roman. Life didn't get much worse. Mieux broke the news later in the afternoon, not that she could make it seem like a surprise or a negative. Yay, she was eating with her fiancé, woo hoo! Big sigh.

Didn't help that Chic, the stylist who'd led her makeover, was waiting at home to talk her through that week's designated outfits. Yes, that's right, the *week* of designated outfits. For both during the day and in the evening. It wasn't enough they'd filled the closet. No, obviously she couldn't be trusted to dress herself. Everything down to the underwear and the earrings were picked out ready to go. She and Roman hadn't crossed paths on the *Undercover Ops* set, but she was sure he was responsible for the strict instruction all the same.

Didn't make much difference to her what she wore, so she went along, doing as told, because what difference did it make?

She put on the dress, the shoes, curled her hair as instructed, and spritzed on the perfume left by accessories in her closet.

Outside in the driveway, she got into the car expecting an impatient Roman, except the backseat was empty. Huh, well, that gave her a chance to check out the fridge. There should be champagne or whiskey… Anything alcoholic would—nothing but club soda. How exciting.

With Roman being an addict, curbing temptation must be a rule. Did that mean no alcohol in the house? No, there'd been wine with dinner the previous night. Wine. Good start. She shifted along the seat intending to run in for a quick shot of something, but didn't get further than the middle.

Roman got in and slammed the door. "Where have you been?" he demanded. "What was the delay?"

Uh, attitude? Oh, wait, this wasn't the reasonable Lowe. This was the unreasonable one.

"I'm here," she said, sliding along the seat to get as far away from him as possible. "Before you."

"I was waiting in the foyer for an hour. I don't wait around for anyone."

Definitely an exaggeration. Petulant actually, like a three-year-old. Wow. What a champ.

Gravel crunched beneath the tires. Good. Go Faster. Every second that passed was one closer to being away from him. That was what to focus on. They'd drive wherever they were driving. Eat. It was dinner. She didn't need dessert or coffee or an appetizer, entree and home.

The point was to be seen, you know, happy, pleased to be with the man she loved. No scandal. No headlines.

Maybe she should have asked for acting lessons.

No, her attitude was all wrong. Everything she knew of Roman was skewed by her first impression of him the morning they met. That was an intense time, high pressure, maybe he wasn't as bad as she thought. Sure, Struan and Mieux and everyone she'd met seemed to agree he was high maintenance. Still, if this was going to be her life, she had to make the most of it.

A good motivator? This man meant something to Struan who meant a lot to her.

"How did you get into acting?" she asked, setting her purse on her lap, determined to find some common ground.

"Have you never heard of the internet? Anything you want to know is—"

"I don't know how long this will last. How long we'll have to see each other, live with each other, but it's going to be more than just tonight. Unless you have some secret plan I know nothing about?" No response. "So we should find something, don't you think? Something we can talk about."

If nothing else, by all accounts, he loved to talk about himself.

Tension in his body pulsed, as though it was his instinct to argue; it quickly deflated again.

"We did it at school," he muttered. "And there was a drama club thing my father took us to. Struan wanted to know how everything worked, the lights, the camera, how actors prepared. I loved being on stage, even in rehearsal, being up there commanding a room felt right."

His typical scowl loosened. She could almost see a glimmer of Struan in him, which was the first time she'd seen either of them in the other. Just because they looked alike didn't mean their souls were the same.

"Is there anything I should know? We're going to dinner together and shouldn't embarrass each other. I know not to order alcohol—"

"I'll order the wine," he snapped. "I'm no drunk." There was that line between his brows again. "You don't have to do anything. Don't say anything. This is an important guy. Ricardo Whey owns half this town."

And CollCom the other half, from how she heard it.

"He's in charge of *Undercover Ops*?"

"His company is. He sits in his office and makes decisions. He's important, very important. Don't be surprised if he doesn't ask your name or remember it. He's not there to see you."

That got her thinking. If Ricardo Whey was so important, why would he take a meeting with Roman Lowe? Given a choice, she wouldn't meet Roman in private. And if she was managing his career, she wouldn't want anyone else to meet him in private either. In private it was too easy to reach for the decanter, to accept one drink and another, increasing the chance he'd embarrass himself.

Putting him in a restaurant surrounded by other people gave them a time limit. Didn't it? Once the food was eaten, they could sit at the table, but would they stick around all night? Surely not.

"How long will it take to get there?"

"What the fuck do I know?" he snarked. "I don't care."

"Do you have allergies? Likes? Dislikes? What kind of place is it? What food do they serve?"

Asking other people questions about the man who'd apparently stolen her heart embarrassed her, embarrassed them, and she didn't want a repeat of that. This guy was supposed to be her boyfriend, her fiancé, shouldn't they know something about each other? He didn't seem bothered about walking in blind.

Was it really a surprise? Was Roman Lowe the type of man to know everything about a girlfriend? A serious, like forever, girlfriend? Maybe his heart was broken. It wasn't with her, she didn't want it, but maybe she should learn something about where it truly lay.

"Tell me about Sway."

That jerked his chin higher. "She's the goddamn love of my life. My woman, my soulmate." She'd never seen him so sure about anything, and with a guy as cocky as him, that was saying something. "We're destined to be together." He wouldn't be so brusque if she truly was a potential love interest, would he? Knowing what she did of Roman, it was possible. "So don't get any ideas."

Ha! He wished. Breathe. Just breathe through it. Laughing in his face wouldn't set the right tone for the night ahead.

"Why did you break up?" she asked, deserving an Oscar for her calm.

"It's none of your business. No tell-all book for you."

Yeah, like that was her goal. Knowing more about the type of woman he could love would help her enact her current role.

"Where is she now?"

"In town somewhere. People in her life are keeping us apart."

That sounded serious. People who meant her harm? Who meant him harm? Surely, if that was the case, he'd be more adamant about catching up to her, about finding her, saving her.

This was the Land of Happily Ever After. Also the Land of Death and Tragedy, Drama, Crime, Sex, and Politics. Hollywood was everything good, and nothing bad, under the perfect sheen of stage lights and heavy makeup. There, everything was translated into sound bites from contrived scripts and pumped out to the masses across the globe.

"Is anything in this town real? How do you have a relationship with someone when there's so much theater?"

"Sway and I are real. We'll always be real."

"Did you talk to her about us?"

"Stop asking questions. We've got this dinner, you'll smile nice, and then we'll be back at my place. This doesn't mean anything; you're not my girlfriend. I know it's a big deal to be seen with me, to be out with me, but if you think I'm going to jumpstart your career…"

Sour, she smiled. "You can't jumpstart your own, buddy. Everyone around you is working overtime to improve your image, and I'm a part of that effort. So yeah, this isn't real, and boy am I glad about that. I couldn't care less about you. Don't forget you're not the only one with power."

"If you even think about—"

"Acting out? Walking away? Telling the truth? Depends on you, I won't take anything off the table. You don't have the most stellar reputation when it comes to treating people well, but I'm your fiancée. You keep looking at me like that in public, you, the great actor who knows and loves his craft so well? You'll give the truth away. Everyone will know our relationship is a sham and they'll ask why."

"Struan. That's why. He fucked up. He caused this. My damn brother—"

"This is not his fault. Yes, Struan and I got close in private. We didn't know about the camera, and we didn't mean to hurt anyone. But if your reputation hadn't been in tatters in the first place, if you'd been a better man, capable of treating people well, none of this would be needed. I could have been passed off as a one-time encounter, a rebound, a moment of comfort in an intense circumstance. The press wouldn't have cared who you snuggled up with. They only care because you've burned so many bridges, and I get it now, because you're like this. That's why this is necessary, because you're so spiteful, you walk around with this undeserved hubris… I wouldn't be surprised if the press, and half of the production companies in this town, weren't gunning for you, waiting for you to fall on your face. I can't tell for sure right now, but it seems to me like it might be deserved."

"Who the hell do you think you are?"

"Look at the way you treat people, the way you treat me, your brother, Magnus, everybody. If you root for people, they root for you. *You* don't do that, you judge and sneer and snap, like you have some automatic entitlement. You look at people with disgust and disdain; I wouldn't spend any time with you by choice."

"Don't let the door hit you."

She smiled. "I made an agreement, and I'll do my part. In fact, I'm curious. Why would Ricardo Whey let his people take a chance on you?"

Whey probably didn't make a lot of day-to-day casting decisions. There had to be a thousand ongoing projects under various WMC umbrellas. Something was different about this leading man, or Whey's relationship with him.

That this dinner was taking place at all suggested one of two things: either Roman Lowe had dirt on Ricardo Whey and he blackmailed his way into the role, or there was some affection between them. Maybe the why would become clear after eating a meal with them. Something had to come of it. If Roman wasn't going to talk about himself, she'd just have to ride the rapids. Probably for the best, could she ever trust Roman to be honest anyway?

FIFTEEN

ON ARRIVING, she and Roman didn't wait for service, no doubt inflating the ego of her date. It sure didn't need any help in the size department, but the moment they were seen, he was gestured over and greeted like an old friend.

Every corner of the restaurant was dressed like it belonged on a movie screen. The lighting, the ambience, the quiet music that bracketed the susurration of conversation. Each nuance was carefully orchestrated. How many deals were being struck in those walls? How many stars being made over caviar? How many careers ended before dessert?

The pleasant smiles and affable manners of those filling its seats told a different story. The restaurant with its elegant tableware and nouveau vintage décor wouldn't be a suitable location for an executive to challenge or end someone's dream of superstardom. Talk about awkward, and, of course, the "money" didn't have time to waste on has-beens.

They quickly zigzagged around tables, beheld by

diners, to one elevated in the back corner. Had to be the best in the house. With a window and advantageous view over the rest of the room enjoying their meals, the position screamed power and status.

"Roman!" Ricardo Whey declared and stood up. How did she know it was him? Just a guess. The woman at his side rose too, smiling and accepting Roman's cheek kisses as Ricardo's attention landed on her. "And you're the secret."

Whatever that meant, but she was kind enough to accept his polite hello kiss.

Roman helped her into her seat. "The secret?" she asked.

"Yes." Ricardo gestured at his companion. "This is Raquel. She's been with me for years." As a wife? Girlfriend? Assistant? Assistant with benefits? What was allowed these days? "Knows all the ins and outs. You can't beat the stability of a good woman. They know how to keep us in check."

"Sure do. Bambi wasn't a secret," Roman said, all easy happiness. Where did that come from? He must've had a personality transplant since leaving the car. "Bambi is not used to the spotlight."

"She should be." Wearing a broad smile, Ricardo checked out her chest and expression. Hadn't he just done that when they met? "She could be a superstar. I could make her a superstar."

"No, thank you." She paired the quick refusal with a self-deprecating laugh. Agreeing to being Roman's fake fiancée unfortunately also meant not trashing the man's career. It helped that trashing Roman's meant trashing Struan's. She wouldn't do that for anything; aversion fueled restraint. "I'm happy where I am at Brooker."

"Ah," Ricardo said. A server hurried over to fill her and Roman's glasses from the bottle already at the table. Another brought a replacement. "That answers my next question."

"Which was?"

"How we met?" Roman's hand slid over hers to twine their fingers together. Quelling the instinct to pull away, she fought to dampen the cringe in her cheeks, concealing it as happiness. "You know what I'm like when I see what I want."

Roman raised their hands a few inches, rather than kiss or continue any fondness, he went for the wine instead. Good choice. A reprieve, though it may be temporary. The wine saved her skin from his lips, but may not save her from his attitude later. What did alcohol do to him? Couldn't be anything good.

"I heard Sway was in town," Ricardo said with a hint of seriousness in the set of his brow. "Are you on speaking terms?"

"Sway and I are fantastic," Roman answered. It was funny to see him say the woman's name without a weight of hatred-tinged passion propelling the word from his lips. "She's happy for me. I'm happy for her."

"Yes, her engagement. To Deacon… something. He plays in your brother's band."

"Yes."

Roman's slight head nod was curbed by another drink of wine. Excellent plan. She lifted her own and tried to be subtle about gulping rather than sipping. Her other hand was anchored on the table by his heavy affection. Immobile under his, neither of them quite knew how to show warmth without some point of connection.

This couldn't be easy on him either. Clearly, he was used to being in control, demanding what he wanted and receiving satisfaction.

With her. It wasn't like that.

He didn't want to be with her any more than she

wanted to be with him.

While pitying his profile, Raquel spoke for the first time. "I heard that's over already. Her and Deacon. Is that true?"

"She struggled," Roman said. "Without me, without us. As I would have done if I hadn't found my true purpose."

A squeeze of her hand preceded his head turning her way in her peripheral vision. Shit, he meant her. She concentrated on smiling at the other couple.

"She's turning down roles," Whey said. "Far as I hear she has nothing lined up. And I hear everything."

"If she thought she was getting married—"

"When the right thing comes along…" Whey cut Raquel off, "Sway'll make her choice."

Roman beamed. "Like *Undercover Ops*."

"Yes, something to give her an aim. A home, a place to rediscover her love of the art."

"Are you an actor, Mr. Whey?" she asked. "I know that's not your stock and trade now, but did you ever feel the call of the stage or screen?"

"Not officially," he said on a warm laugh. "Though some may argue what I do every day is pantomime."

The table's laugh felt genuine, perhaps the first she'd heard since meeting Roman Lowe.

"It's a difficult town to adjust to. I'm never sure what is real and what's pretend."

Whey leaned a little over the table. "None of us are," he murmured, still smiling. "That's the secret natives hide. Want to get along in this town? Follow the money. If the dollars are moving from their account to yours, you're doing the right thing."

That's what it was. Amassing money. Acting, directing, producing, distributing, every single avenue of entertainment media was measured by how many zeros were added to the check at the end of the day. Whether that money was coming from big studios or little kids' allowances blown on lunchboxes and action figures, it was all about the money.

"It's instinct. Those who cut their teeth in LA around stars and moguls and world-renowned names, we take it for granted. You understand how it works, what's important, who to ingratiate yourself with, and who to ignore. It's a gut feeling. You get a sense of who'll make it and who will fail."

"It can't be taught," Raquel said, gazing lovingly at the man who didn't look her way.

"What you've got to know in this town, sweetheart, is you're only as good as your next deal. Success can slip like sand from the fingers with one bad choice."

Like Roman, oops, maybe not a nice thought. Anywhere else she would have said it aloud, but not there.

"No more of them." Roman projected his voice as he puffed out his chest. Yes, he was Mr. Big Shot, in his own illusions anyway. "No more bad choices."

What was it he wanted?

Addicts wanted their next fix.

The way he guzzled the wine suggested, perhaps, a dependence. It couldn't be nerves, could it? Roman Lowe nervous? Nope, funny, not the man she knew. He'd claimed alcohol wasn't his drug of choice, that he didn't have a problem with it. Except, for a time, he'd wanted the high more than his career. He'd almost lost it in lieu of chasing the dragon. Did that drive ever truly go away?

Where did Sway fit into it?

They'd never met, but already she was fascinated. Did the woman crave attention? Play to it? Perhaps take advantage of it? Or was she like almost every other person in Roman's life, eager to be free of the exhaustion he bred?

"The past is the past," Ricardo said. "Yeah, you've made shitty choices, but the public still want you."

"They want him to succeed," she said, though it was more of a question than a statement.

As the girlfriend, fiancée, she should want her partner to succeed. Though, in truth, she didn't get it. Why were audiences still interested in a man uninterested in their adoration? A man who prioritized his addiction over their fidelity?

"You've got it or you don't," Roman said, reaching for the wine to top off his own glass, ignoring everybody else's.

"That's what they say, but a star can be made, if it serves a purpose."

"Why go to the trouble?" Roman sat tall. "Everyone is hungry."

"There's always someone waiting to take the place of anyone who falls from grace," Ricardo said. Was there a thread of warning in that tone? *Undercover Ops* was a big deal. "I'm taking a chance on you."

"It's not a chance, it's a guarantee. The role was written for me. You won't regret this. It's fate, and this is only the beginning. Pilot's going great, soon we'll be out there on location. I'll dive deep into the soul of this guy. I see it all. I see the future. Movies, books, online opportunities. This is going to be big! Its own action franchise!"

Nowhere else but in his own head so far.

"We're here tonight so I can look you in the eye. Your mama meant something to me, and Magnus owes me big for this. He tells me you're clean. Are you clean?"

"Yes."

Could be Roman was just a good actor, but she believed that too. Though his inability to attend the event where she met Struan suggested maybe he wasn't all that free and clear of his issues. She and Struan needed to talk.

Had Roman been drunk that night? Was there more to this man than she knew? She'd asked Struan if she could trust him, if he would tell her the truth. She'd stand by Roman if it meant saving everyone's jobs, Struan's job, but she didn't want her name next to an asshole's, not for anything.

"I believe in taking a man at his word. The way my dad did deals, and his dad before him. Industry standard doesn't matter. A man has integrity or he doesn't. I'm here tonight, looking you in the eye. Roman. Tell me you're not going to fuck this up."

"I'm not going to fuck this up."

Adamant though he was, she suppressed a snort. Without Magnus and Struan, and God knew who else, this guy wouldn't be able to tie his shoes in the morning.

"What's your priority? Is it this contract or will you fold if it gets tough?"

"It's this. *Undercover Ops* is my priority."

"No more fucking off to tropical islands with dozens of babes?"

"That was a means to an end."

"Yeah, and one you fucked up. You said that online contest bullshit would win us fans. Instead, it brought scandal, all the wrong type of scandal."

"Worked for Lomond."

Ricardo growled and snatched up his glass. "Don't say that man's name to me."

Touchy. What scandal had the island brought? Was it the same island Mieux and Struan spoke about? What went down with that? And Lomond? Another question mark. Who was he?

Again, she needed answers. And Struan was the only one she'd trust to give them.

SIXTEEN

UNFORTUNATELY, SHE DIDN'T see Struan. Not after dinner or the next day at work. Withdrawal made her twitchy. His lure tempted her in like a siren to the shore. Going without him wasn't part of the deal. Maybe she should've been more explicit about that. Except she hadn't known how hard it would be to be without him until enduring the anguish.

Oh, and guess what lay ahead that night? Another date with Roman. Yep, another one!

Okay, maybe if she'd thought about it, she'd have figured being fake engaged meant going out on dates with the pseudo fiancé. But every night? Seriously? Every single night? No reprieve? None at all?

The dressing up and fancy perfumes might mean a little more if she were looking forward to the evening ahead. That night it was some kind of industry party, she didn't know more than that. Mieux recited details, but she hadn't been listening. It truly didn't matter.

She put on the clothes, the jewels, the plastic smile, and would follow through on her promise. Whey put it the right way. Industry standard doesn't matter. A man has integrity or he doesn't. That went for *wo*man too.

Pep talk, come on. Another night with Roman. She could do this, smile, listen, react appropriately. Note that: appropriately, not honestly.

Though it hadn't been the point of the exercise, living as Roman's other half was a crash course in Hollywood etiquette. The truth, not the façade. A valuable education she likely wouldn't have got any other way, not so quickly. By the end of the week, she'd be a pro.

Descending the stairs to the foyer, her new heels hadn't been broken in and pinched at the back of her ankle. Hopefully this would be a fun night that wouldn't involve much standing around. These patent leather beauties were at least an inch or two higher than she'd worn thus far. Suppose it was something that the shoes gave her a focus beyond the man she desperately wanted to ignore.

Alone, again, she opened the large front door, went outside, and stopped. The limo was parked in the same position as the previous night. Except this time there was a man next to it. Not the driver, nor the man she expected.

"You're not Roman," she said to her addiction.

He exhaled a laugh. "That a problem?"

The smirk on his face betrayed he already knew the answer.

Glee was instant. And the pain in her foot? Forgotten in a heartbeat.

Hurrying to him, just like that, her attitude flipped and excitement for date night flourished.

"Get down here."

With a quick tug on his lapel, she forced him to stoop and kiss her.

Quick to withdraw, he showed more control

than she could boast. "Better keep me cool or we'll be going upstairs not out."

She'd be okay with that. Too forward? After all the effort she'd put into getting ready—who was she kidding? She'd strip naked for him in a heartbeat. Right there in the driveway if he demanded it. Oh, she wished he'd demand it.

He opened the car door and with the union of their hands, helped her into it.

"This is a treat," she said as he joined her and they got underway. "Are you my reward for good behavior?" He smiled, but the discomfort behind it, behind the amiable, polite expression, dulled her excitement. "This isn't for me. This is for him."

"I'm here because I want to be."

"What did Roman do? Is he drunk? High? Off somewhere wreaking havoc?"

Specifics may be vague, but it wasn't exactly a leap to picture Roman being a selfish thrill seeker. Was he out there cheating on her? Not her, her, the construct of her, of them. Not something she should focus too heavily on while her own hand rested so high on his brother's thigh.

"I want to be here," he said again, and scooped up her hand to kiss her knuckles. "For the first time, a night of playing my brother isn't such a bad prospect. Maybe the second time."

His next smile reminded him, reminded her, of the night they met.

"I don't care about him. I care about you. If he's out there being an idiot, or on twenty-four-hour watch so he doesn't choke on his own vomit, it affects you. You're who I care about."

"Do you know about tonight?" he asked, apparently eager to change the subject or, at least, not dwell on his twin's position. "Where we're going?"

Was it to save his own sanity? Roman's behavior had to be laborious in its repetition. Given he'd dealt with it his whole life, Struan could just be over it, or was he genuinely concerned and in need of a distraction?

"No. After Chic put my clothes out for the week, I stopped asking. Figure as long as there's no stripping or karaoke involved, I can handle most anything."

"I'm with you on the karaoke. On the stripping..." he drew out the word, raising his brows like he wouldn't be averse to that idea. Providing it was them together, alone, she wouldn't be either. "Don't worry, you're safe. It's a party, something for the studio. Bigwigs getting together, rubbing shoulders, crowing about their latest multimillion dollar deal, or the last billion dollars they made at the box office."

So she may be standing around. "Easier than dinner. If it's a party, we don't have to stay too long with any one group."

"No." He curved an arm around her hips to pull her even closer. "And there's dancing; I'll be allowed to put my arms around you."

Tipping up her chin, she leaned in. "You're always allowed."

He kissed her quick. "Just remember my name tonight."

Talk about extinguishing the passion. "I'd rather refrain from using any name at all than call you him, call you by his name."

"Whatever you decide."

He took her hand to his lips again. Would they ever be them, just them, without Roman's specter spoiling every moment?

"How long have you had to do this? Have you been out with other women for him?"

"Sway, but she knew the deal. Anyone less committed didn't get an explanation. His worst years were with Sway. I don't know how she put up with him. I honestly don't."

And, at the same time, she questioned how he'd done the same thing his whole life. "I'm curious about her. And there are things I... I hoped we'd get a chance to talk, but didn't see you at work."

"Me and the guys were off-site, preparing for Vancouver."

"Is that where we're going on location? What's the plan?"

"You'll have a place to sleep. I'll keep a spot warm for you, don't worry about that."

She feigned a swoon. "My hero."

"Just looking out for you, baby."

"I'm happy you're prepping, confident in your ability. If it was anyone else, I wouldn't be so sure."

"You're biased."

No denying that. "And proud of it."

"You're taking UO by storm."

"UO?" She frowned. "*Undercover Ops*? I am?"

"Yeah, everyone's impressed, confused how Roman bagged you."

"Something else he can thank you for."

"You assert yourself and still make friends. You're doing really well."

"I refused to be put back into isolation. I might not have experience filming TV shows, but I can muck in."

"That's what I'm hearing. No job too big or small. People like you... which puts them in an awkward position."

And that she got in an instant. "Because they don't like Roman?"

"They don't know him that well yet. Most aren't sure how to approach him. Those who've tried never know which Roman they'll get. Happy, personable, humble—"

"Humble? Ha!" She laughed. "Humble? I've never seen that side of him."

"He can pull it off, he's an actor."

"Don't I know it. During dinner with Whey I kept reminding myself. He was so different from the man I knew."

"You did well last night too, sorry I wasn't there."

"You can't be running around after me every minute. I understand your brother can be tedious, but he's never endangered me." Yet, the word stayed in her head. Roman had done little to suggest he was any kind of predator, yet she never quite felt completely safe with him. "Why did Whey give him the role in *Undercover Ops*?"

"Ricardo Whey doesn't make casting decisions on—"

"Are you giving me a scripted answer?"

His laugh at her offense only tightened his hold. "He had a thing with our mom a million years ago, before we were born. Never asked for the details but Magnus knows, something anyway, doubt he went past the broad strokes. Why would he want to wade in like that?"

He wouldn't with his own sister's sex life. "Whey said Magnus owed him big for this."

"He does."

"Shouldn't it be Roman who pays any debt?"

"If he pulls this off, it works for everyone."

And if he didn't...

"Who's Lomond?" she asked while she had him.

His frown came to her in curiosity. "Zairn Lomond? They talked about him?"

"Once. As soon as Roman said his name—"

"Let me guess, Whey lost his sense of humor?"

Their fingers coiled and played, stroking between each other, rising occasionally to his mouth.

"There's bad blood there?"

"It's a long story."

"Who is he?"

"Zairn Lomond? Owns clubs, entertainment venues, a whole bunch of everything. Billionaire out of New York. I've known him a long time, he's a good man."

Even having never met this Lomond, she trusted Struan's evaluation of his character more than Roman's, and what was suggested by Whey's reaction to the name.

"Wait…" she said, reaching for the glimmer of a memory. "Lomond. I've heard that be—Lomond's Delight."

"His fiancée, Roxie Kyst. Yeah, same Lomond."

Huh, so there was a connection between them. During that conversation with Mieux, Lomond's Delight had been described as a friend.

"Will Sway be at the party tonight?" she asked. "I'd love to meet her."

"Doubtful. I can text Tripp and find out."

"Tripp? Is that who she's with now?"

"No, him and Roxie have been looking out for her since we got back from the island."

Being with a man like Roman must be devastating. How did someone free themselves from that?

"Raquel, Whey's companion at dinner, thought Sway was engaged to a Deacon."

"Sway and Deacon were together years ago, before she got with Roman. After her and Roman split when he was in rehab, her and Deac found their way to each other again. Don't know how it happened. Logan might."

"Your other brother?"

He nodded. "Things kicked off when Roman found out they were engaged and there was drama in

Hawaii. It's a mess of crap." As was Roman's theme. "It's not important."

"Is she okay?"

"Sway Sheridan is stronger than everyone gives her credit for. The bullshit she put up with in her family far outweighs anything she probably had to endure with Roman. But I don't know. I'm not the guy she'd tell about that. Tripp's on it. Everybody talks to Tripp."

The curl of his lips was proud, and maybe a little amused.

"Everybody?"

"Everybody. Why do you think we call him 'Priest'? Anyone can confess anything to Tripp Breckenridge. He's more trustworthy than your priest, your doctor, your therapist, your spouse, everyone combined, and never breaks his vow."

"Is he religious?"

"No. Far from it." That came with another whisper of a laugh. "In a family the size of his, there's always something going on. He listens, watches, he cares about people. When someone needs to get something off their chest, he's there for them."

"I'd love to meet him too. He means a lot to you. I can tell."

"Yeah, Tripp's put up with it from me, and then some. There aren't a lot of outlets for the Roman stuff, the rehab, the relapse. With my brother it's drama after drama, and Tripp always picks up the phone."

"I can be an outlet," she said, freeing her hand from his to slide it high on his inner thigh. "If you want me."

Bowing, he rested his forehead on her. "Fawn, I don't know how I got through the days without you." Yet he bristled. "It's not easy that you're with him."

"I'm not with him. And never would be. I'm doing this for you." Didn't he get that? "Because you asked me to do it."

"I know I didn't mean—the world thinks you're together." He straightened to meet her eye again. "I hate they don't know the truth. For the first time, I really resent the shit out of it."

Would there be a way to navigate this? For them to be free of Roman and maybe explore what was between them?

Would they always be private? Secret? A dirty indiscretion never to be discussed?

"I'll be better," he said. "More present. When you came out that door tonight, Jesus, baby… looking at you, everything else fades away. You're everything."

As he cupped her cheek, she relaxed her head into his palm's embrace. "It's important to me that you don't forget. Promise me you won't forget."

"Forget what?"

"How this started. Why this started. How we found ourselves in this situation."

The tape? No. Their predicament was nothing to do with the video, not exactly. And he didn't need that spelled out.

"In that basement," he murmured.

"In that basement," she agreed and closed her eyes as his lips descended to hers again.

SEVENTEEN

CHAMPAGNE AND SMILES. Everyone was charming. In the moment. Neither the faces or conversations stuck with her.

One simple kiss in the car had become a make out session that ended with her dry riding him through his expensive slacks. Oh, she should be ashamed, but how could she be?

Right then, his hand was in hers, left hand to left hand, because his right was on her hip, holding her body against his side. They hadn't broken contact for a moment all night.

The people were whatever, the music, whatever, the point of the night, or whatever they were talking about, nothing measured up to the gentle possession his hands betrayed.

Could she call herself his after such a short time?

Whatever words fitted or didn't, sensation told a different story.

Whenever she spent time with Roman, she rued this crazy set up and wished to be anywhere but with him. That night, she rued the location and event, but not the man.

"Are you okay?" His lips moved in her hair, and the people they'd been talking with were gone. She'd missed the conversation. Was it important? Had she contributed at all, or was her first impression bimbo dumb?

"Hmm?" She coiled his arm around her waist. "Were those people important?"

She'd be damned after going through all this just to ruin Roman's reputation anyway. That was not a crime her shoulders deserved.

"You're the only important person here."

Caught in the shield of his body, he navigated them through people and onto the dance floor again.

She laughed. "We've spent more time here than anywhere else tonight."

By rote, her arms coiled around him, beneath his jacket, and closing her eyes, she rested her cheek against him.

"It's my favorite place to be," he said, his strength as calming as it was arousing.

Even then the music didn't compute. He led and she moved with him. By outward appearances, they were a couple, enjoying each other like dozens of others were at that moment. With her eyes closed, she could believe they were alone, that it was just them and nothing else existed. No Roman. No con. Just them.

"Are you ready to go home?" he asked.

If it meant leaving his embrace, no, she didn't want to go anywhere. How long had they been dancing? The night wasn't close to over, was it?

Time didn't pass the same with him.

"I want to stay here." She squeezed all her muscles. "Right here, beau, nowhere else."

Fate wasn't smiling on her.

"Roman!" someone exclaimed, shattering the moment. Her date was forced to release her. "You haven't been returning my calls. All about Whey now?"

"No, Mr. Wrigley, definitely not."

"Richard. Richard. Call me Richard." The guy smacked a hand to Struan's bicep and swiped up his hand to shake. "Have to admit, with a beauty like this, I would be distracted too."

"Richard Wrigley, this is Bambi Bennett, my fiancée."

Hummina, that sounded good on Struan's lips.

"Yes, the whole world knows that," the man said, laughing again. Jovial though he portrayed himself, wariness prickled. Her female intuition wasn't taking this guy at face value. "We need to get together, there are things to discuss."

"I'm shooting every day. I don't have a lot of time to myself these days."

"Yes! You're on the rise again. That's what we need to talk about. I have some interesting opportunities—"

"If you'll excuse us. I have to get Bambi a drink."

Again, holding her, he directed her to the bar to order more drinks.

"Who was that?" she asked.

Struan sat on a stool and guided her into the vee of his thighs. "A sycophant. You get used to them. When you're on the way down, no one knows you—"

"On the way up, everyone's your best friend?" It would be galling if it wasn't so ridiculous. "How do you live in this town? Honestly? How do you do it?" Turning to relax her back on his chest, still in the circle of his arms, she scrutinized the room. "There are so many people here, and I don't know any of them. I don't think I've met a single genuine person in this town, except you."

"Some of the UO crew are good people."

She conceded that. "Maybe it's the small-town girl in me. I'm used to everyone helping everyone, to them meaning what they say."

"No such thing as small-town gossip?"

Her grin quickly became a laugh. "Oh, God, people talk about each other all the time. There's always whispers and always judgment, but at the end of the day, if someone needs help, your people are there for you. We might whisper in our own circles, but if anyone dares take on someone we class as our own…"

"Do you miss it?"

"Sometimes I miss the people. I miss knowing exactly where to go if I want peace or the best latte in town. Knowing where I'll be guaranteed a listening ear, or a gentle nudge."

"You've got that in me, Fawn," he murmured against her.

And he felt so good. "I love my home, but it's not the whole world. I know people who are born and live and die in Wishbone and barely leave its limits. There has to be more to life than that. Doesn't there?"

He'd swept her hair from her shoulder and was trailing gentle kisses down the side of her neck and along her shoulder.

"Thank you for leaving its limits," he whispered, his breath fogging her skin on his mouth's return journey.

She flattened her hands on his to twine his arms further around her. "You have to stop doing that."

Her mouth spoke words her body couldn't back up. Her head tilted and her lips curled. The heat was more than electricity. She struggled to take even short, sharp breaths. His solid form held her up, cradled her in a safety she'd never known. In that strange place, surrounded by these unusual people, she had found her home again, and not in the geography.

"Come here."

He snagged her hand and rushed from the bar. What happened to their drinks? Oh, who cared about drinks?

Struan swung her around into a corner, past a shelving unit and indoor trellis to a shadowy alcove.

"What are we doing?" she called in a laugh as he picked her up to seat her on something. "Beau!"

"Your feet hurt."

Mm, yeah, sure. Suspicious, in a good way, she doubted her discomfort was the root of his emerging inner rascal.

"How do you know that?" she asked filled with the ecstasy of a teenager finding her first love, lost in a haze of passion and hormones.

Everything she was depended on what happened in the next few minutes. The kiss, the thrill that could be forever. What was the potential with a man so full of life? An honorable man who treasured her? He kissed her, cradled her face and toyed with her hair. The light trace of his fingertips tickled down her spine until he elevated her hips, pressuring her back, deepening their kiss, pressing her skull into the wall.

Struan was everything she wanted, her adventure. Her body responded without thought. There was no mental process. The certain pressure of his lips and the firm nature of his tongue sent silent signals on how to respond. A wordless dance. His hands wouldn't stop roaming across her body, and when he dragged her dress up her thighs, she didn't hesitate to raise her knees higher around him.

Love hadn't been on the agenda. Maybe it had been somewhere in the distant background, but it wasn't why she'd left her home. In LA, she'd been doing her job, living her life without thought of establishing romantic relationships. Not yet, maybe somewhere down the line...

People said love found those who stopped looking for it. Love didn't have to mean settling down forever, barefoot and pregnant, locking yourself away. Not with Struan Lowe. Something in their connection granted her freedom while keeping them tied together.

"Struan," she gasped when he kissed her jaw and forced her head back with his own to taste her neck. "Is this a hotel?" Shelves didn't do much to conceal them from partygoers. Salacious ideas definitely required privacy. "Baby..."

When his mouth rose, she kissed him again. Cupping his jaw, she anticipated his tongue only to be left wanting. He hunkered down, snagging the elastic of her panties to drag them down her thighs.

She laughed. "What are you doing?"

Question? Yes. Curious? Yes? Concerned or reluctant? Not a chance. Her fingers supported her weight to lift her hips and grant him access.

"You want adventure," he said and kissed her knee.

Their eyes stayed locked on each other as he trailed those lips up her inner thigh, then he scooped her to the edge, plunging his tongue into her.

Oh, God, her body arched instantly, clenching in carnal reaction to the delightful delectation of him devouring her.

He knew just how to convey his own need and satisfy hers. The former was such a huge part of her gratification, she'd never felt so desired, so special, so appreciated. He pampered her, spoiled her, granted attention few men would and certainly not first.

Arousal wasn't just about nerve endings and sparks of endorphins, heat and pressure and need and want.

Her power, the true, overwhelming nature of this sensuous naughtiness came with the knowledge that it was all about them. He got pleasure from her pleasure. This was gratitude for giving him the same meaning she felt in him.

He wanted her, needed her, and had found something he hadn't been expecting either. How did she know? The way he held her, the delicate pressure of his lips, the glide of his tongue around her clit. Her nails dug deep into the wood beneath her, and she gasped, teetering closer to the edge of release.

"Baby…" she stuttered. "Oh, God, beau…"

Another cry. Not hers. A gasp and a shriek opened her eyes. Struan rose in a twist enough to cover her modesty, but yeah, they were being watched.

Not by one or two, but by ten or fifteen, and at least a few of them had cameras.

Shit. Why hadn't she thought about there being press at the event? Of course there were members of the mass media present. And many who wanted to impress them.

She caught his hips and he laced their fingers together.

"I'm sorry," she whispered against his back.

In a second, he faced her. "That was just a snack," he said, kissing the back of her fingers, left then right. "Entrée's coming soon."

He wasn't sorry. Defiant, he'd owned her, and didn't mind the world knowing it.

EIGHTEEN

"I DON'T EVEN KNOW what to say," Magnus said, failing to recognize that in itself was a statement.

He threw the newspaper onto the living room couch next to her.

"Wow," she said, picking it up. "I didn't know people still got these."

"When your name's in them, we have no choice. What were you two thinking last night?"

Roman was uncharacteristically quiet. Without a word, he strode the width of the front window back and forth, hands clasped behind him. Rich of him to think he could pass judgment on anyone.

"I don't understand why it's a problem." Her intention wasn't to aggravate the already inflamed tension, she just didn't get it. "Yes, okay, maybe, from a human standpoint, a relationship standpoint, I wouldn't want my intimate life splashed across the papers, but this started—"

"This started…" Roman declared, marching up behind Magnus, "because you two were horny fucks who couldn't keep your hands off each other, and here we are again."

"Why is that a problem?" she appealed to one man then the other. "Didn't we fix that mess by telling the world we were getting married? So what's the problem? In those pictures, we're two soon-to-be-married people physically enjoying each other. What's wrong with that? This isn't the forties. Even if it was, the world knows by now we're living in sin. I've been staying here since the story first broke."

"How do we fix this?" Roman asked Magnus.

Was he listening to her at all? Was anything getting through? Did she even matter? It was a wonder. They'd waited for her to wake up before planting her in the middle of the couch and demanding an explanation.

After being caught in the throes of whatever they were doing, as a fully consenting adult couple, Struan excused them to the limo and finished what he started.

She yearned to ask him to join her in bed, but already felt brazen for being caught red-handed… rather red-faced and not in shame. Look at her. Yes, there were pictures, right there on the couch in newsprint, head back, eyes closed, body presented to the man on his knees worshiping.

In the newspaper. In goddamn print!

God, she dreaded to think what was online where censors wouldn't have their way. How long had they been watched before the exclamation intruded?

"You're taking her out tonight," Magnus said, interrupting her chain of thought. "Dinner. Somewhere quiet. Somewhere we trust so we can manage the visuals."

"The *Making of…* guys want to interview her."

"Not today," Magnus said in full control. "She stays here. You both should. We all should."

"In shame?"

If the man pleasuring her was her actual, supposed fiancé she'd be ashamed all over the place. Not that it would ever happen, unless she was super drunk, mortifyingly inebriated, to the point it would be assault not consent. She shuddered at the thought.

Anyone should be embarrassed to be caught with Roman given the mess of his life. If he wasn't so damn cocky, she'd say anyone taking advantage of him would border assault too. The guy was strung out all the time. Had to be if Struan kept stepping in to cover his ass. Maybe not on drugs, but Roman Lowe did not have his shit together, not even close.

"I'm going to set," Roman said. "I'm not unreliable. I'm not letting the world think that I'm up to this kind of crazy shit." Again. "I bet Struan's already there."

"Struan's already where?" The voice of the man himself prompted her to grab the back of the couch to look over it just as he wandered upstairs from the kitchen. "You guys having a party without me?"

She smiled and rolled her eyes. "I'm getting chewed out," she admitted and slouched against the back of the couch as he came around it. "For being slutty."

"Whoa, then I missed something, because you were sleeping alone when I checked in on you this morning."

Oh, now that was hot.

Did he really creep in her room at night to check she was okay? That she was alone? Huh, it was hot until the question: why wouldn't she be alone?

Did Struan worry his brother, or someone else, would sneak into her room at night? Good to know. Yep, she'd be locking the door from then on.

He dropped onto the couch next to her and scooped up the newspaper. "I didn't know we still got these." She stifled a laugh. "What's the problem?"

Picture down, he discarded the paper. Not because he was ashamed of it, to protect her modesty while sitting in that room with that judgmental pair.

"He can't be doing shit like this." Roman marched closer, pointed finger at the floor. "This is not your fucking job."

"It's not like you were fighting me for it last night, or the night B and I met. You can't decide when you want it and decide when you don't, just pick her up and put her down as you see fit. If she agreed to marry you, you should be a stable force in her life, someone she can rely on, someone she can—"

"Fuck around with in public at parties?" Roman cut his brother off. "Great. We've already established her and me are going out tonight. Should I bring protection or are you on the pill, Sugarlips?"

Struan shot to his feet. "If you so much as think about—"

"Everyone calm down," she said, standing more slowly, threading her fingers through Struan's, hoping to ease tensions. His focus stayed on his brother. "We've upset the status quo." Seeking answers in any of them was fruitless. "I admit I don't understand why there's a problem, but I don't know this town. There's obviously something I'm missing. If you need us to apologize—"

"No one is apologizing," Struan declared, his fingers clamping deeper between hers. "Everyone at that place thought I was you, Ro, and she's supposed to be engaged to you. What's the problem?"

"I would never do that," Roman snapped, pointing toward the inverted paper. "I would never—"

"Please the woman you're supposed to love? Says a lot about you, brother."

"Both of you put your tackle away," Magnus said, finally finding a spot in the middle. Man couldn't have got as far as he had with the brothers without being used to a little compromise. "It happened, and it's in the press. No, nobody died. These are not the kind of party boy headlines we need right now."

That's what it was? Back in the throes of his hedonism days had he cheated on Sway? Had there been pictures and headlines and scandals falling left and right around the woman? Why would she put up with it?

Her sympathy for Struan was a given. It was automatic. She didn't know how he kept it up. Always clearing up after his brother, but Sway? How did the woman manage to wake up to Roman every single day?

Roman was a nightmare, and as far as she knew, he was sober every time he was in her company. Imagine having to deal with him while he was on drugs, high, spaced out, erratic. She scoffed. More erratic. That was where the wariness came from: his volatility. The air vibrated around him like he was a guitar string wound too tight, on the cusp of snapping. And him, or someone, kept on turning the tuning pegs.

"Bambi's staying at home today."

"You're benching her?" Struan's outrage was flattering. "You can't keep her locked up here like a prisoner."

"Do you want her answering questions?" Magnus snapped. "Do you, Stru? Want the press taking her picture and banging on the limo windows? Screaming her name? Isn't this why we brought her here? Why she agreed to be here? So we could protect her from that circus?"

Hmm, fuzz, guy had a point.

She swung her and Struan's joined hands a little toward her ass. "I'll be okay here," she said. "If that's the price for what happened last night, I'd pay it every minute, and you know it."

His chin dropped, landing his eyes on hers. "So would I."

"What the fuck is this?" Roman barked after they'd been gazing for goodness knew how long. "I say it and it's a problem, he says it and it's not?"

That was his grievance? Her agreement? Roman was the only man she'd ever met who'd be capable of starting an argument in an empty house.

"Then it's settled. Ro's going to work today and Struan will be needed."

"Yeah, and there's no reason for me not to be there." No one knew he was the man in the pictures. "But we're towing a 'no comment' line. Nothing gets said about the picture, the past, or the future, without Bambi's agreement."

It hadn't occurred to her they could say what they wanted while she was locked up in the palace walls.

"The break gives you a chance to look through some of the requests. Decide if there's anything that's safe to do. It won't be now, but maybe when things have settled…" These interviews again? Appearance requests? She just nodded. "Mieux will come over with everything you'll need. If you want to write up any statements or comments, she'll pass them on to us for approval."

Somehow that last word implied, while Roman's side sought to approve whatever was coming from her proverbial mouth, in return, she'd only get consultation. Forewarned before they threw any grenades. Did that mean she needed to be forearmed? Her arsenal wasn't exactly packed with options.

This would have to end sometime, and her exit strategy…? Nonexistent. The reason for that was at her side. Of its own accord her body relaxed against his, just a little.

"Exit" suggested away from Struan. That was not somewhere she wanted to be.

"Chic will let you know if there are wardrobe changes."

Because whatever was supposed to be on the calendar would now be canceled or rescheduled? Surely one outfit was as good as the next for a social occasion. They wouldn't be going to a pool or a costume party. Though with this being LA, she wouldn't bet anything on that assumption.

Struan would go to work, Roman and Magnus too. At this rate, all she was good for was going back to bed. She'd only just got up and ready for the day, and already she was eager for it to be over.

Oh no, wait, she took that back. The ultimate punishment would come before bedtime. An intimate evening with Roman Lowe, smiling nice for the cameras, just what would that entail exactly?

NINETEEN

TO GIVE ROMAN his due, he'd been more charming through that evening's meal than he had on other nights.

"Struan's not used to being the fuck up. That's the problem." Unfortunately, with the subject continually returning to his superiority over his brother, Roman was no less insufferable than normal. "He knows how to fall in line, how to do what he's told. He can take instruction, direction. This is him acting out or a sign of his ability to make stupid decisions." Roman snickered. "I think it's a signal he's better staying in his lane."

Her position was impossible. Impulse demanded she argue and defend Struan, that she point out he hadn't fucked up or made any bad decision. He'd simply followed his own desire for once. And, yes, that desire might be sexual, in this case, but that didn't diminish his right. Choosing her, from what she could gather, was the first thing he'd ever chosen for himself.

The meal was lovely, neutral, polite, she'd done her duty, right? No waves. No opposition. She'd nodded along and let Roman listen to his own voice all night long.

"It's getting late."

"Do you want dessert?" he asked, sliding a hand to the middle of the table, his fingers beckoning hers.

Damnit, she'd have to reciprocate.

Every muscle clenched as she forced a smile to her lips and allowed him to hold her hand there near the edge of the table. Just because she hadn't seen press didn't mean they weren't there. Everyone had a camera these days, and in LA especially, most all wanted to make a name for themselves somehow.

Magnus said they picked the restaurant to control the visual. Did he mean they were surrounded by friendly people influential enough to spread the tale of what they'd seen in the right circles? Would that straighten out what Roman classed as Struan's mess?

Holding his hand didn't feel right, neither did gazing into the smile on his face. Smug was the only word that came to mind to describe it. Did he feel like he was getting one upon his brother?

She definitely didn't want any part in that pissing match and would always choose Struan. Still, not rocking the boat made his life easier.

"It's getting late," she said, "I'd like to get to bed."

"No argument here."

He stood up, hand still in hers, and helped her onto her feet.

"Shouldn't we ask for the bill?"

"It's covered," he said, still bearing that cocky arrogance.

Maybe she should punch him in the face. Right there. How would that be for a visual?

He led her out, nodding and smiling at those who caught his eye as they passed.

Yeah, those were his people. The brownnosers.

Sycophants, Struan called them. He recognized their falseness, did Roman miss it? Maybe he just didn't care. She'd put money on him being the same in return. If only there was an Oscar for fawning.

In the back of the car in the dark, in shadow, his hand crept onto her knee. Her thigh actually, not exactly indecent, but not welcome either.

On an inhale, his head turned her way, words couldn't have been far behind—his phone rang, granting her a reprieve.

Thank God! If she had to put up with him prattling on any more about how wonderful he was or how wrong Struan was, she would lose it. Through the years, mortal folks heard tales of celebrities going crazy.

Now she better understood why.

Maybe it wasn't the adoration of fans or the long hours and stressful work conditions. Maybe it was the egos, those who knew little screaming about how clever they were, how valued and loved and welcomed.

She wanted to be valued by one man.

Damnit. She had to stop thinking that way.

Roman fished the phone from his pocket and answered with a, "Hey, buddy," so exaggerated, it betrayed she'd be secondary for a while.

Good.

Not just a while it turned out, the call passed second by second, minute by minute… Whoever was on the other end deserved her gratitude, honestly, she'd pay the caller every cent from her bank account if it saved her discovering just why that hand was there, still on her skin.

The car stopped at the front door and she got out. Sometimes there were people there to open doors, sometimes there weren't, but she never waited. What was the point when she was fully capable? Why pander to an extreme that should have gone the way of the petticoat?

Roman could enjoy his call as long as he wanted.

Was it rude that she hadn't said goodnight? Probably more wrong that it hadn't occurred to her until she was at the top of the staircase, just a few feet from her bedroom.

Loosening the clasp from her hair and removing her earrings, she shed the wares of the night. Shower? No shower? She couldn't be bothered drying her hair, which she'd have to. Morning, she'd get up early tomorrow.

"Hey." She'd just clicked on the bedside lamp and didn't have to look to know the visitor was unwelcome. "Sorry about that."

An apology? From Roman? Unusual.

"It's fine, I know you're busy." Now leave. "I had a nice time. Thanks for dinner."

The words tripped off her tongue, like an *I'm fine* after someone asking how she was. They weren't genuine. Honestly, she didn't mean them, and just stood there, waiting for him to excuse himself.

He didn't.

In fact, he did the opposite and stepped inside, pushing the door though it didn't reach the frame. Oh, shit. Alarm thrust her shoulders back and her chin rose a little, armor required. How much wine did he drink? Did it matter with an addict? Why was that her first thought? Didn't the man deserve a clean break? If he'd gone through the program and come out the other side, he was renewed, right?

Excuses and self-criticisms ebbed and flowed, fading to nothing as he came right up close. If she were a cat, this would be the point she'd pin her ears back and sink her head into her neck to hiss.

"This has been hard on you too. You thought you were getting into something, and it became something else. There was a promise of something maybe. And then it got complicated. You're a beautiful woman, Bambi." When his fingertips touched her jaw, her molars clamped tight. "You don't have to be alone in this. Don't be afraid. If I intimidate you—"

"You don't," she said and backed up a step only to be caught in the angle of the nightstand against the edge of the bed. "You don't intimidate me, and I am not alone. I am, however, tired, so I'd like to get some sleep."

"I know what you want." And there it was, a phrase so many women heard on lips just like his the world over. "You can have what you want."

As he bowed, she dipped back, planting a sure hand on his chest. "I don't want that. I don't want you. I want to go to sleep. And if I'm not allowed to do that here, I'll find somewhere else to do it."

"Don't be like that," he said, fingers curling to strengthen his grip around her skull. "Don't worry about anyone else. We're here, and this is right. Take advantage, baby…"

Of his time? His presence? His presumption? No, thank you. He tried again, and without thought of discretion, she shrieked.

She pushed hard and he reared back. "What the…"

The pin from one of her earrings had pierced his shirt. The other earring and the hair clasp fell to the floor while that one stayed put, not fully in, but enough for him to react. Except he only grinned.

"You like it rough?"

God, no! He grabbed her arms and pulled her closer, another scream burned her throat. Objecting, tugging left, right, backwards, forwards, she struggled for freedom. He laughed and pulled her tight against him.

"No! Roman, don't!"

The second she hit the bed, she expected him to follow. Instead flesh thwacked flesh and someone tumbled to the floor. Spitting hair from her mouth, shaking her head to clear it from her eyes, there was Roman on the floor with Struan standing over him.

"Out!" The upright brother glared at the prone one. "Get out of here now!"

"You fucking asshole!" Roman leaped to his feet, provoking Struan to pounce closer.

"Give me the excuse, brother, I'll give you a left to go with the right. Don't kid yourself, you know how this ends. I'll play if you want to get dirty; you won't win. Get the fuck out of here. Now!"

Struan wasn't to be messed with.

Muttering under his breath, Roman stomped on out and slammed the door, probably to punctuate his anger. Who cared? She was pleased of the barrier, the shield beyond, and the guard who'd defended her without hesitation.

"Bambi," he said, whirling around.

"I'm okay," she said, running her fingers through her hair as she sat up. "I don't know how that—"

"I'm sorry. I promised nothing like that would happen, that you'd be safe here—I'm sorry. Come here. Let me look at you." He grabbed her wrist to tug her onto her feet. When her body bounced off his, he stopped and raised his hands in surrender. "Shit, I'm sorry. I shouldn't have—you don't need another guy pawing and manhandling—assaulting, that's what—"

"You're not another guy," she said, capturing his wrist to direct his arm around her as she went up close to rest against him. "You're *the* guy. Beau, there's no way for me to express—I don't know how that would have gone if he'd—if you hadn't been here..."

Ridiculous that terror could visit in such an upmarket place with such a well-known face. These things weren't supposed to happen in nice neighborhoods. Rich folks were supposed to be well bred and mannered. Did economic status matter? No. At the end of the day, predators were predators.

The calming words he whispered into her hair, stroking it from her crown down her back, clued her into the tears, her tears. She'd acted—no, reacted. At the time, she didn't feel sad or emotional, just on edge. Survival instincts came from the very depth of a person, all the way from their most basic roots. Fight, flight, or freeze. And she'd gone for being rescued by the right twin.

Her arms, nestled between them, shifted so she could wipe the tears from her cheeks.

"Sorry. I don't know where that came from," or how long they'd been standing there possessed by it.

"Do you want the law? We can call—"

"No, no, you know what he's like."

Funny she should be saying that after only knowing the man a few days. Every minute with Roman was a lifetime she wanted to end. With Struan…

Eyes wet, she blinked up at him. "I'm tired."

"Yeah, it's late," he said. With an arm still around her, he shuffled their position to reach over and pull back the covers. "Do you want me to lock the bedroom door? There's a key—"

"I want you to stay." She clung to his hand, possessed by that brazenness again. For the first time, tension held a fear of potential rejection. "I feel safer when you hold me, beau. Would you lie down and put your arms around me?"

Her heart raced, thumping hard until, with a single nod, he granted her wish.

Without looking at him, she unzipped her dress and shimmied out of it, discarding it there on the floor as she crawled onto the bed.

Already in just sweats, he joined her and tucked the covers over them, spooning her against him. The heat of his chest met her back, and immediately she felt stronger, more in control. He kissed the top of her head and tucked it beneath his chin.

She closed her eyes.

This was what she needed. After Roman, she'd never have been able to sleep under that roof without the man holding her close. He'd never let anything happen to her. He'd stood up to his own brother to protect her. Nothing but him would touch her, and that was exactly how she wanted it. From then until…

TWENTY

THE WARMTH OF HIS mouth roused her from sleep.

"Mmm," she moaned, tipping her lips higher.

He could have all the access he wanted.

"Go back to sleep, Fawn."

Another kiss.

When he scooted away an inch, she grabbed his arm. "Where are you going?" she mumbled, eyes open to slits.

"I'm getting up."

"Getting up? It's still dark out." Eyes closing again, she wriggled closer. "You're not getting up." Still half asleep, she frowned. "Are you sneaking away? Did I ask too much? Am I being clingy and in—"

His kiss silenced her. "I get up at four thirty every day, babe."

She heard but didn't understand. "Why would anyone do that on purpose?"

"It's my job."

In the face of his amusement, she was just confused.

"Your job to get up and—" She blinked, seeking his gaze in the shadow. "You're going to the gym?"

"Basement fitness suite, but, yeah."

"You're getting up out of bed at four thirty in the morning to go get shredded?" The angle of his brow didn't seem certain how to respond. "Man, you're dedicated." Laying a hand on his cheek, she rose to kiss him. "Come lay down with me again when you're done. If you have time; if you want."

"I'll be around when you wake up."

"Good." She pulled the covers to her chin. "I'll dream about you getting pumped and sweaty."

His next kiss proceeded a snicker. "You do that, B."

Ah, bed. Yes, the man was incredible, but the gym at four thirty? Talk about stamina. Hmm, nice, another nuance for her dream.

***

UNFORTUNATELY, THOUGH THE dream had a happy ending, her bed was empty when she woke. Well, the guy had been there when it counted last night, she'd forgive him his dedication.

And it wasn't so disappointing to go downstairs because he was in the kitchen, chopping, dicing, blender on the counter, back to her.

She crept over, given cover by him hitting the blender button. Darting closer, she smacked his ass and leaped to the side. With barely enough time to register her, he whipped around, scooping her up with one arm to dump her on the counter.

Her laugh was lost in the depth of his kiss. Right there, in the middle of the kitchen, she wound her legs around him, clamping him tight to her. Not that he was going anywhere, he held her head when his lips teased hers, but those hands descended to her ass as their passion grew.

"I want to taste your parsnip," she breathed.

His head rose in a tilt. "That's a new one."

On a laugh, she socked his arm. "Your smoothie."

Was that really better?

"Ah," he said, admiring her lips. "You've got to share yours first."

He kissed her mouth, her chin, and bent his knees to—ah, no, she wouldn't let him sneak down on her again.

"I need you here, beau."

Clasping his jaw, she joined their mouths, once again basking in the divine and devouring.

"What the hell!" Magnus came stomping in. "Are you two insane? What if I was someone else?"

"Someone else who?" Struan asked without releasing her or changing their position. Wow, he really was happy to own her. "Mieux's the only other person who might stumble in and it won't be a shock to her."

Magnus blustered. "You told her?"

"No. But Mieux is Mieux, she divines things. And don't kid yourself she's not walked in on clients doing worse than this."

"You are not her client and shouldn't be doing anything with anyone. Aren't you due on set?"

"Not for a while."

Finger-combing her hair, Struan matched their gazes again. She could sit there all day and be satisfied. And damn, she wanted to kiss him. Why did Magnus have to interrupt?

"No more private dates," Struan said, proving what concern was on his mind: her. "Roman got too handsy last night."

"Too handsy?" Magnus squawked. "They're

engaged! There's no such thing as too handsy."

She laid a hand on Struan's arm for support as she leaned back to take in the man at the perpendicular side of the counter.

"Whoa, okay," she said. "Let's unpack everything that's wrong with that statement."

"I just meant—"

"I know what you just meant, Magnus. You're lucky you're responsible for raising this guy too." Her eyes smiled on his. "Because you got him just perfect."

"Whatever this is, you two have to cool it. If the media—"

"The media are not what you're worried about," Struan said. "And what did you think would happen locking the two of us up under one roof?"

They weren't prisoners, but the man had a point. This started because they couldn't resist each other, now they lived together.

"I thought you would respect your brother's—"

"Let's talk about my brother and respect." That was the catalyst for separating them; Struan went around to confront his uncle. "He put his hands on B without consent last night. He's lucky he's not in the ground."

"He's your brother—"

"Doesn't give him the right. He's got to know where the lines are. If he can't respect those lines—"

"You think you can spout this shit? How is it any of your business?"

She sensed Struan biting his tongue. He did have a right. She'd said he was the man when he held her last night and meant it. Except they'd never talked about them, maybe he didn't want the role long-term. That wasn't the moment to define their future. Everyone was due elsewhere.

"It's my place," she said. "This isn't exactly the most hospitable environment, and there's a lot of politicking I don't understand. Yeah, I'm a small-town girl, and everyone smiles and pats me on the head, but I'm not actually disposable. I am a human being. And if Roman chooses to forget that, or thinks about violating any boundaries—"

"I get it," Magnus said, proving he didn't just by interrupting.

The flat hand he held up screamed of dismissal.

"She won't be paid off or hushed up, if I have to stand with her—"

"Okay," Magnus said. "Geez, what wound the pair of you up this morning? Roman's Roman, he's just the way he is, and—"

"Excusing him like that has caused this whole situation. You're not doing him any favors," she said. "You have to understand that doing it now with me, in the privacy of his own home, is one thing. If he's allowed away with it once, predators escalate—

"Predators?" Magnus barked. "Where did that word come from? No. No. No. No. We're not using that word. Don't use that word."

Why did she bother? What a waste of words. Yes, she was outraged and affronted, but what she was saying was true, and it would cover their ass too. But, no, Magnus didn't see that she was actually doing him a favor by bringing it to him.

"What's the situation with his sobriety?"

"Situation?"

"When we go out, he drinks."

"He's not an alcoholic."

"You know he shouldn't be drinking," Struan backed her up, "it's part of his recovery. One step leads to—"

"So what's the guy supposed to do? Take out a double page ad declaring to the world he's no longer capable of socializing?"

"It's possible to socialize without consuming alcohol." Okay, that came off a little bitchy. "If refraining from it helps him, I'm willing to do it too."

She wasn't a big drinker. Though the wine did take the edge off her irritation, she assumed. Perhaps it didn't, perhaps alcohol inflamed her negative feelings. Going sober a few nights might cast Roman in a new light.

"If the booze causes shit like last night," Struan said, "it's trouble waiting to happen."

"I'll talk to him." She sealed her lips and silently sighed. Everyone seemed to proclaim how ready they were to talk to Roman like it made the damnedest bit of difference. "There's nothing on tonight. Everyone can relax, take a breather, reboot. Let's just get through today."

Another day on set. Providing no one pushed her in the direction of her bullshit beloved, she may just get through it.

"Are you ready to go, B?" Struan asked. "It'll take me two minutes to mix this and there's a car—"

"No," Magnus interrupted. "I'll take her, you travel with Roman." Did that mean even their uncle, their guardian, didn't want to spend time with Roman? "We can't afford getting mixed up in any more sordid stories, so like I said, you two kill it, here, out there, everywhere."

She got assaulted and still got a talking to the next day? Nice. Clutching the edge of the counter, she threw one leg up then the other, boosting herself onto her feet again.

Okay. She'd rather travel with Struan, but Magnus did have cause for suspicion. She conceded privately, like super privately, only in her own brain privately, that if she and Struan got into a car together, she couldn't guarantee hands and mouths wouldn't wander.

Struan approached like he intended to say goodbye, but Magnus hurried past him and shoveled an arm around her to rush them out into the car.

"How do you do it?"

They'd been on the road maybe five minutes. She'd been quite happy with the silent agreement to avoid discussion, although apparently that agreement only existed in her head.

"How do I do what?" she asked Magnus.

"Struan. I've never seen him with anyone else the way he is with you. Roman's always been his priority and somehow you have Struan threatening to ruin him. His own blood."

"I don't do anything. All I heard was a man saying he'd do the right thing, any decent person would do the same."

"They need each other. Struan gets strength from taking care of his brother, supporting him."

"You don't know what Struan needs. This has been his life for so long, sometimes I wonder if it's just muscle memory. You've conditioned them both and orchestrated this life… Roman likes the attention, Struan doesn't, he was the natural choice for stardom, I get that. Can't you see you've wrapped everything Struan is up into his brother? It maybe works for a while, but Roman's inherent volatility doesn't make him the surest bet. You're in this web too. Everyone's livelihoods teeter on the thread of Roman's mood. I know he went to rehab—"

"He did, and he worked hard."

"That's great. He deserves a second chance. If you believe in him I'm sure he'll prove you right. I don't have that same faith. I don't know him well enough."

And what she did know scared her a little.

"But you know Struan well enough?"

"They're different. There's sincerity in Struan. It's who he is. He isn't always honest, I get that, he protects his brother. Who protects him? You have to figure out how to get tighter control, or find out what Roman needs to get that control for himself. Is it about Sway?"

"Don't bring her name into it." With an elbow on the door, Magnus cradled his brow, covering his eyes. "Forget you even know it. Forget you heard it."

"Why are you afraid of her?"

"Because, as you've seen, any mention of her affects Roman's mood, which affects his ability to do his job. He needs to get into the swing of UO, to find the track, to set himself on the rails, and, it's like magic when he does what he does. When he's engrossed in a part and focused on the art… he deserves to do this, he's good at this."

"At what cost?"

Magnus's hand dropped to his lap, his expression of forlorn wonderment tracked outside.

If he wanted what was best for them, if he truly believed it was this job, and that their lives were the way they were supposed to be, she didn't envy him what lay ahead.

Her fear for Struan could be blinkered because he was the one she cared about. Maybe she shouldn't be so hard on Magnus. What was the uncle's alternative? Struan wouldn't want to walk away from his brother, and, she hoped, Magnus wouldn't want to walk away from either of them. Though if it came down to a 50/50, choice, he'd bet on the payday, he just had that aura about him.

They could agree to disagree while it was intellectual, she just wished Roman showed a little more gratitude. If he understood and valued what his blood family did for him, she wouldn't necessarily judge him so harshly.

Neither said another word, even when they reached the set. Magnus hurried away and she was quickly waylaid by Renata rushing up at her side.

"This is a big day!"

"A big day?" she asked, her eyes still on Magnus as he disappeared around a corner. "Why is it a big day?"

"They want to interview you and take another second—"

Wait, what? What did she say?

"What was that?"

"The guys, our *Making of...* guys, they want to interview you!"

"For what? I'm not part of the show."

"You're the biggest part of the lead actor's life!"

Shit, those kinds of questions? About their every intimate moment? Given the watershed last night, this wasn't the best day to spout opinions about her fake lover.

"No, I don't want to talk to them."

"You have to." Renata caught hold of her to stop her walking past. "It'll help, see, humanize him and answer some of the questions everyone's desperate to ask."

"What questions?"

"How you feel about his work, and how you support him. How you supported him getting this role, when he told you about UO, when you met, when you fell in love."

Yeah, that was exactly the path she didn't want to walk down. They still hadn't come up with a backstory for their relationship. Really showed how much everyone cared about her being put on the spot.

"I'd prefer to keep running back and forth doing errands, helping out, like I have been. I barely know my way around—"

"That doesn't matter." Renata scoffed. "You can't get lost. Everyone knows who you are. You don't even need a security card. The rest of us can't go pee without six guards stopping us. You can go wherever you want."

That was almost awe. Renata had five, maybe ten years on her. She looked fantastic, no matter her age. Fantastic in the LA way. Perry loitered in the background of the moment, smiling at this person and that, she was a woman who knew how to seize opportunities. They hadn't spent time getting to know each other. How could everyone know her? Everyone?

When Mieux suddenly appeared, Bambi brightened up, gesturing her over while extricating herself from Renata's grip.

"Let's go over those interviews and appearances," she exclaimed. "That important list. You know, the things they wanted me to do?"

Her colleague wasn't on the same page. "We covered that the other day."

"I want to look again," she said, taking Mieux's arm to tug her away from the silently begging Renata. "Let's look at that list and see if there's anything we can organize today to get, you know, to get, to get the wheels in motion." Her smile didn't move, even when they were out of earshot. "Let's just walk away, please."

Mieux laughed. "Oh, we're avoiding something."

"A curse," Bambi said. "I'm pretty sure as soon as I got to LA some ancient Hollywood starlet I insulted in a past life put a curse on me."

"Everyone in LA feels that way. There's no in between, you're on top or yesterday's news."

"Let's find a corner to talk about yesterday's news, because I want to stay out of tomorrow's."

TWENTY-ONE

STUNT REHEARSALS MESMERIZED her every time. Try as she might not to sink into the view of—okay, so, yeah, the stunt part was interesting, but she was really just drooling.

The sun had set. All were still there for some two minute night shot. Still no pro, even she knew "two minutes" didn't mean two minutes. They'd probably be there when the sun rose again.

Updating the schedule according to the handwritten notes she'd been given, this wasn't an assignment she could fuck up.

"Come here." Someone caught her hand, yanking her from the chair and around the corner of the nearby building into a narrow alley to plant her back on the wall. "You've been driving me crazy all day."

Her laugh disappeared into his kiss, but he quickly withdrew.

"Beau…" she whispered, sinking into the sensation of his lips on her throat, running her palms back and forth across the width of his shoulders. "Baby, where's your trailer?"

Both of them knew the answer. And what she was really asking. Though the kissing stopped, the light in his eye didn't dim.

"I'm fucking addicted to this," he murmured, cupping her head to kiss her again. "To you, Fawn." Even though it went against every ounce of good sense his uncle tried to hammer into him. "I've been thinking about you all day. You're right here and I can't…"

He wasn't alone in his frustration.

"Trailer," she murmured, her fingers curving around the sides of his neck. "Right now. And you can."

Risky? Yes. Better than doing what they wanted to do right there in the alleyway.

The smile that touched him joined his fingers threading between hers. "This way."

They didn't get two strides before a shout stopped them. Not directed at them specifically, but elsewhere, close by—there was another exclamation. Struan stopped, turning to glance over her head, concern written all over him.

"Go," she said, tugging his arm once before letting go.

He snagged the back of her head and scooped her forward to kiss her quick, then rushed back the way they'd come.

Hmm. Leaning against the wall, she folded her hands at her back. The man never got a second to himself.

"Bambi?" Mieux's voice drew her attention to the mouth of the alleyway. "You okay?"

"Yeah," she said on an exhale. "What's going on?"

"I don't—I probably shouldn't—Magnus said I should take you home."

"Why?" she asked, intrigued by Mieux's

reluctance. "What did he do?" Because it could only be Roman. "Disappear? Runaway? Get caught in some compromising position with—"

"No! Oh, no, that's not… He's just not happy."

What a surprise. "Then let's go back to the house."

Home it was not, but she'd rather be there than exist under the potential someone may assume she'd have sway with the man tormenting the crew.

Mieux joined her on the journey back, but didn't stay long. She didn't mind. Mieux was entitled to her own life.

Besides, alone time was overdue. And she had work to do.

After snagging some crackers from the kitchen, she went upstairs to finish the task. When complete, she saved the file and tossed her headphones onto the bed.

Was it too early to go to sleep? The house was quiet. Whatever happened with Roman, she wasn't interested. Well, she was, because it impacted others, but she did not want to give a tantrum the time of day. And, yes, she fully believed that whatever his issue, Roman was blowing it way out of proportion. The man had so many troubles that he couldn't control, he grabbed for the stick any time he thought he'd get away with it.

After midnight was a normal time to go to bed, she'd just climbed to her feet when the front door downstairs opened. She stopped. Who was coming in? Was that—

"You didn't have to come over here," Struan said.

"Are you kidding? I've had her on a leash," another male said. "What the fuck is this bullshit?"

"Don't swear at him like that," a female said, much more fawning. "Oh, Struan, sweetie…" the woman's voice stayed so calm, like a mother talking to a child. "What the fuck is this bullshit?"

Struan laughed. "Rox Out just can't be anything but Rox Out."

"You're welcome," the woman said. "Why aren't we having this conversation at the club? I've been waiting all week for you to show. Your little brother's blowing up my phone."

"We're keeping Roman away from Crimson."

"Good. Saves me turning him away at the door. I'm sure you didn't hear me inviting him. He can line up at the main entrance like the more valuable people. And if he gets in, Z will punch him in the face, because, let's be honest, it's overdue. I'm not so sure I want to work my magic restraining my Casanova anymore."

"Rox…" the unknown male warned.

"Okay, geez, if it's not you, it's Logan. I so don't get what everyone sees in this man."

"Is that helpful?" the unknown male said. "I said you could come if—"

"I could come—oh, baby, you don't know me if you think I need permission from any man for anything."

"Except you didn't know the address."

"I do now," the woman said, sly in her delivery. "So what do I need you for?"

"Half the female population of Manhattan," Struan said. God, it was nice to hear him relaxed. "Percentage is probably higher out here."

"Mm, right, without his mom looking over his shoulder."

"If you think geography matters, Rox Out, you don't know my mom."

Curiosity took her to the bedroom door, she snuck along the upstairs hallway, concealed by the wall.

"You want a drink?" Struan asked.

"Yeah, I do," Rox said. "In my empire. Grab anything you need, the car's still warm outside."

"I'm not going out."

"Why not?" Rox said, boastful. "We get cell signal at the club."

"Or so she's told. When was the last time you charged your own phone?"

"And I said the money wouldn't change me."

"It didn't. You never did it yourself before, now your guy pays someone to do it."

"Not exclusively. Though that's been a tug of war between us since—why are we talking about me? Come on, we're leaving."

"I'm not leaving," Struan was adamant. "I won't leave her alone in the house with him."

"Thought he was out."

"Yeah, but he'll come back eventually."

"Like a bad smell. Get her and we'll all go. Is her name really Bambi or is that a sex thing?"

"It's her name, not a sex thing," Struan said, confused. "What kind of sex thing involves animated characters?"

"I don't know," the second guy said. "Ask Lola Bunny."

"He doesn't call me that in bed," Rox said, almost sneering. "Or maybe he does, I don't know, I keep my earbuds in. Playing Pink Floyd on repeat is the only way I have of getting off."

"Let me guess, 'Money'?"

"Anything hotter? You wouldn't understand, Trust Fund Brat. Why are we talking about my relationship again? Let's talk about yours, oh, wait, you don't have one because your penis will explode if it visits the same pussy twice."

She smiled. Rox, whoever she was—wait, Rox, like... Pressing herself to the wall, she slid just a little further along to peek down into the foyer below. Three of them. Struan, Rox, shit, that really was...

"Are you really that bad in bed no woman will lay down with you twice?"

"Your guy had you sign an NDA before you fucked. What's that say about him?"

"That Lomond secrets will remain Lomond secrets, and he's put a ring on my finger just to make sure."

Rox… Roxie. Was having Roxie Kyst there the same as having the press around? Why would Struan trust her there with everything that was going on?

"And we'll all be paying for that forever."

"Oh, boo hoo," Roxie said. "You'd be heartbroken, you can't stay away from me, Priest."

"Priest." Oh, God, that was—now they were all looking up at her, had she—shit. "Uh…"

"Hey!" Roxie called, separating from the group, arms open. "Come here." She glanced at Struan who shrugged. "I've been taking lessons from Jane. Trust me, I'm better at this…" Rolling her wrists, the woman gestured her down. "I'll be gentle."

Okay, she'd revealed herself, what choice did she have?

Going down the stairs, she spent more time looking at Struan than anyone else. And not just because he was her anchor.

Roxie came over to meet her at the bottom and immediately pulled her into a hug.

"B, this is Roxanna Kyst and—"

"Tripp Breckenridge," the guy said.

Shaking his head a little, a smile threatened Struan's somber lips. "Ignore that, he can't help it."

"Can't help what?" Tripp asked.

"Your swagger's worse than my guy's," Roxie said before pulling back to meet her eye, hands still on her arms. "Are you okay, honey?"

"Am I…?" Another glance at Struan. "I… yes."

"So you're the waif from Wishbone," Tripp said, checking her out with an interest that wasn't close to a come on. Roman could take lessons. Somehow there was actual respect in that gaze. "You don't disappoint."

"I... I'm what?"

"Lot of talk about you."

"Talk, when? Why—who?"

"You were special requested for the Lighting Darkness event." That stunned her into silence. "Guess you didn't know that."

"I didn't."

"Neither did I," Struan said. "Who?"

"From the top."

"All the way—"

"Yep."

"And now you've sufficiently freaked her out..." Roxie said, looping their arms together. "Drinks all round! I don't have my ace bartender with me, but the understudy's been practicing."

"I know you're not talking about Tripp." Struan led the way toward the living room. "Getting wine from the bottle to the glass taxes him."

"Well, you know..." Roxie held their link closer. "It involves him taking his hands out of her bra..."

"Shows what you know." Tripp exuded only pride. "Getting rid of the bra is step one."

"Before the drink?"

"Way before."

Struan stopped by the couch. "You want to sit out back?"

"Is Roman afraid of the dark?" Roxie asked. "If so, yes, and let's turn out all the lights."

Tripp dropped into the furthest armchair. "That's the woman's fiancé you're talking about."

When her horror rushed to Struan, the last thing she expected to see was his smile.

"Relax, B, they know it's not real."

And just like that, all the tension rushed out of her body. In some possessed moment, she grabbed Roxie into another hug, tighter, and way more sincere than the last.

TWENTY-TWO

"AWW, HONEY," Roxie cooed. "Were you worried I thought you'd lost your ever-loving mind to be attracted to a cretin like him?"

"Still Struan's brother," Tripp reminded her in the background. "And Sway's ex."

"That was Stockholm. No one will convince me different," Roxie said, stroking her hair. "No, you can talk freely here, Bambi, honey. Tripp really would explode if he betrayed anyone's confidence. And Struan's loopy-lou for you, honey. There's no denying that." Stated as fact with a neutral expression like it was no big deal, Roxie glanced left and right. "Where is my drink again?"

"Wait 'til you see this," Tripp said, slouching low in the seat, resting muscular forearms on the arms. "This is where Roxie rights the wrongs of the world."

"I don't right the wrongs. I just call it like I see it. And this is a complete clusterfuck." To calm herself, or maybe to soothe, Roxie guided them to the couch and seated them close together, arms still entwined. "You should've called me earlier."

"I've never called you in my life," Struan said, somehow knowing the woman meant him.

"Well, you should've. I shouldn't have to hear this third hand from Tripp."

"Third hand?"

"She was eavesdropping. She eavesdrops," Tripp said, looping her in. "Roxie meddles."

"I don't know how I've been tagged with this label."

"You denying it?"

"No, but don't you think you should let people figure it out for themselves?"

"There's only so many hours in the day, Rox Out. Sometimes skipping the first few pages is a good thing." Switching it up, Tripp leaned forward to rest his elbows on his knees, cradling his glass in both hands. "Here's what you need to know about Roxie Soon-to-be-Lomond." He winked at Roxie and the woman tsked in return. "She's a Chicago girl who takes loyalty seriously. She works hard to get things done, and almost as hard to hide that truth. She came from her regular girl life to her current billion-dollar status by way of a TV talk show contest that sent her around the world with the man now betrothed to marry her. God knows how drunk he was when making that decision. He's always been staunchly anti-drugs, but I guess he could've been spiked or whatever."

"Tri—"

"She's smart, vicious when she needs to be, she's astute. She talks too much and there's nothing, honest to God nothing, that she wouldn't do for someone, anyone, in need. Unless that someone wronged her, which means, yeah, pretty much everybody."

"There are people I wouldn't go to any lengths for."

"Yeah, the people who wronged you, I just said—" Tripp shrugged. "Okay, I take back astute. She has the attention span of a gnat."

"*My* attention span's—I'm sorry, how many women did you pick up on the way here?" Roxie asked. "And we came in a private car! How did you even manage to get that blonde's number?"

"That blonde, this blonde, any blonde, I'll take a brunette and a redhead too. I'm an equal opportunities fornicator."

"Maybe I should tell Bambi what she needs to know about Tripp Breckenridge."

"Maybe the two of you…" Struan said, coming over, holding out glasses to each of the women, "should stop sniping at each other and tell us why you came."

"Not for nothing, Struan, baby, but in the movie, Bambi is a boy," Roxie said for no reason she could fathom. "Everyone thinks he's this cute, little, innocent fawn, but by the end of the movie, he's a hot, horny stag I'd ride all kindsa ways."

"Okay. Should I send out a press release?"

"I'm saying Bambi is not to be underestimated, perception doesn't always tell the whole truth." Roxie accepted her drink. "And he has excellent taste in friends."

"Friends?"

"Thumper," Tripp explained. "The rabbit. Like Lola Bunny."

"That's what you came to tell us? The deer and the rabbit will be friends?"

"You know why we came. It's all over the place out there. Roman Lowe meets the woman of his dreams, moves on from the tragic mess that was his life. People are all over Sway. We've got folks camped outside the house."

"Nothing new there," Tripp said, accepting a

glass from his friend. "What food have you got around here?"

"What do you want?"

"It's after midnight," Roxie said. "Maybe you two put a kibbutz on your feast and lose a few pounds while we straighten out some kinks. Pay close enough attention, you might learn something."

"Don't kid yourself, Rox Out."

Tripp caught the bag of whatever Struan threw over their heads. He opened it to scoop a handful of nuts into his mouth.

"How can you still be hungry anyway?" Roxie asked. "You ate right before we came out."

"A couple of times," Tripp said. "Twins are twice the effort." He pointed right at her. "Bambi knows what I'm talking about." Ew. "A man needs to keep his energy up."

"Okay," Struan said on a snicker, seating himself at the opposite end of the couch, nearest his friend. "If the goal was to freak Bambi out, I think you've achieved it. We should kick you out, she'll want to get to bed now."

Putting it in that way reminded her of the previous night.

"These situations aren't easy even when everyone is on the same page," Roxie said, arching a brow, sipping from her glass. "Not bad."

"Never going to beat your man in this house."

Roxie's smile became sly. "Never gonna beat him with your bank balance either."

"Money means squat to you, Roxanna," Tripp said. "Stru would run rings around your guy in the gym, then who'd take you home?"

"Ha!" Struan raised his own glass. "I forfeit. Roxanna Kyst is way too high maintenance for me."

"How is Sway?" she asked, recalling what had

been said about Roman's ex. "Is this hard on her?"

"She'll bounce. She's a tough cookie."

Roxie's next drink was more generous. "And silently thanking the gods, I'll bet. But this is going to explode soon. What's the exit strategy?"

Tripp and Roxie had manners enough to glance at her first, but Struan was their ultimate focus.

"Are you looking at me? You think I make the rules around here? You think if I made the rules that things would go the way they always do?"

"Roman's way?" Tripp said. "He doesn't make the rules or follow them. He makes it up as he goes along. Maximum destruction, that's what he cares about."

"That's not true," Roxie said, lowering her glass to her thigh so an opposite fingertip could touch the surface of the liquid. "He cares about his ego, his reputation, his good looks. He cares about being popular. He cares about people liking him—no scratch that, he doesn't. He wants people to worship him. He cares about his supposed supreme entitlement—"

"Okay, okay," Struan said, tossing back half his drink. "We know where you stand."

"Yet no one knows where you do. This is why Thea got into it with you too because you fail to look beyond the next twenty minutes. Suppose it's something you and your brother have in common. You got this girl into this mess and now you want to turf her out into the world when you're done with her? Just randomly tell the press one day, 'hey, it's over,' and hope they don't eviscerate her? You know Roman will never take the blame. He'll never be grateful. He'll throw her to the dogs and won't even care that—"

"Magnus said I was protected from the press here."

"Here? Maybe, but, at some point, tomorrow, the next day, six months from now, will you still be living under this roof pretending to be Roman's girlfriend? Excuse me, fiancée?"

"Roxie—"

"You know how I feel about Z and I doing our thing to cover those who deserve it. I don't know much about this girl. Maybe she doesn't deserve it, but I honestly feel immensely sorry for you, Bambi. I can't imagine having to spend five minutes smiling in Roman's company, let alone doing it through a whole meal."

"I won't be here in six months," she said, shifting position to get a better look at Struan at the other end of the couch. "Will I? Will I be here in six months?"

What was she really asking? Would she be playing Roman's fiancée in six months? Would they still be sneaking around making out and copping a feel wherever they could? Seemed juvenile when she put it like that, but she couldn't imagine being away from Struan if given half a chance. Except he lived with his brother, his obstinate, demanding, prima donna brother. Would Roman give her up? Hand her off to his twin? Forget about the press. Was anyone allowed to choose someone over Roman Lowe, in his eyes?

"From the blank stares and slack jaws. I'm going to assume there is no exit strategy."

Tripp laughed. "Come on! You're Queen of No Exit Strategy.

"Ah! Ah!" Roxie raised an erect forefinger. "Empress of No Exit Strategy. I'm going to guess as well that Roman doesn't treat Bambi with much respect." There was that questioning brow arch again. "Am I right?"

Diplomacy eluded her, instead, she aimed for contrite. "I try not to spend too much time with him."

"No one wants to spend time with him, honey. I could tell from the pictures online he's an asshole to you. Since getting with Zairn, we've been kind of lining them up and knocking them down when it comes to friends and acquaintances pairing up. Seen a lot of love this year, a lot of respect, a lot of decency, seen a lot of heartbreak too. Fundamentally, Roman doesn't care about you. It's written all over his face and I'm not even talking about when he's looking at you. I mean that's obvious in itself, but it's—"

"The little things."

Roxie gestured with her drink. "The little things. Exactly. He holds your hand like you're an accessory. He doesn't walk in front of you to protect you, he does it to put himself in the lens. He wouldn't let anyone steal the show and you're far more interesting. Everyone knows Roman Lowe's story, where he's come from, where he's going, or where he wants to go, which may be two completely different places. What you need is a wing woman."

"She does not need a wing woman," Struan said, shaking his head fast, leaning over to put his glass on the coffee table.

"You're afraid of me," Roxie taunted.

"If he's got half a brain, he's afraid of you. I'm afraid of you." Tripp swallowed more from his almost empty glass. "Can we get a bottle over here? We're professionals."

Struan got up to go fulfill his friend's request. She supposed anyway.

"Then a wingman." The future Mrs. Lomond was tenacious. "Let Tripp stick with her."

"Not a chance."

"You trust your best friend with your girl. They shouldn't be either if you don't."

"I'd trust them both naked, alone, and drunk out of their minds, yeah. That's not why it's a bad idea."

Even Tripp was shaking his head. "You know, Rox Out, I never walk away from a woman in need, but do you think I'll make the situation better? Me in close proximity to Roman? How long ago was it I challenged him to a bareknuckle fight on the beach?"

"Hmm." Rox's head dropped to the side. "Good point. Well, if we can't stay here, she's coming with us."

"I'm coming with you?"

"Excellent! That's agreed." Whoa, that was so not what she—did Roxie ever give up? "Magnus said you were safe here because they'd look after the press stuff for you. I can do that at Jane's."

"Jane's?"

"It's where Zairn and I stay when we're in town. Most times. Jane's our best friend and wedding planner. Tripp and I are staying there. It used to be Knox's house, and then it was kind of Kintyre's, but him and Lilya are on honeymoon at the moment, so we have plenty of extra room."

"No, I wouldn't want to impose on your friend. She doesn't even know me, it wouldn't be right to invite me—"

"No worries." Tripp returned to his slouch, glass aloft when Struan appeared beside the chair to top it off. "She does it all the time."

"What happened on set today?"

Oh, Roxie. As Struan sat again, he paused halfway to the backrest, absorbing the exact question he'd wanted to avoid.

"How do you know anything—"

"Because I have my sources."

Tripp's amused lips curled around the rim of his glass. "She eavesdrops."

"I didn't eavesdrop this, Priest. I heard it direct from an eyewitness. He had a tantrum and threw something at a producer."

"Sound technician," Tripp corrected.

"Oh, Mr. Breckenridge, sound technician, excuse

me, that makes it okay then." The blonde didn't hang on to her sarcasm. "Do you know how dangerous that is, Stru? Your brother getting violent? With crew? When he's supposed to be sober and—"

"I don't need to be lectured," Struan said, his hand leaving his leg. "I didn't throw anything at anyone."

"Yet you're the one getting heat whenever he does something wrong," Roxie said. "Every single time, and every single time you put up with it."

"What do you want me to do instead? Throw you out? I'm not the one who's done anything wrong."

"Try focusing on the person who has and see that he's not good for you."

"So he should throw Roman out?" Tripp asked, maybe enjoying stirring the pot just a little too much.

"I don't care what he does with Roman. I wouldn't put up with it. I have an annoying sister whose mooching boyfriend is banned from calling my guy because he's such an entitled jerk. I have zero patience when it comes to people screwing with those I love. There's no law that says you have to live with your brother. Why not just leave?" As Struan answered, Roxie chanted along… "Because you won't leave Bambi here alone."

Somehow, Struan kept his good humor. "If you know the answer, why ask the question?"

"Okay, well problem solved, she comes home with me and Tripp. Everyone gets a breather. For the record though, you were here before Bambi got here. Your life is entwined with his."

"I've heard this before."

"And it never gets through. One of these days you'll care about something enough to listen and see that what we're saying is right."

His unenviable position wasn't made any better when the front door opened and bodies barreled in.

Bodies? Magnus and Roman. Damnit. Caught.

"What the fuck are these people doing in my house?" Roman demanded.

TWENTY-THREE

"HAVING A GOOD TIME," Tripp muttered. "Until you showed up."

How did Roman not see what his attitude did to the atmosphere? What a different life he could have if he was just a little more aware.

"I didn't give you permission to be here."

"Nobody asked," Roxie said. "Especially you. I've seen enough of you to last me a lifetime. You're just a scared little boy."

"Insults don't get us anywhere," Magnus said, putting himself beside Roman. "They're just having a drink. They're friends."

"When it suits them," Roman said. "They're hangers-on. Wannabes."

"Said the washed-up has-been," Roxie retorted. "And I don't know if you've noticed, but my press is way more favorable than yours. And way more widespread. I have the world, and you can't even get the zip code. I came here because I care about Struan. Just like Tripp. And we care about Bambi. She doesn't deserve to have you foisted upon her. You should be kissing her feet for putting up with this to save your skin. Are you kidding?"

"Roxie…" Magnus warned.

"Okay, I know. I'm sorry. I'm poking the bear, I'll stop. Subject change? What happened on set today?"

"Roxie," that time it was Struan warning the blonde.

"God, a woman can't get two words out without getting in trouble from someone."

Roman sneered. "How does Lomond put up with you?"

"I'd tell you to ask him yourself, Roman, but I wouldn't advise you get too close to him any time soon. My man still owes you an ass-kicking."

"Like to see him try." He thrust an arm toward Tripp. "And what is he doing here? I don't want him anywhere near my sight. Show up to man up?"

"I already invited you to have your ass kicked." Tripp exhibited no concern. Ease seemed to be his specialty. "Offer's open-ended if you want to go now…"

In the middle of the living room in this multi-million-dollar mansion?

"Where is she?" Roman demanded.

"Sitting right there," Tripp said, nodding toward her.

"Not her. You know who I'm talking about. Where's Sway?"

"Not here," Tripp said. "Bambi is the one you should be focused on. Isn't she your fiancée?"

Did Roman know they knew it was bullshit, or were they back to perpetuating the lie?

"I've been calling her," Roman spat, "sending messages. She's not responding. You won't let her, will you? Can't back up the cocky playboy stuff when there's a better guy on the scene, can you? She'll never pick you."

When Tripp laughed, everyone tensed… except

Roxie. "She didn't pick you. Regardless of her brief circle back to Deacon she's not the type to travel old ground. A hot ass babe like that doesn't need to pick up old trash."

"You fucking asshole!"

Magnus grabbed Roman's arm to haul him back. "No one's fighting! Sway's not here, is she?"

"No, and she won't come within twenty miles of this place," Roxie said. "Personally? I'd make it fifty, probably fifty states, but she's scrappy, she knows what she's doing."

"Where have you got her locked up? With Knox Collier? You got her tied up with him? On a leash? Collared?"

"Jealous?" Tripp asked. "Never trusted you enough to engage in that kind of play. Guess some, trustworthy, men bring out the kink in her. I wouldn't trust you to collar a dog."

"Tripp, man," Struan said, still holding ground on the couch.

Given the buzz in the air, if anyone moved too fast or too far, the lid would blow off the can and all kinds of worms would spill out. The permanent kind that couldn't be put back or hidden away.

"He brought her up. You know damn well Sway's better off without him. Bambi would be too. Guy needs to get himself in order. You know…" When Tripp shifted to the edge of his chair to dump his glass on the table, the tension pounced a few notches. Except he wasn't getting up. Just adjusting his position. "You used to be okay, Roman. Back in the day. Way, way, back in the day. You always thought too much of yourself. Though arrogance isn't short in our crowd, could be contagious.

"But, Sway, the way you treated her. They way you are now, the way you were on the island, and since rehab. You're losing your grip, man. This isn't even the addiction."

"I'm clean," Roman asserted.

"Maybe that's the problem. Because whatever's going on with you, it's not about Sway or Bambi. You have a chance at getting your career back. All you have to do is show up and do your job. That's it. Struan's doing all the heavy lifting. Just make the faces and say the lines. That's all they need you to do. Why are you still so hooked up on Sway? Why can't you let her go?"

"Because she's mine," he barked. "You don't understand, you don't get it. She's my soulmate."

"Then you've spent too long in this town. Because happy ever after is a rare thing. Even rarer when it's unrequited. Sway is moving on with her life. Take a breath. Go to some Thai spa retreat, whatever it is you need because you're putting too much on her."

"You're only saying this because you want her for yourself. What did you do to her? You don't screw around on a woman like Sway Sheridan, stick your dick in her and then take it to the next 'ho at the party."

"Sway is not a whore," Roxie stated, clear, concise, and extremely unimpressed. "I'd go so far as to say no woman is. There's no such thing. If males are so rarely held to that standard, why should women be?"

Roman scoffed out a snicker. "Guess your guy's got his work cut out for him. All those late nights in the club, how many guys you take hard and fast in those dark corners? Do you even know their names? Shit, I'd be surprised if you even looked at their faces. You take any guy who'd bend you over and ram his cock inside you."

"I wouldn't take you," Roxie said, cheerier. "Not in a million years. In fact, when it comes to you and me, I'm the exact opposite of a whore. You can consider me a goddamn nun. I'm Mother Teresa. I'm the Virgin Mary. That goes for me and all my girls, which I'm sorry to say for you, includes Sway."

Roman pounced a stride toward the blonde. "You have no right!"

Struan rose in a half crouch, ready to move, but Magnus got in front of the actor.

Roxie laughed. "Until you work on your boundaries, this conversation is over." When the beauty slammed her glass on the table and stood up, she took Bambi right along with her. "Tripp."

He got up a flash before Struan.

"What the fuck is happening?" Roman asked.

Tripp came around the back of the couch to close in on her other side. His long arm encompassed both her and Roxie as they beat a path toward the front door.

"We're getting out of here."

"No, no, I don't fucking think so," Roman said, rushing to put himself in their way. "She stays fucking here."

"If she wants to go, she goes." Struan's voice—firm, a little impatient, and a lot resolute—brought them all around. "Get out of her way, Roman."

"You're going to let these fuckers take my fucking fiancée?"

"She's not your fiancée and she's put up with enough shit from you this week."

"We had an agreement—"

"No one's cancelling anything," Roxie cut Magnus off. "We're taking her to a safe place to be surrounded by people who actually give a damn about her needs." Roxie showed Struan her hand. "And I don't give a down how many times you felt her up or stuck your tongue down her throat. The fact that she's still here and he's still standing means you prioritize your brother. Which means she's not as safe here as she should be. I will not leave a woman in jeopardy. You can let this happen quietly. We'll walk out the door without incident and go from one private driveway to the next where no one knows who's getting in or out the car. No one's busting open your secret, or tarnishing your so-hard-won reputation that you clearly care so much about." Not. "But if you want to make this difficult, we can do that too. I'll call Ballard. It's no trouble, I have him on speed dial."

"I'll call Ax," Tripp said.

"What's your brother going to do?" Roman snickered with ridicule. "He's in New York."

"He's not, actually, but his location doesn't make any difference. You don't think he has agents everywhere?"

"So which is it to be?" Roxie asked, finding the diplomacy Bambi hadn't been able to muster. "We walk out. Everybody's smiling. Or we bring a goddamn army and half the world's press? You know I have the Colliers."

"You know I have the Wheys," Roman countered only to be startled by Roxie's laugh. "What the fuck?"

"Oh, you think Ricardo Whey's going to save your ass? He cares about his own far more, darling, believe me. The shit I know about that man. That Knox Collier knows about that man, that Caspian Collier knows… Want to play fast and loose? Shake those dice? Place your bets. Let's just see. If you light the fuse, I'm more than happy for the dynamite to blast your pathetic little life to shit."

"Roxie…" Struan again.

Her eyes met his. She didn't want to be separated from him, but Roxie's description of this being a clusterfuck couldn't be more on the money. All she wanted to do was curl up somewhere with him and learn everything there was to know about the man who had her hooked.

Roman kept coming between them and after last night…

Said man stomped off like a petulant toddler. No surprise.

"Get the fuck out of here," Magnus snapped.

After another glance at Struan, she was guided in the huddle of her new protective friends into yet another limousine.

What just happened? "Did I just leave him?" she asked when the static white noise cleared from her ears.

"You're welcome," Roxie said, popping open a bottle of champagne.

"We're celebrating?"

"No, this is what they stock the car with by standard," Tripp said, reading her mood and retrieving flutes. "This is a rental."

"Because we couldn't be in a car anyone in the press might identify as ours," Roxie said, pouring slowly to maximize liquid and minimize bubbles.

"We're about to drive through them," Tripp said, shifting to put his back to the door as Roxie pushed her head down.

There was a clamor and some shouting and less than a minute later, it quieted.

Roxie let go and Tripp put a flute in her hand. "You'll get used to it."

She gulped the alcohol. "So people keep telling me."

"You didn't leave him, either of them," Roxie said. "Unless you want to, we can facilitate that too."

"I don't know you. Either of you." Why was she in that car driving away from the one person in the state she did care about? "Why would you help me?"

"Because right is right."

"You really hate Roman, don't you? What did he

do to you?"

Roxie and Tripp touched glasses and drank.

"Hate's a strong word," her new friend said. "There's few people I'd apply it to. I strongly dislike him."

Tripp tipped his glass her way briefly. "She hates DA Ackley."

The beauty carried on. "I don't like anyone who takes advantage of women or anyone who thinks they're better than anyone else. I haven't known Roman Lowe for long."

"She's known his younger brother longer," Tripp added.

With a smirk, Roxie peeked over her shoulder at him. "Would you stop?"

"Facts are facts, Rox Out. Logan Lowe got closer than the rest of us."

"You were never interested. Dry your tears, playboy. I was never broken enough for you and never will be. He has a hero complex. He likes to save women. For a limited time."

Which explained, sort of, why they were there and their current predicament.

"Does your friend know we're going to appear at her house?"

Uninvited.

"Jane? She's in bed already, and Knox wouldn't appreciate the interruption. She left the club a couple of hours ago."

Club? Crimson?

"You were at Crimson?" She gasped. "You left the club to come here? Oh my God, I'm so sorry!"

"For what?" Tripp asked. "We live in the club."

"In New York, we live in the club," Roxie said. "Here it's more of an evening retreat. A place to get Zen."

For them. What about others? Sway wasn't with the duo, and she didn't blame the actress for staying away from Roman. She'd never got a straight answer on Sway's reluctance.

"Is Sway still in love with him? With Roman?"

Roxie scoffed.

Tripp smirked. "Not a chance."

Amusement faded to a curiosity until the blonde asked, "Do you care? Are you worried she might want him back?"

"No! She can take him. She can have him," she said maybe too quickly. "I worry with the way he's fixated on her… She could be in trouble."

"She's not the only one."

Bambi shook her head. "I think Roman will be happy when this is over. As happy as I'll be."

"Don't count on it. He likes the attention, and to have as many people in his orbit as possible."

"It's causing damage. I can see it."

"Damage?"

"To their relationship. Him and Struan."

"They're brothers, twins, have been through their whole lives together. Trust me, you're not causing any harm that wasn't there already."

"Struan doesn't deserve this."

"So we keep telling him," Tripp said.

"How do we help? How do we stop it?"

"All we can do is be there for him. He has to make his own choices, his own mistakes. At some point, maybe now maybe in fifty years, it will combust and Struan will realize what life with Roman has cost him."

"Will it cost him you?" Roxie asked. "You could be enough to make him see—"

"I'm not."

"You've asked him to walk away?"

"I'd never do that. He's stood up for me. I know

he cares. But this is temporary, it's not enough. When I'm gone, the record will keep spinning."

"Don't worry, girlie, we got him."

Would that be enough to alleviate her guilt about walking away? Struan had people in his life who cared about him. People who hadn't been able to convince him to leave his brother's side in all the years they'd known him. Was she doing damage? Was she making it worse? Would the brothers' relationship survive this, or would the abuse continue?

He'd be okay without her, wouldn't he?

TWENTY-FOUR

SHE OBSESSED ABOUT it, about him, about them. They needed more time to communicate, which was why she snuck into his trailer not long before he called lunch on the stunt rehearsals.

The stunt crew would be shooting that afternoon.

Roman liked as few people on set as possible, to maintain the illusion, she supposed. So she wouldn't be allowed to watch.

In the trailer, she sat there, waiting. Her fingers tucked beneath her thighs before they touched her neck and ran through her hair. With a thud, her head fell back against the wall behind the couch.

If Struan walked in with anyone else. What possible reason could she have for being there? He'd come up with something. He was better at this than her.

When the door opened, she held her breath until the door closed behind him. Alone. They were alone. She exhaled.

"What's wrong?" he asked concern immediately

etching his brow.

"Nothing."

"No? I saw you sneak off." Had he expected her to be there? "Are you okay? Did something happen last night?"

"Nothing, Roxie and Tripp took good care of me. I didn't see much of the house, but it seems like a beautiful place."

"I've been there." Struan stomped over to sit next to her, that groove still worrying his features. "I didn't want to send you off. I didn't want it to be like that. Like I didn't want you around. I thought after everything that happened with Roman, you'd be calmer, happier, there."

"Calmer, maybe, but happier? I missed you."

When she tried to take his hand, he curled his fingers into a fist, away from her touch. "I can't stand the way you're tossed around," he admitted. And the pain of his rejection ebbed when that same hand cupped her jaw. The pad of his thumb moved slowly back and forth on her cheek; with that simple connection the world was safer, brighter. "You shouldn't be enduring any of this. I'm sorry."

He'd apologized before. Didn't take then and it wouldn't take now.

"You're tired." She lay her hand over his. "You didn't sleep."

The corner of his mouth reacted. "You were too far away."

"What happened after we left?"

"Took Ro a while to calm down but he ran out of steam eventually."

"It's so complicated, I don't understand it."

"Understand what?"

"You and Roman. The dynamic between you. You're so calm and together. He's the complete opposite. I see the strain. How the threads of your sanity are stretching. Mine would too. Anyone's would."

"Let's not talk about that. Let's not talk about him. You look beautiful today."

Flattered, her grin was automatic. "You're gorgeous every day. How do you feel? About this afternoon. Are you ready?"

"Piece of cake. We've been going through the motions. We've got it down. I trust my guys."

"Set seems a lot quieter today. There's less tension in the air."

"Roman's off set. He did a couple of hours this morning."

That might mean… "Can I watch?"

"Yeah, come check it out. Set's mine. When it's up to me, you're always welcome. Might throw me off my game though."

"You?" she said, leaning in, hand trailing up his thigh. "Didn't peg you for the performance anxiety type."

"Don't jinx me, baby. Hasn't happened yet. But if there's one woman I'm terrified to disappoint, it's you."

"Not possible. I'm impressed. Always impressed. Have been since the minute we met."

"Yeah?" he asked, relaxing when she climbed over to straddle his lap.

"Yeah. I don't worry about the physical with us." Her fingertips met his cheeks as she bowed forward to breathe him in. "I just wish we had more time to be ourselves. Talk about all the things I want to do with you. All the places I want to take you. What we could be."

"Take me? Around the world?"

"No." She laughed. "I've barely left this coast for more than a minute. I want you to see my home one day. You welcomed me into your life." Against his will or not, she was definitely in deep. "I want you to know where I came from, to introduce you to everyone, to show you off."

"I'm the one who'd be showing you off. Long as you stay mine, the rest of them can look."

Her nose brushed across his before their lips met for the scarcest of moments.

"Take you to Elda's for cake. All the way up to the summit of the Crest, if it's warm enough, I always wanted to make love in Lover's Crag, I never did that. Never wanted to before you. Now it's all I think about. Being alone in there with you, completely alone, just us, where no one else can find us."

"Never did it with an ex?"

"God, no, I'd never… You bring it out in me, I guess, my wild side." She laughed. "I say that until we get caught and shame my family forever."

"Let the town come watch, they can drag me away, long as you finish."

"Me?" she exclaimed. "We!"

"You. If I got that chance, there's no way I'd leave you unsatisfied."

"Am I crazy?"

"Not crazy, Fawn, it would be my honor. Then where would we go?"

"I don't have my apartment anymore, thank God. It was so tiny, you would never fit. But I'm not sure my dad would be wild about us sharing my childhood bedroom either."

"In case I sully his little girl?"

"You could try." Oh, it was so easy to be happy with him. "The walls are paper thin, we'd corrupt the whole block.

"I accept that challenge." She kissed him again, then he rested his head on hers. "What is it, baby?" he murmured, stroking from her hips to her waist up to her shoulder blades and down her spine. "What you thinking about?"

"How I want you to always think of me like this. I want us to remember each other like this. Like in the basement, and in my room in, and here. When it's just us alone. The things we do to each other, the way we feel… However it turns out, it's real. Please don't ever hate me."

"Hey, Fawn," he soothed. "How could I hate you?"

"Because we don't know what long-term damage this could do to your relationship with Roman."

"It's just us here." He pulled her mouth to his. "Just us, baby. Be just us."

Permission? Excuse? Whichever it was, she gave in and did just that. Oh, to be nothing but his. The sweet texture of his lips moving on hers and the cool touch of his tongue suggested they had all the time in the world. They had to live like that. In a fantasy bubble, believing nothing else existed, because that was when everything was okay. When they kissed and touched and lived in each other, nothing about them was wrong.

She didn't hear the door open. Just Magnus's exclamation. "Jesus!" Tearing herself away her attention flew around to him. "How the fuck can you two—" He stopped himself and got away from the door to nod toward it. "Out!"

"Hey! Who do you think you're—"

"Out! Now, Bambi. Go. Struan and me need to have a talk."

Despite his annoyance, Struan nodded. She fixed her skirt, climbing off his lap, and trailed out of the trailer like a scolded schoolgirl. It wasn't fair that Struan would face all of Magnus's wrath, but she'd got between him and too many of his relationships. She had to let him handle this one alone.

TWENTY-FIVE

YES, SHE GOT to watch stunt filming, but there wasn't much time for talk. And every time Struan's eyes met hers, she looked away, fearful the truth of her feelings would show.

In the car with Mieux that evening, she couldn't stop thinking about him. The authority in his voice, guiding others, stopping and starting, patient, composed, taking the time to ensure everyone's comfort and safety. He made it look so easy to get the needed shots without the usual tension or anger.

They slowed as the gate opened. It was only as they went through that she even thought to look out the window.

"Roxie's?"

"Yes, I heard that was the plan. Would you rather go somewhere else?"

"No."

Whatever the plan, it was her responsibility to stick to it. Though she'd be sorry not to see Struan again that night. Two nights in a row without him was just too much.

Throughout the afternoon, she'd worried he might regret their brief interlude in the trailer. Whether he did or not, she thanked God they'd had at least that time to be alone. Wasn't much, no, but cold turkey wouldn't be good for either of them, they needed glimmers of togetherness if nothing else.

Mieux led the way inside past a floating staircase and partition wall that concealed a massive open plan space. Outside, a sunken lanai and pool perfected the epitome of indoor-outdoor living. Had she really spent the night there?

"Hello!" Roxie leaped up from her stool at the kitchen island to hurry over. "We've been waiting for you. How are you doing?"

We? So far all she could see was the blonde. Bambi never thought of herself as a hugger, as such, but Roxie's openness and desire to comfort were reassuring in the current mess of her life.

"Okay."

"And my Mieux." Roxie went to do the air kiss thing before giving Mieux a short, tight hug. "I've missed you."

Mieux laughed. "We talk on the phone all the time."

Warm hospitality was just Roxie's way. As expected, the woman shrugged off the remark. "I miss your face. You should get into the video call thing."

"I don't have time for video calls," Mieux said, clutching a tablet and leather binder to her body with one arm while the opposite hand held her cellphone.

"Woman doesn't know how to take a vacation," Roxie said. "How to relax. All that time together on a tropical island, and I never saw you drink one drop of alcohol."

"My whole life is a cost benefit analysis." Mieux's

lips stayed curled. "The costs of alcohol far outweigh the benefits."

"Then you haven't been doing it right," Roxie sang, dipping her head a little closer only to then straighten up and throw her arms in the air. "Ah! The man himself!"

No surprise who that would be. Tripp stayed there last night, so why wouldn't he still be present?

Except the tall, dark-haired man who walked by them wasn't the same ruffle-haired rake who'd brought her there last night.

"Surprised to see me?" The stranger's arm lunged out to snatch the blonde against him. "Shouldn't be. I'm always following you, Lola."

"Not always," Roxie said, sort of sly as she straightened her arms and the man came down to join their lips.

"They could be like that for a while." Mieux took her waist to direct her around the couple toward the kitchen. "Are you hungry? I can order in. What is everyone in the mood for?"

"Stop the presses," another male voice boomed from somewhere and she wouldn't be caught unawares again. God knew who else might creep out the night. Except this time, it was Tripp. Hmm, radar was off. Tripp didn't pay her, Roxie, or the other man the slightest bit of attention. "Did I hear Mieux Penrose's voice?" For the first time, Mieux paled like she might not absorb or rebuff whatever surprise might come her way. "I did!"

Roxie pushed away from her kissing partner and batted his arms to win her freedom. "Wait, wait, wait, I hear attitude. Definite tone and attitude. What's going on here?"

"I was going to order food," Mieux said, ignoring Tripp whose focus stayed absolute as he moseyed up to relieve the young woman of the tablet, folder, and phone. "Whatever you—"

"I've ordered food," Tripp said, snatching Mieux's hand now her shields from the world were on the kitchen island, unable to save her. "Come here."

Mieux yelped when he yanked her hard and sped them out of the public space.

"What don't I know?" Roxie landed suspicion on the man she'd just been making out with. "Casanova?"

"That you're my reason for living and breathing?"

Roxie tsked and rolled her eyes. "Duh!"

"The sun which my world revolves around?"

"Not about us, Skippy. About them."

The guy smiled and tossed an arm around his woman. "Bambi Bennett," he said. "I'd say 'I assume' but I know who you are."

"Right, right. Yes." Roxie patted the guy's stomach. "This is Z. Zairn, my Zairn."

"How many Zairns are there?" he asked.

"I don't know. Don't you and Tripp know everyone between you? Count them."

"You're engaged." Man, she was slow. "You're her—"

"My Casanova." Roxie rested her head against him for a brief second.

"I'll get drinks."

Zairn kissed Roxie's hair and went outside.

"This is an incredible place."

Roxie swept up her hand, using the loose connection to guide her over to the couch she been sitting on when Bambi came in.

"I'd say thank you, but it's not mine."

"Jane's. You said it was Jane's. Is she here?"

If she didn't meet the woman to say thank you, continuing to squat would be inappropriate. She didn't want this Jane to think she was rude. That and, you know, her mom would disown her.

"Dinner with the in-laws. Which is just as well because Jane's all about the romance. She'd love your star-crossed lovers thing. Did you speak to him today?"

"Struan? For a minute. It never seems like enough."

Roxie hooked an arm on the back of the couch to support her head on the heel of her hand and folded her legs up at her opposite side, holding them there with the other arm.

"Z and I have been together for almost a year, officially/unofficially, depends which version I tell. I have full access to him anytime I want him. And I can tell anyone in the whole goddamn world that he's mine. I can walk into any room, do anything to him. Touch him, kiss him, whatever I want." The woman's smile grew. "But I still feel exactly the same way about him." The joy quickly faded. "I'm so sorry you're going through this. I can't imagine what it must be to…"

Zairn came in, three glasses grouped in his hands. Roxie took the first and she took the second. Somehow, though there wasn't exactly much space, he sat between Roxie's back and the arm of the couch.

"This girl time?" he asked and kissed Roxie's head again as the woman adjusted to let his free arm curl around her waist.

"It never seems like enough," Roxie said, semi-turning her chin his way. "The time we have together."

"This another dig about me going overseas?"

"No," Roxie's retort was a high-pitched rebuke. "Stop flashing your ego at our new friend. We were talking about Bambi and Struan, how little time they get together, because no one can know about them."

"We've been there."

"Have we though?" Roxie said. "We were a

secret because it was a bad idea and you and your whole, 'best suited to ride your cock' thing."

"And after New Year?"

"I was oblivious, kidding myself. And it might not have been enough for us, but I didn't belong to anyone else in that time. Struan has to watch her with Roman. Imagine if you had to watch me with one of your boys all the time. What if I was going out to dinner with Ballard and the entire world thought we were in love?"

"You never could've sold that."

"We could've sold it," Roxie said on sort of a sneer, which cleared in an instant. "I can't even imagine it now, being near you without having you, without owning you."

"This supposed to console our new friend?"

"I'm commiserating, validating her feelings. Saying it's okay to feel the way she feels."

"Thank you," Bambi said, looking into her glass without any interest in tasting the liquid within. "What makes it harder is…"

Roxie leaned forward and, on instinct, Zairn's arm strengthened to give her counterbalance when she touched Bambi's face. "You never have to worry about saying anything in front of us, Bambi. We will always keep your secrets."

From the world or from Struan? Wasn't a plethora of trustworthy and sympathetic ears around. May as well take the risk, who else did she have to talk to?

She exhaled. "I don't know much about your relationship, but being two single people, you at least had the prospect of being together. How are Struan and I ever supposed to consider doing this for real?"

"You can give it a shot."

"How? It's not possible. It's not just that I can't be with a man I care about, it's that I'm with his brother and they live in the public eye. Yes, you were right, there's no exit strategy, not one I know. Even if there was, it would separate me from Roman. Great. Fine. That can't happen fast enough."

"But it separates you from Struan too." In understanding, Roxie sank back against her lover. "Have you talked about it?"

She shook her head. "I know it's not real. We all know it's not real, but what kind of woman moves from one brother to the next? I don't want Struan painted as the bad guy, I don't want any of us hounded by the press, but I also can't trust Roman to support us or tell any version of the truth other than one that paints him in the—"

"Best possible light?" Roxie said. "Imagine all those victim points. 'My brother stole my fiancée.' He'd be golden."

"In the public eye," Zairn said, proving he was listening.

He sipped from his glass, then rested his lips in his woman's hair. The couple touched, they felt, their physicality appeared natural. Impulse brought them closer. Each could read the others form and provide exactly what was needed. If she didn't already envy them their ability to be together, public and proud, she envied the security they had in each other.

"I'm no fan of Roman Lowe," Zairn continued. "If I got a say, I wouldn't have Roxie within a hundred city blocks of him."

"You get a say." Roxie pushed back a little against his mouth. "I just don't always listen."

"I can't blow smoke up your ass, Bambi, and imply that it's going to be okay and love will overcome the odds. Because you and Struan together could be the worst thing to happen to the Lowe family, to the industry, in quite a while."

"You haven't seen them together." Roxie laid her forearm on his to press her palm to his knuckles and squeezed tight; they oozed chemistry. "Who the hell do you think you are to say someone else can't fight to have what they want, Skippy? You did. How did that work out for you? Huh?"

"Don't get snippy with me. I am not diminishing what they have, I haven't seen it, I don't know. This is a warning from a friend, from a well-intentioned place. Think less about what this will do to Roman's career and more of what it will do to Struan if his brother loses everything."

"If Struan left his brother—"

"He loves his job."

"How could he keep it when the truth comes out? Even if they could hire another stunt coordinator, would anyone else put up with Roman's bs for more than five minutes?"

Not many folks, that's for sure. Maybe Magnus would help him hold it together if the brothers were forced apart.

"He's lost Sway and has been looking for an excuse to return to the crutch that got him in trouble in the first place."

Losing Sway, his brother, his job… would that send him back to his addiction?

"You can't put that on her." Roxie was quick to defend, as was always her way. "That's not Bambi's decision or Struan's. Don't make them accountable for Roman's bad choices. Tripp and I were just telling her last night how Struan never listens when we point out how little respect his brother shows. Struan doesn't need you dumping on him too."

"I don't disagree with you," Zairn said, composed as he sipped from his glass. "I'm just saying it's not necessarily going to be a bump-free fairy tale ending. You both have to decide how much you want this, what you're willing to sacrifice. Being together is an option, Bambi. It's always an option. There's nothing I wouldn't give up for Roxanna, and that's my choice. No relationship or job is worth more to me than she is."

Sacrifice? Like it or not, the guilt would burden Struan. He always took responsibility for his brother's mistakes.

"We'll support you," Roxie said, pushing her shoulders back. "If you want to do this, if you want to leave, throw down the gauntlet, issue the ultimatum—"

"Because that never causes problems in relationships," Zairn said, smirking. "Maybe try open communication first?"

"Mr. Know It All. We don't need you, Skippy," Roxie said. "I'll support Bambi without you."

How could she…? "Don't you live together?"

"What does that matter? I can help you and live with him simultaneously."

"I don't want to cause issues in your relationship. You've already been so generous."

Roxie laughed. "If we can overcome the issues *I* put in our way, we can overcome anything. This is nothing. He knows I'll do anything to protect my girls and wouldn't leave me for all the money and pussy in the land. So if you want to tell Struan you're ready to make it real, your guy just has to step up and do what's right. *My* guy will always show up for me, that's a given. Don't you worry about anything except your heart. I've got everything else covered."

She'd never met someone so certain or selfless. Zairn's head rose, drawing their attention to Tripp and Mieux joining them again.

"Good! Now the gossip," her blonde-haired friend exclaimed.

Mieux swatted at Tripp's hand when he touched

her waist.

"No gossip," Tripp said. The look on his face was far too satisfied to be absolutely meaningless. "Unfinished business."

"I'm not worried," Roxie declared with confidence. "We have a full bottle of your favorite Johnnie Walker behind the bar. And I might be in the mood to dance."

"I'm in," Tripp said.

Zairn snickered and downed the rest of his drink. "To which?"

He shifted forward on the couch, hand open in anticipation of Roxie's glass as she gulped its remaining contents. They might be able to down this strong liquor like it was nothing, she wasn't as practiced.

"Food's on the way. You said—"

"They'll redirect it." Glasses in hand, Zairn went back outside.

"I probably shouldn't go out tonight. I don't know if there's a plan."

"If there's a plan, it will find you," Roxie said, easing the glass from her hand to cast it aside, somehow aware of her reluctance to drink. "They'll bring food to the club, or box it up here for us to eat when we get back."

"Ask them to multiply everything by ten and send it to the Sigmore Shelter," Tripp said. "Hundred percent tip, put it on my tab."

"The homeless place?" Mieux asked, scurrying to the kitchen to retrieve her combat tools.

Roxie's grin was both proud and mocking. "Momma's boy."

Slipping his hands in his pockets, he shrugged.

This was happening? They were going to Crimson? "I might have work tomorrow."

"Thank goodness it's still today!"

Had Roxie ever met an objection she couldn't counter?

On Mieux's return, Tripp flopped an arm around her, yanking her to his side.

The assistant's body didn't respond. "I won't—"

"You will." Tripp was confident in his smile. Man was always confident. "Alcohol's optional."

"Anything goes at Crimson," Roxie said, tugging her onto her feet. "Come on, you have to visit. Otherwise it's like refusing to look at my beautiful child."

"Your beautiful what?" Zairn asked, sauntering up to them. "When did you get one of those?"

"Right about the same time you gave me that purple envelope."

"Luck of the draw," he said. Roxie took his arm in a mutual, probably unconscious, move. "What were the chances?"

And there was Bambi, lost. "Purple envelope?"

"You know," Roxie said, "I always wondered…"

Zairn offered Bambi his other arm. Her Bambi. Like her! This insanely hot, successful businessman with—who said this town wasn't a dream-maker? To hell with it. If she was going to get mixed up with anybody, better it be the involved one than the singleton. Though she wouldn't mind riling Roman by cozying up to Tripp, it wouldn't win her points with Struan. Choosing to play nice, though she'd get no acknowledgment for it, she slid her hand into Zairn's elbow.

"Wondered what, Rox Out?" Tripp asked, teeing Roxie up.

"If Jane and I had sat in opposite seats, would we still be here today?"

"Jane would never have broken the rules."

Roxie's shrug joined them on the way out to the car. "Toria then. Toria doesn't care about rules. She'd have got you drunk and jumped you for sure."

Tripp reached for the champagne the moment the door closed behind them. "So probably not."

"You think Tori would be in my place?"

"She'd probably be in jail," Tripp said. "Woman doesn't know the word decorum. She'll grab a guy just about anywhere."

"Z wouldn't press charges. You wouldn't press charges, would you, Casanova?"

"A man can be sexually assaulted too," Mieux highlighted, which provoked her nod.

"Absolutely, yes," Roxie agreed. "Toria knows things."

"Blackmail things?"

"Sex position things. She could teach my guy a thing or two. And the finger thing works on him, she likes that."

"Mmm, I'm intrigued," Tripp said. "Toria fancy a trip to LA?"

"Oh, little one, your eyes are too innocent for her wonders." That got a laugh as Roxie winked at him. "Besides, you know the rules, you want one of my girls? Pick carefully. She'll be the last of them you're allowed to touch."

"Rules," Tripp scoffed. "Like you follow rules."

"This one's law." Roxie tossed her hair. "You want to hang in my club, you obey my laws."

What kind of night awaited them? A club? No, not "a club" like it was just anywhere. Crimson was the most exclusive club in the universe, especially the sections these guys would hang out in.

Feeling inferior, a little self-consciousness visited. "I can't go clubbing in my work clothes."

Roxanna Kyst batted that objection out of the park too. "They'll bring us clothes there, don't worry. I'll look after you."

Yeah? From a woman who said "anything goes"

that wasn't particularly reassuring.

TWENTY-SIX

PARTYING SEEMED TO be on this gang's agenda every night of the week. Tripp's description of them as "professionals" was apt. How was anyone supposed to keep up? She surrendered to their superiority because what else could she do?

Roxie grabbed her and Mieux as soon as they got to Crimson. Not just anywhere in Crimson, right past the main dance floor, up a private staircase to the VIP floor. As if on cue, a stylist appeared to take them into a side room and dress them up for the night. Damn, she was getting used to the instant access thing. Not because the money mattered, no, but so many choices would be exhausting if she didn't have someone making them for her.

When they were freed from the fashion bonanza, drinks were brought to them and Roxie's favorite tracks were played. Though, with Roxie, every tune seemed to be her favorite. The hostess knew every word to every song.

Zairn sat on a couch in the same space, in a dark

corner occupied only by him. Others sat in adjacent seats, but no one dared touch the sofa. Was that another of Roxie's laws? More likely to be Zairn's; Roxie wasn't the jealous type. She'd never met a couple so secure in their relationship.

As soon as a glass was empty, another drink was put in her hand. Roxie had a gold medal in this clubbing thing, a platinum medal. If this was a sport, the woman would have a trove of trophies, no doubt about that.

At the other extreme, Mieux refused alcohol without anyone batting an eye, and her drinks were topped up just as quickly, even being virgin. With her friends at opposite ends of the spectrum, she could set her own pace. No one called her out to drink more or stick to alcohol. Every variation was accepted there.

Access to such a private world was mind-blowing. She still hadn't figured it out. In addition to their dance floor, private pods split this side of the VIP area from another. Some in darkness, others light, they hadn't ventured into them yet, maybe they wouldn't. Who knew?

Roxie tumbled her way to plant a kiss on her cheek and kept on dancing as she altered course to head for her man. Mieux came to take her hand. Not something the woman would normally do, but with the music so loud, it was difficult to get anyone's attention without physical contact.

Her colleague called into her ear. "Do you want to sit down?"

She nodded though could've kept on dancing. With the loud music pumping her endorphins, and the alcohol taking just the slightest edge of awareness from her consciousness, she lived in the moment. The environment, and company, made such a difference to her nerves, to her needs.

Roxie's suggestion to toss their worries into the

wind seemed wishful and ambitious until they were there, surrounded by friends, in the heady humidity and graciousness of Crimson's walls. There she could feel safe, like she would back home. Roxie was right. If this was her child, it sure was beautiful.

Mieux led her toward where Roxie was draped against Zairn. The beauty tempted her man's mouth to hers and he surrendered for a few beats. On breaking the union, he coiled an arm around Roxie's waist and lifted her as he stood, leaving the blonde's feet dangling a couple of inches from the floor before he set her on them. Roxie stayed that close and side-nodded with a point that prompted Mieux to adjust their trajectory.

Tripp was somewhere, had been somewhere. He'd flitted around until she lost track. In any other circumstance, she'd know where every member of their party was, so no one would get lost or hurt. That seemed unlikely in Crimson; Tripp should be fine.

The most central glass chamber lit up to reveal what was effectively a living room in the middle of a nightclub, and, ah, mystery solved: Tripp entered from the other side.

"Having a good time?" Tripp asked, wearing a grin that knew the answer.

Hers was maybe just as exuberant. "I've never been a VIP anywhere in my life."

"Get used to it," he said, dropping into the furthest armchair and smacking his thigh. "Mieux, babygirl, I've saved you a spot right here!"

The woman snickered and sat on the opposite armchair. "No, thank you."

The two shared a smile, maybe it was a private joke no one else got, but it was fun, not predatory.

Tripp moved on from Mieux's rejection fast. "You got the guys coming over, Z?"

"Soon."

"Cool. There's someone else here who needs a minute."

Zairn sat on the end of the couch closest to Tripp, guiding Roxie down with him by her hips. The blonde crossed her legs toward her love, and he draped an arm across her lap. Ah, swoon, their intimacy—the walls darkened, blocking the view of beyond.

Tripp's door opened—Struan.

He could be the last man on Earth or her first and only savior, she'd never been so pleased to see someone. She hurried over to throw her arms around him, it didn't even occur to her she should hesitate given he wasn't his brother. Or was he? Who was he playing?

"I'm so sorry about—"

Music started. Not loud but when she glanced back, Roxie was smiling and gave a single nod before returning to distracting her fiancé. The music gave them some cover to have an at least semi-private conversation.

"I was surprised you came here, Fawn. Are you okay?"

"Yes, but I've been worried about you. What did Magnus say today? I'm sorry if he reamed you out. He shouldn't have. You should have put it on me. I was the one—"

"Magnus is family." He stroked her arms and rested his palms on her shoulders. Fondness still bloomed in them but there was a reticence too. "We should talk about—"

"We have to stop," she said, reading the truth he didn't want to utter.

Knowing it didn't mean she wanted to hear it either.

"Yeah. At work. I agreed at work we would keep our distance. It's too difficult when so many people know us both."

"I understand." Finding errant sanity, she

dropped her arms and stepped away. "I'm sorry, I shouldn't have…"

"This isn't me. Tell me you know this isn't me."

"I know." The door opened again to someone else, a stranger the world knew. "Sway Sheridan."

"Sway, baby!" Tripp called, tipping his head back. "Saved you a spot right here!"

Much as Mieux did, the woman smiled and shook her head. Tripp was already conversing again, proving he hadn't expected a positive response.

The smile faded when Struan stepped aside. "You wanted to meet her. Bambi, this is Sway. Sway, Bambi."

"Hi."

"We have a lot to talk about."

Toward the back of the room was a high table with tall stools, Struan guided them over, then left them alone to join the others. Okay, so she had a private audience with the woman of wonder, and one question tumbled from her mouth without any thought.

"How did you do it?"

Sway smiled. It wasn't a broad or enthusiastic expression, somehow it betrayed that the question was anticipated.

"You must think I'm all kinds of crazy."

"Actually, I think you're the strongest person I've met. You know the truth, Struan told you?"

"He didn't have to, but, yes, I know the truth. I'm one of a select few who can understand exactly what you're going through. I've been in your shoes, Struan and I used to do it all the time. Especially when it was really bad, before rehab." The same role, yes, with one super important difference: Struan was her guy. Going home to Roman wouldn't be such an optimistic prospect. "You're lucky you have Struan to lean on. He's a good guy; he'll look after you."

"He tries," she said, pausing long enough to watch a server come in and distribute drinks. Not all conversation died, but people were certainly wary of new ears in the room, and only fully relaxed when the person left. "Roman's not an easy man to direct."

"Rome can be overwhelming. He is overwhelming. Don't believe everything he tells you. He can get cruel, abrupt. Some of the things he says… he only wants to hurt you."

"I'm less worried about me and more worried about Struan."

The actress touched the rim of her glass on an exhaled laugh. "That's a tangled web. They have a complicated relationship. Struan loves his brother very much. In his own way, Roman loves his brother in return. He just doesn't know how to show it. They never had a healthy example of a relationship to follow. Didn't have parents to watch—the closest they got was sleepovers with their friends most of whom lived in broken homes."

Most everyone did these days. Even in her hometown there were plenty of broken hearts and divorce agreements that came with bitterness and visitation arrangements.

"I just can't believe you did it for so long," she said, awed by the glamorous woman. "Or that you did it at all. I'm only pretending to be with him. I don't have to spend any time alone with him in private, yet I already feel like I'm going insane. I can't even talk to him; he doesn't seem reasonable. Feels like we're not on the same planet. My reality isn't his reality and there's Struan bumbling along, going with the flow, accepting every insult his brother throws, absorbing each body blow, and just continuing on."

"At some point, these things will take their toll. You think he's nearing breaking point?"

"Maybe not. I'd say so, but what do I know? I barely know Roman. It's unfair."

"It is, but none of us can make the decision except Struan."

Which was exactly what Tripp and Roxie told her.

"I tried to talk to Roxie about it. She says she'll support whatever I choose."

"Roxie is an incredible woman with a big heart. You can trust her completely, a hundred percent. She's shown me nothing but kindness and opened her home to me. It doesn't matter that I broke off my engagement to Deacon, which causes Logan issues. Roxie knew him first, but she still protects and supports me."

"Logan? Lowe? Roman and Struan's brother."

"Yeah. Truth is, if it hadn't been for Roxie and Tripp, I don't know how I'd have gotten through this. Roman's not the easiest man to rebuff. I can hire security and lock myself up, except then you end up isolated and afraid."

"You shouldn't have to live your life like that."

"Without their support, I'd have lost my mind or given in to Roman. Getting away from him the first time wasn't easy. Your relationship might be fake, but don't underestimate him. You're in his orbit now. He likes that, likes having people around him, people he can control and manipulate. You and Struan caring for each other gives him another avenue of torture. Don't expect him to graciously say goodbye and let you go, there's no end to this, he'll want you to stay close."

"Why?" she asked. "There's nothing invested here, no feelings. This only started because of Struan and me. It's a short-term arrangement, the relationship. Just to give Roman enough leeway to build his reputation again."

"Except he's already screwing that up. I heard

about what happened on set."

Everyone else knew more about it than she did, Hollywood was its own kind of small town. It certainly seemed that way with the amount of gossip and backbiting.

"Something's not right with him. Do you think he's using again?"

"I don't know, Struan doesn't think so. He's got people keeping an eye on his brother to make sure it doesn't happen again. But you can only keep someone safe as long as they want to be safe. If he chooses to go out there again, there's nothing any of us can do to stop him."

"He has it in his head that you two are meant to be. He talks about you all the time. Asks Roxie and Tripp. He gets frantic, worked up."

"I know, I have the voicemails to prove it. Another reason I'd probably be back there by now, if it wasn't for Roxie."

"You still love him?"

"As horrific as this sounds, it's guilt. When I hear him like that, and he's telling me I'm the cause, that he's in that state because of me, that he's thinking about using and can't survive without me... I think of all the people who rely on him. Friends. Family. Other actors, crew members, everyone connected to UO. If the one thing he needs to keep him steady is me, isn't it selfish not to give him that?"

"You deserve your own life as much as Struan, and you've broken free. If you go back to Roman now, you're showing Struan it's not possible to get out."

"Roxie tells me not to go back. She keeps me steady. I don't want him in my life. If I get pulled back in again, that's it, I'll never get out."

"You left for a reason. Was it the addiction?"

"Our relationship had been falling apart for a

while. And I say all this but, in truth, Roman's the type of man who's never satisfied. If I went back, I'd be rewarding this negative behavior, proving he can get what he wants if he holds his breath long enough."

"Should we be helping him? This has to be deeper-seeded."

"Rehab was supposed to help. Shit, for what it cost they should've brought him back with a brand-new soul. There's therapy and meetings and things he's supposed to deal with. We spoke about bringing in one of the top-tier life coaches, people who can really help, but he doesn't want any of it. He doesn't do any of it."

"Don't they say the aftercare is just as important as the residential stay itself?"

"Yeah, it's never a permanent state. You don't wake up one day cured, no longer addicted to your drug, whatever it may be. It's an ongoing process, in the same way it's an ongoing process for all of us with mental health and trauma. We have to be willing to admit we're not perfect. And no one can convince him of that."

"So why did he go to rehab in the first place?"

"I begged him to get clean for years and he never did. Maybe it was the work drying up and the whispers in the community. He was blackballed because he was just so damn unreliable. I told him I was leaving; he never accepted it. Maybe some part of him thought if he did it, I'd stay longer. Maybe I should have."

"He's a grown man."

"Yes."

"He shouldn't need all of us wiping his chin and patting him on the head."

"I'm sorry you got drawn into this, Bambi. Though I'm happy that Struan has someone at last. I'm sorry you're something else he'll lose for his brother. Because at some point you have to make a break for it, Bambi. You have to decide to go, and you have to run.

As fast as you can; as far as you can. And don't ever look back."

"Exactly what I've been telling you, Ms. Sheridan, for weeks!" Roxie appeared suddenly, slapping a hand on the table as she put an arm around Sway to squeeze and lean against her. "Regifting my advice?"

The women shared a smile.

Sway raised her drink. "Can we bring Bambi with us?"

Struck by freezing panic, just as she gained a support system, she could be losing it. "Where are you going?"

"Home," Roxie said. "New York."

"And you're going with them?" she asked. Sway nodded. "I've never been to New York."

"It's a wonderful city."

"We'll look after you there."

She just shook her head. "Not sure even Magnus could sell that one to the media. Me and Roman's former love elope to the Big Apple together?"

"Hey, you said you couldn't run away with his twin. Isn't his ex the next best thing?"

Roxie's joy encircled them. Yes, there was pressure and negativity and all kinds of drama piling up around them, but they were in Crimson. A place she was learning was the happiest on earth.

"What happened to the music?" she asked though it was still playing. "Doesn't it go any louder in here?"

"Now, that's my language," Roxie said, whirling on the spot. "Casanova! Where is our cellphone?"

TWENTY-SEVEN

WHENEVER HER EYES flitted to Struan's, he was already watching. They were in a VIP pod in Crimson with other people. Yes, people… with eyes. Although the walls were opaque, flaunting what they were, what they had, even in this elite group, wouldn't be smart. There was such a thing as tempting fate. It wouldn't pay to get too used to access to each other.

Roxie and Zairn sat so close not a sliver of light broke between them. They whispered to each other and there was the occasional maybe-too-familiar caress, but they couldn't feel the same as she did in that moment. No, they had each other, owned each other; frustration and isolation clawed at her.

She rose. "Going to the restroom."

Yes, it was true. She needed a few silent moments without the pressure of desire squeezing her chest. All she wanted to do was climb into his lap, seek his lips, to feel his hands on her body. Alcohol and desire tended to overrule restraint, and she was close to her limit.

"Get it together," she whispered to herself in the

cubicle and went out thrusting her shoulders back.

In the mirror, as she washed her hands, she practiced conveying determination in her gaze. This was easy, no big deal, just exist in the same space as him without mounting him. Easy. Easy? God, she didn't even believe it in her own head.

Staying in the bathroom forever wasn't an option. Talk about drawing attention to herself. And she didn't want to worry anyone by cowering until the sun rose.

Get back out there, Bambi, come on. Few alternatives lay before her, so she dried her hands and exited. Difficult as it may be to check herself, she didn't want to go home if that meant going back to Roxie's and spending another night without him. She could do it. She could go back to that pod. Listen to conversation. Contribute. Be a regular member of the group. Socialize. Friendship.

On the cusp of admitting defeat, someone appeared in the hallway up ahead: Struan. He went through the door nearest him with a sort of semi-side nod that indicated she should follow. Is that what he meant? Was she getting the signal or about to embarrass herself?

Not a restroom. The door said nothing and was just a little off the latch. Was it security protected? Could that mean privacy? She tiptoed in, ready to apologize for being wrong. Suddenly, she was yanked aside and planted against the wall. His hand propelled the door back into its frame, then glided over to rest just by her crown, his forearm supporting his weight.

"You've got to stop doing that."

"Doing what?" she asked, breathing segueing to a pant.

"I can't quit looking at you. How the fuck am I supposed to leave you alone at work when you're all I think about? I'm obsessed. Addicted. For all the crap I give Roman about his issues, I'm no fucking better; I need to get my own shit together."

When her hands skimmed up his torso, he gritted his teeth, hissing like flames traveled in their wake.

"I don't want you to get over it. I want you obsessed. I need you addicted to me because I'm addicted to you. You, Struan, I need you, beau."

Snatching her head in both hands, he stooped to slam his mouth on hers.

There in the shadows, isolation gifted privacy. The music hid each mew and whine seeping from her throat. She couldn't control the sounds, the writhing, the need. Yearning drove her, owned her, in desperation for a satisfaction only available in him.

He shunted her hips along the wall and up on to a hard surface. That was better. Being higher she could tilt her pelvis and push the want burning at the apex of her thighs against the solid ridge that complemented it.

Her hands on his shirt weren't enough to break the fever. Even in spite of the tantalizing wall of his muscular chest, she wanted more than what they'd had before. His fingers combed through her hair, tightening in a brief fist at the back of her neck to angle her head higher, then they went across her shoulders and down to her breasts. He wanted more too. His pain was hers.

The flash of scorching flesh on hers betrayed he'd rid her of the straps of her dress now pooled somewhere around her belly.

She could do the same, open his shirt and kiss his body until they were stolen from each other again. It always ended that way. Each moment they shared was fleeting. They weren't living together and weren't allowed to play, or even engage, at work. Where else would she get the chance to…?

The decision made itself.

Undoing his belt, she was quick to open his pants. A rumble of primal want escaped him, though she didn't know if it was appreciation or reluctance. She needed to feel him. Too many times he'd been pulled away. It wasn't right. This was hers, he was hers. She coiled her fingers around his shaft slowly, one by one. Tightening each preceding digit as the next took up its place. Arching her body, undulating herself, she used the head of his cock to stimulate herself through her panties.

It wasn't enough.

That heat was meant for her, that desire, that broad evidence of what they were had a home it never visited. He snatched her head again, tighter this time; his mouth barely left hers even as he clenched his jaw.

"Don't tease me," he hissed.

Maybe there was reluctance there, but it wasn't because he didn't want this.

"No more teasing," she gasped in a panted whisper. "Have me."

Forcing her shoulders against the wall, she crushed her breasts against him and tipped her chin as high as it would go. He had to know what he did to her; that she wasn't ashamed or uncertain of them. Although her eyes were closed when his hands ran down her body and squeezed her breasts, she felt every aching nuance of his admiration.

"Yes," she repeated her urgency when his fingers drifted down the midline of her stomach to insinuate themselves into her panties. "Yes."

Kicking her heels on to whatever was beneath, she raised her hips to move with him as he slid a finger inside. Her slickness held no secret, no doubt or reluctance. She wanted him.

Under the pressure of the clock, his fingers disappeared and hesitation vanished. They didn't have the luxury of basking too long in foreplay. That message wasn't lost on him either. He wasn't withdrawing to leave, he was—he plunged into her. All the way. Deeper than expected. He hit hard and she grabbed for stability in him, allowing her body to absorb its new playmate. The electric shock of sheer satisfaction zinged and tensed at the same time.

Mmm, nothing could've prepared her. This wasn't a joining of bodies like any other. Digging her nails deep into his trapezius, she rose, eyes closing, moving with and against him, widening her legs, squeezing him tight within.

"Struan," she whispered his name, aching with the whine of want compressing her chest.

How could she have existed without this? Now he was inside her, she wouldn't breathe without him. Friction came with speed, with heat, with a tension that pulled at her jaw. She dropped as her hands climbed higher to the back of his neck.

"God," she gasped. "Baby…" Her long whine switched to a pant of vowels that somehow built to the crescendo of orgasm in a powerful wail. "Struan!"

Her being snatched his so tight it provoked his growl as he smacked a fist on the wall, absorbing his own release.

Surrounded by the bass from beyond and the fog of their love, she relaxed her fingers, skimming them up into his hair to hold herself closer.

Still it wasn't enough. When he came lower to give her more, he slid from her body. Damn, and she'd been ready to keep him there forever.

"It shouldn't have been like that," he grumbled against her in an exhale. "Shit, baby, I'm—"

"It was perfect," she said, laying a hand on his cheek to ease him back and find his eyes. "Our start wasn't conventional. It's right our first time wasn't either."

In other circumstances, with more liquor and less restraint, they'd have closed the deal in that basement the night they met.

"It's hard to believe you're real," he said, driving his fingers into her hair by her ear. "You deserve the whole world, you know that?"

As long as he was the one to give it to her, she'd take it, and fight to give back more.

"That mean you'll sneak me into your bed tonight?"

"No." Disappointment was instant, though he greeted her with a grin. "Is there space in yours? Tomorrow's Sunday. No work until Monday. Tomorrow's Halloween, I guarantee Roxie and her crew will go out."

They'd be alone. In a safe place. Whether Roxie remained concerned about her safety at Roman's, her friend's worry wouldn't extend to Struan. And no one explicitly said she couldn't have friends stay over.

"For you, and only you, always."

Always wasn't long enough. They'd found each other by accident and couldn't lose each other. She wouldn't survive it. Any world that existed without him wasn't one she wanted to live in. Except that decision may be made for them.

TWENTY-EIGHT

"DID WE EVER find out who it was?" she asked, lost in a haze of half-sleep, fending off encroaching slumber to luxuriate in every moment alone with Struan.

Roxie hadn't batted an eye when he joined them on the ride back from the club the previous night. She appreciated her friend not making a big deal of it, for his sake. She, on the other hand, was so excited to spend a night with Struan, she'd have crowed about it, to the highest limit of her friend's patience, if asked.

When they weren't making love, his heavy hand spent most of its time on her hair. She liked it there. With her head on his chest, and the shadows all around them, they were the only two people in the world.

During the day, others moved around beyond her bedroom avoiding their den of sin. No one had bothered them. Since their friends absconded to the Crimson Halloween party, the house had been blessedly silent. Struan left the bedroom for sustenance at one point before sunset, but all she needed was him. Work would steal them both in the morning, they had to make the most of these precious moments.

"Who it was?"

"Who leaked the tape?" she asked. "Magnus said he'd investigate then I never heard about it again."

"I don't know."

"We should find out," she said on a sigh, lips curling. "Send them a thank you gift."

The rumble of his laugh warmed her cheek. "You want to thank them for putting us in this position?"

"This position isn't so bad."

"No, it is not, Fawn."

His tone was enough to betray his thoughts. He may like being there with her, but, like she'd said to Roxie, it wasn't enough. This wouldn't last. They wouldn't.

"Are you sorry?"

"About what?"

"This," she said and sat up, crossing her legs, tangling them in the sheet, thus revealing a little more of his delectable body. Reaching over, she covered him again. She couldn't be expected to have a conversation without drooling on him if he didn't give her a break. "Are you sorry that we're here?"

"I'm sorry this is the best I could give you. I'm not sorry we met."

"And the tape?"

"I hate the tape," he said. "You should never have been disrespected like—"

"Are you embarrassed?"

"No," he said and sat up. When the sheet fell again, she closed her eyes. Guy was trying to kill her. "To be with you? No. I want to shout it from the goddamn rooftops."

With a hand on his chest, she pressured him to lay down again and dragged the sheet across his pecs.

"The tape put us here, beau." She linked their

hands. "Here, together. We wouldn't have got this time if it wasn't for that tape."

"I was going to call you."

"You didn't have my number."

"With a name like yours, I'd have tracked it down."

Maybe not in LA, a city that made its money on stage names. Anyone he asked who didn't know her might assume he was looking for a hooker. A frequent comparison she'd lived with growing up… and into adulthood.

Could they be together? Independently of Roman? Was it possible for Struan to have a romantic relationship of his own? Even with her working on set, they barely got any excuse to be alone; always in proximity, they were teased with each other all day. It would only get worse now they were supposed to ignore each other.

Outside work, would he have time for dates and sleepovers? What if Roman needed him?

"Zairn said we could still do this. Be together." Putting it on him wouldn't be fair. "I understand why we can't."

"Fawn—"

"I would never do anything to hurt you or your brother." Because one meant so much to the other. "And I do think about it sometimes. That night was kind of perfect on its own."

"You wish we'd left it there?"

On a shrug, she conceded. "It depends on my mood. Sometimes I tell myself it was wonderful fate forcing us to confront this special energy between us."

"And other times?"

"I think fate's laughing at us. What were the chances of that room having cameras? It didn't even occur to me, I didn't think to check."

"Neither did I."

"And why were they working? The power was out—"

"I know the answer to that one because most security systems follow the same rules these days." He waited for her to raise her brows before carrying on. "Terrorism. If someone breaches the building, they might try killing power to the security system."

"But the owners still want to get their eyes on who is breaking in."

"And it stands as evidence if a case gets to court. Security systems, Dysaic security systems anyway, hold backup power on an isolated system that runs off renewable sources."

"You really do know a lot about it."

"We've hung out."

"We?" she asked. "We who?"

"Zane Dyce, his was the island we were on in the Pacific. He's a good friend of Zairn and Roxie's." He paused for breath. "Oh, and my cousin."

Now that was something to note. "Your cousin? One of the richest men in the world?"

"It's a convoluted family thing, but, yeah."

She laughed and bowed to snuggle against him again. "Is there anyone you don't know?"

Again he cradled her head. "The good people of Wishbone."

Hadn't taken him long to come up with that response.

"Why would you care about Wishbone when you have Hollywood and Pacific islands?"

"They didn't give me you."

Being his was a dream that would never come true. Worrying her lip, she couldn't decide whether to say more. They could disappear down the rabbit hole of what would never be, but it wouldn't do either of them any good.

"That night, the night we met, would've been special to me, even if it was all we got."

"Ah, don't want me to visit home anymore?"

Slipping her hand beneath the sheet, the warmth of his skin reassured her. "Talking as if this is forever breaks my heart. I have to be honest with myself and just hope we come out of this as friends."

"Friends? That all I get?"

"You can't date your brother's ex-fiancée. I know you're not stupid, you've played this through just the same as I have."

"I'm not ready to give up on this."

And, boy, did she understand that. They were trudging to the gallows through the howling wind. Leaving the path was a choice; one neither of them would make.

"And if we get caught again?"

"We won't be caught here. And Roman can't get in, we're safe here."

"We can't live here forever."

"Roxie will be gone all night."

"Roxie's not the one asking us to cool it."

No, that was Magnus. And Roman was the one saying no to their relationship. Except he wasn't, and it wasn't fair to put it on him. The man might be guilty of a lot of things, their predicament wasn't one of them.

"Just at work," he said. "People know us there and are more likely to know the difference between me and Roman. For one thing, they'll know where each of us are supposed to be and—"

"And we're here rather than in your bed because…"

Roman would cause drama. Related to them or not, Roman would storm through with his usual destructive force and waylay everyone from their own lives. Struan's lack of an answer was expected. There was nothing he could say to better the situation. And although it was heartbreaking, she didn't want to fight.

She changed the subject. "Sway seems nice."

"She is."

"Have you known her a long time?"

"Only through her relationship with Roman."

Which was the equivalent of going to war together, or it would've been pre-rehab. "She's going to New York with Roxie. She broke off her engagement to Deacon."

This was just as bad. Her talking as though she had any right to his life. As a couple, these things mattered, and without that relationship…

"I got something for you."

Easing her aside, he vaulted from the bed to snag his jacket from the chair by the window. Man, he was something to look at. It was almost worth losing him at four thirty in the morning when this, when he, was the result. How could someone with such a good heart, sense of humor, and integrity also be so ripped? It wasn't fair to the rest of the population.

He fished something from the pocket and tossed it to the bed as he turned. Fumbling through the sheet for the packet, she'd just raised it up when he dropped beside her.

"Gummy bears," she said, laughing and holding them to her chest. "I love them."

"The liquor wouldn't fit in my pocket."

"There's a bottle of Tripp's favorite Johnnie Walker behind the bar."

"Superb," he said and kissed her shoulder before getting up again. "Get to work dividing them up. I'll be quick."

He glanced back and they shared a smile. As he disappeared, she exhaled. Recreating the night they met with a happy ending. How was she supposed to stop herself falling for him? Oh, who was she kidding, she was already sunk.

TWENTY-NINE

ON MONDAY, Mieux had work to do at Brooker, so they spent the day at the agency, possibly to give them a breather from the UO set. Her a breather. It hadn't been put like that, but after what happened on Friday, distance wouldn't be a bad thing. Mieux was a helluva considerate. Roman flipping out may be on him, that wouldn't stop the crew avoiding or judging her though. At Brooker, she didn't have to face animosity.

Mieux closed her laptop. "Okay, we have to go."

She lifted her heavy head from the heel of her hand. "Go where?"

The club again? All day she'd been dragging. Partying at Crimson on Saturday night was a great idea at the time. Not necessarily so great that she wanted to be out all night on a weekday and carry a hangover to work.

"Chic is waiting at the house."

"Waiting at the house? What house?" Dumb question. "For what?" she asked, forced to stand when Mieux pulled out her chair. "I'm wearing the designated outfits."

Okay, so, that was a lie. Saturday night was

someone else's clothes. That day, she wore Roxie's. Given she'd woken up in the woman's house, already late, they hadn't had time for modesty. She'd only just got dressed before Mieux arrived at the front door with the car.

"Where are we going, Mieux?" The assistant piled up their things, slipping some into a satchel while holding her usual binder, tablet, and cellphone in one hand. "Is it Crimson again? Is Roxie outside?"

"Roxie wouldn't wait outside." Thinking of the woman put a smile on everyone's face. Everyone but Roman's anyway. "Haven't you figured out Roxanna Kyst doesn't wait for permission by now?"

"She doesn't have clearance for Brooker's."

"She's Roxie Kyst, Bambi. In this town, a name means everything. Roxie's famous and hot right now."

"With her stream?"

"And the documentary. There's also talk of bigger and better things coming along."

"Bigger and better? What does that mean?"

They went outside and got into a car. Mieux was talented. She hadn't wanted to go anywhere and asked questions. Yet without ever raising her voice or being forceful, Mieux got her to do exactly what she wanted.

"Have you heard from Roxie today?"

"You can call Roxie anytime you want. Be prepared for Astrid or one of the other assistants to answer."

"Because she never charges her phone?"

"Yes, Zairn has her line diverted to others in case of emergency. Not that if anyone had an emergency they would call Roxie. She's a wonderful woman to have around when things are tough. Answering her cellphone though… that's hit and miss."

"Do you have Tripp's number?"

Mieux's chin rose an inch, her eyes narrowing. "I

can give you Tripp's number. I don't think Roman will like it."

"Roman already thinks Tripp is sleeping with Sway."

"Yeah, so how do you think you'll feel about his current fiancée calling him up too? If you want to speak to Roxie, call, someone will pick up. Maybe. But you won't have time for Crimson tonight. And Roxie's not Roman's biggest fan, so it might not be an idea to take him to the club without, you know, explicit permission. Without him, within earshot, because no offence, but if your fiancé hears no, he'll only want to go even more. And that puts the Lomonds in an awkward position."

Uh huh, because Struan was allowed in and there had been talk of Roxie being friends with the younger Lowe brother: Logan. Could they refuse Roman without causing a scandal? Geez, everything around that guy was a scandal.

"I'm still unclear as to where we're actually going or what we're doing," she said, aware of the woman's haste and intent.

They weren't just finished for the day and going home, if Chic was waiting at the house, something specific was on the agenda.

"There's an event tonight, a movie premiere."

Glam and enticing to many, yet she remained wary.

"A premiere? And you're going to this premiere?" The question was sort of facetious, not sort of, okay, it was kind of rude, though she now understood the woman's reticence. "Roman wants to go?"

The apology written in Mieux's expression was sympathetic. She really did have a way of knowing things.

Could the brothers switch out? That really shouldn't be her first thought.

"So I'm going home to get prettied up?"

To smile and spend the night on the arm of a man who wanted to throttle her.

"Red carpet," Mieux said, "cameras."

Okay, so she was a little grateful for the prettied up part, if her face was going to be plastered all over the place… again. Better that it match Roman's magnificence than be captioned, "commoner after a day at the office." All she could hope was the cameras wouldn't capture her reluctance, or the aversion to her fiancé that vibrated her every atom.

No negativity. Be positive.

Roman was her fiancé. She'd sell it. For Struan. The wonderful, incredible man she'd been bathed in for two nights and a day. Not long enough. She'd picture him. Imagine he was with her instead of his brother, if she could. One was a poor substitute for the other, and she wasn't looking at the scandalmonger.

THIRTY

BAMBI NEVER WANTED to be an actress. Not even when she was a little kid did she dream of fame and fortune. It had never been part of her repertoire to stand up in front of people as the center of attention. She didn't necessarily shy away from public speaking, though it wasn't like she had much experience.

With Chic, it didn't matter. The guy was nice and polite but was either so bored with his job he ignored the client to save himself from small talk drudgery, or so full of himself that he didn't think the client deserved any input. Maybe she wasn't famous enough for him.

She wouldn't lose any sleep over not being his best friend.

Just like before she went along with everything and was told there was a car waiting in the driveway. Down she went, without excitement or anticipation, regardless of their exclusive destination. The driver opened the door and she slipped inside the empty vehicle.

No, she didn't want to wait around, especially

with her shoes pinching her feet, but she'd rather sit there in a vacant space than be faced with Roman.

Unfortunately, that wasn't a future she could put off forever. Quicker than expected, the door opened again and Roman got in. His loose expression quickly became a scowl. She couldn't bring herself to care, not that she didn't care in a bitchy way, it would just be hypocritical to engage him like she didn't feel exactly the same way toward him. Yes, she'd rather he was his brother and wouldn't deny it.

Maybe that's how Struan felt his whole life, that wherever he was, people would rather he be his high-profile brother. Anyone who knew the men's personalities would have to prefer the stuntman to the superstar. Hands down.

They'd been driving a while before he opened his mouth. "You're not going to say anything to me?" he asked with an expectation that put her on the spot.

"What would you like me to say?"

They both knew the truth and didn't have to make this out to be anything other than it was while they were alone.

"We're going to a premiere. This is a big deal for someone like you."

"A mere mortal? A small-town girl? A simpleton? Can't call me a bimbo, my rack isn't big enough." She resisted spitting in disgust. Just what did he think of her? Actually, she'd be surprised if he thought of her at all. "If this is for my benefit, we don't have to go."

Though she couldn't believe he'd do something generous of his own free will.

"We need the pictures. It's been too long."

Ah, the ulterior motive. Too long since they'd showed up as a couple, or since he'd been at something like this? Wasn't likely this was about their relationship at all. Good PR was what he needed, and showing up with her at least changed the conversation. Why was his name being whispered again? Oh, yeah, she remembered…

"I can't help that you threw a fit at work the other day. That's on you. Maybe keep your pistol holstered next time, quickdraw."

The words came out and in the same beat, she couldn't believe her own audacity. Hadn't she already decided to sit quietly and let him be, rather than provoke him into any kind of mood?

"You don't know anything," he said. "You don't know what happened."

Was violence ever the answer? "You're on the defensive. Tells me all I need to know."

"Who do you think you are to talk to me like that?"

"Your fiancée," she said and actually flashed a smile. "Hard as it is to believe I don't wish bad things for you. I don't know why you're so angry or why you're on this crusade of self-destruction. You mean something to people I care about, that means something to me."

"Struan," he said and shook his head, "you have no idea."

Maybe she didn't, but given his history of paying attention to others, or lack thereof, she wasn't sure Roman was much more in the know.

"Why do you do it? Why do you push people?"

"Guy like me has to know who's real and who's not. If someone disrespects me, I disrespect them back."

"Don't you see that most of the time you're the instigator. You're hurting people before they can hurt you."

"I don't need you psychoanalyzing me."

"Okay, then we can sit here quietly."

And they did for another few minutes.

"Struan would do anything for me," he said,

apparently unable to contain himself. "Anything at all. I don't even have to ask and he's there at my back. He's never fucked up like this before."

"And that's upset you? Are you upset that it wasn't actually a fuck up at all? He just made a decision for himself for once. One time. You haven't cut him any slack. We didn't know we were being recorded, and he didn't tell me who he was. He kept your secret, had your back. You have to see he loves you."

"You don't know anything about the pressure on me. The pressure I live with every day. Every person in our lives relies on me. And if I can't rely on him—"

"You can. You can rely on him."

"Yeah, and how is this going to play out? You going to stick around and marry me?"

There was a question with an obvious answer. For the first time, it came from the lips of the relevant party: her fiancé. How far would the ruse go? At what point would it end? And what would be left? Maybe Roman was more astute than they'd given him credit for. They'd all known this would have to come to some sort of climax, what would it look like?

Roman was afraid. That's what the anger was: fear. Without answers, they all lived with a dose of that.

The car slowed. "Get ready to smile."

A mass of people outside, bright and glowing and beautiful, stole every other concern from her life.

"I've never done this before," she said.

He threaded their fingers together. "Just smile. Stand with me a minute, then I'll walk you off to the side. Wait there. They'll take a few more pics, and then we go inside."

Wow, so the guy could be patient when he wanted to be. She'd never heard him be so… gentle.

The door opened to a hail of intrusive sound; a melee of madness waited to consume her. No going back now. She filled her lungs and widened her lips. Thank God she wasn't the star; that didn't mean no one would be looking at her.

They were doing this together.

If she'd thought the day outside her apartment, when Magnus came to get her, was a frenzy, that was nothing to what felt like thousands of people there, crammed behind barriers and security guards. Fans screamed for autographs, flashes went off, and reporters held outstretched microphones and smart devices toward them.

People screamed for Roman.

Really screamed.

Fans and reporters alike.

He was kind enough to slow and sign a few autographs. Then he took her hand again, and just as he'd said, they went to stand in the gallery. Putting an arm around her waist, he held her other hand loose in front of them.

She wanted to believe the contact was his way of reassuring her, reminding her he was there with her, supporting her. Yet the slight moves this way and that to improve the angle for the paps painted a different picture.

Although it was probably less than a minute, it felt like a lifetime. Not soon enough, he led her to the other side, near the door, and returned for a few solo pictures. If the presses wanted to go with the latter shots, she'd be happy for that. More than happy. Elated.

He came back and scooped her in at his side. Thinking it was over, she was ready to exhale and relax.

Except rather than go inside, he walked them straight over to a pool of reporters, heading for one woman in particular.

"Roman! Oh, wow, you look fantastic."

"You too, Cassie, how you been?"

The woman blushed, not that it mattered, the guy holding a camera over the woman's shoulder was more interested in them than his colleague.

This was bad. Oh, so bad. All she could do was hold her smile in place. Smile. Smile. Smile. Everything would be okay.

"Me? What about you? Wow, the Pacific agrees with you, Mr. Lowe. How did you ever tear yourself away?"

"Well, you know." With a hand on Bambi's hip, he gave her a shake like maybe she was somehow involved in that decision. And why would that be? Because he couldn't keep away from her or because she was the jealous nag back at home telling him to put down the silicone boobs in bikinis? "Duty called."

"Yes, *Undercover Ops*, we're all so excited to see you in action. How is the set?"

"Full of great people. This is going to be a smash. You'll love it!"

"And love…" Cassie said, still smiling as she gave Bambi the once-over. "You fell fast."

"When it's right, you know it." Another shake. Oh, no, this wasn't going well, what was he doing? "She's the love of my life."

"Oh, that's so sweet."

Yeah, except—his hand slid onto her face, tipping it up as he came down and—she froze the moment his lips touched hers. Every atom of her being wanted to shove him away, to slap him in the face, to scream and run.

She couldn't. Why? Struan. Except he was exactly the reason this was so wrong.

When he retreated, she still couldn't move. Something else was said between him and the reporter. Her ears rang as he guided her past others calling his name. They continued in and up some stairs.

"Okay," he said on a brusque exhale. "Now we find the bar."

***

SO IT TURNED OUT that going to a premiere didn't actually mean seeing a film. She didn't even know what film it was, or if he was in it. They'd gone to the bar, which seemed quite full given they were supposed to be there for an event that didn't include drinking.

She'd been sitting on a barstool for probably around twenty minutes while Roman lapped the room, ingratiating himself with everyone he believed to be important.

When her phone rang, she popped open her clutch, trying not to admit she wanted Struan to be on the other end.

"Hey, honey," Roxie exclaimed. "You coming to the club tonight?"

"I would love to." Bambi sighed. "Unfortunately, I'm at an event."

"Oh, the premiere thing. We weren't sure if Roman would stick around or just go straight out the back."

"Is that an option?" she asked.

Roxie laughed. "Guess if you're talking to me, you're not sitting in a theater watching the movie?"

"Nope." She touched the base of her wineglass. "Sitting at a bar, smiling at no one, trying to pretend it's no big deal that my apparent fiancé has ignored me since we arrived."

Glancing his way once, she twisted on the stool to put her back to the room and ducked her chin a little closer to her chest. "Should I be worried?"

"About what?" Roxie asked. "That people will speak to you, or someone will hit on you."

"I think the people here are smart enough to know I'm a nobody. That's not what I meant." She didn't dare lift her eyes, in case the bartender thought she wanted attention. The opposite couldn't be truer. "He's drinking," she whispered. "The night Struan and I met, he was stepping in for his brother because Roman was wasted. Does the man know when to stop, or am I headed for a full-on collision?" Her friend's lingering silence wasn't encouraging. "Roxie?"

"I'm already dressed and Zairn is on the phone."

What did that have to do with her question? "Okay."

"I'll get him in the car. You…" Roxie's voice seemed to move. "Yes, you, Casanova, give me your hand, we're leaving."

Until then, Roxie had never been the type to avoid an issue.

"Have fun at the club."

"Not going to the club, Bambi, honey. Not anymore," Roxie said, then her voice faded a little. "We're leaving now, Lover. We're going to save a damsel in distress. Big night for you."

"Rox, I don't—"

"I'm talking to Zairn. We're on our way. We'll be there as quick as we can."

With that the line died.

If they'd been invited to the premiere, or had any interest in attending, they wouldn't have avoided the red carpet. Her friend asked about the club, suggesting there'd been no intention for them to come to the movie theater.

Roxie hadn't answered her question explicitly about Roman's drunkenness potentially leading to calamity. Whether it did or not, the woman had become her beacon of stability. Having Roxie at her side changed the game. She wouldn't need to control the situation or control the man. The Lomonds were professionals in this arena. They owed Roman nothing. They wouldn't be there to keep him out of trouble. They'd be there to make sure that trouble didn't hurt her.

Once again, she was awestruck, humbled.

Calling Struan for support wasn't an option. He'd come if she did, but that would be disastrous. On a good day, that would be disastrous, if her guy had seen the kiss… Oh, please say he hadn't seen the kiss.

If it wasn't for Roxie, she'd be on her own dealing with whatever nightmare Roman dragged them into. Even Magnus showing up might raise suspicion, it would suggest she expected Roman required handling, which would then doom them to descend that path.

Roxie and Zairn, a super-hot couple who were massively popular, Mieux was right, they could show up pretty much anywhere they wanted. Having them close wouldn't be suspicious. As to whether it would help… The support would help her; her date maybe not so much. If Roman was drunk and Roxie impatient, the fireworks may be more inevitable than before.

Only they'd potentially save Roman from embarrassing himself, her, and trashing his career. Instead, they'd feed the Hollywood Gossip Circle. In short, the Lomonds were saving her ass and Roman's, yet, somehow, she knew the man wouldn't show gratitude.

THIRTY-ONE

EITHER ROXANNA KYST was a practicing Wiccan, or she'd made a deal with the devil somewhere along the way. Less than an hour after they'd hung up, someone approached the bar. Wasn't unusual, except this time, the guy pointed to the small wall-mounted TV in the corner.

"Are they here?" Glancing up, she wasn't surprised to see Roxie in front of a camera, Zairn at her side, holding her against him. "Can you turn it up?"

"…I know nothing about that," Roxie said, smile broad, every inch the glittering starlet.

The woman may not be an official actress, but she'd never met a role she couldn't fill. Zairn, on the other hand, was almost the trophy husband. He fished his phone from his pocket and scrolled, all the while keeping hold of his treasure.

"It's your wedding! Come on," the reporter asked, "give us something. Tease us. You decided not to let the cameras in, why—"

"We decided not to let *your* cameras in."

"Oh, now, hey, that's something. You got an

exclusive deal?"

On a laugh, Roxie curled closer to her guy to splay a hand on his chest. He just kept on typing. "Marriage means exclusive. It'll be tough for him, but a deal's a deal."

"Who ever thought Zairn Lomond would settle down!" The reporter relished the interaction. "You confident he'll give up the babes—"

"For the ultimate babe," Zairn muttered, still doing something on his phone.

"What was that?"

Zairn tucked the phone away. "Guys don't catch women like Roxanna Kyst," he said. "Most guys. She takes a special kind of care, one I work on every day. Rox is the sun which my world revolves around."

And this time, the reporter laughed. "You've used that line before."

"Yes, we have," Roxie said and moved away. "You take it easy now."

The reporter, and others, called after them. Zairn went with Roxie without letting an inch of space grow between them. Either they'd been practicing or they were used to this schtick. Was it possible two people could share instinct like that? Did they anticipate each other like it required thought, or was it all intuition? Whichever it was, they proved love existed.

The bartender turned the volume down when the picture switched back to their on-site guy.

"You did this," Roman hissed, materializing at her side. "You brought them here."

"I didn't bring anyone here." Should she be facetious and tell him the couple were dying to see the movie? "Roxie just happened to call. Be happy it wasn't your brother."

"What does that mean?"

She wasn't really sure. Just that after spending

time alone with Struan, her need for him had only deepened. Throughout their time locked up together at Roxie's, any time "they" came up, she might've told him she understood his loyalty, but he hadn't said it himself.

"You know how Struan feels when you hurt me."

"What the fuck did I do to hurt you?" Okay, yeah, she had to give him that. Ignoring her was more of a blessing than a slight. He got the concession right up until he signaled the bartender. "Give me two doubles—"

"The lady's drinking—"

"Did I ask what the lady was drinking?"

The guy was nice enough to look at her, though he didn't say anything else.

"Good plan, Roman." She raised her wineglass. "Get sloshed, that'll make Roxie like you."

"I don't want that bitch anywhere near—"

"Should my ears be burning?"

Roxie's sweet voice brought her around with such joy, the blonde lived up to her online handle: "Lomond's Delight."

"Roxie…" She threw both arms around the woman to hold her tight. "You're here."

"See this is why real people are better than showbiz people," Roxie said, smoothing Bambi's hair when she pulled back. "That was a genuine welcome, not one of your Hollywood mwah-mwah things."

When Zairn stooped, she raised her chin to accept his cheek kiss. "You look beautiful, Bambi."

"Thank you."

That was more attention than her date gave her.

"Try to put your arms around me, Kyst—"

"Oh no, Roman, let me contain my disappointment," Roxie said, deadpan.

Zairn wasn't in the mood to play around. "You're lucky you're this close, Lowe."

Did Roman know what playing around was? Or that doing it with fire never ended well?

Best probably to leave the men's beef be.

"I'm surprised you haven't been mobbed," she said. "Even up here."

"See that guy standing with his back to Zairn?" Roxie asked as her fiancé helped her onto a stool. "Yeah, he does a growly thing that keeps people at bay. What are we drinking?"

She pointed at her glass. "This is just the house white."

In front of Roman were two empty glasses. She hadn't seen the bartender bring the doubles, but those definitely hadn't been there before. No mystery where the liquid ended up.

"And that's the downside of small-towns," Roxie said, accepting Zairn's jacket over her shoulders after he removed it.

"The downside of…" Her head went almost all the way around, then snapped back to follow Zairn's progress behind the bar. "Is he going to—"

"He's good at it. And if we force him to stay close to Roman for too long, it'll get ugly."

"Yeah," the actor griped, "for him."

Roxie slapped both hands to the edge of the bar; the beauty looked at her then him. "Let's open a discourse," the blonde announced. "We have to fix this."

"Fix it?"

"This attitude Roman has with everyone. What is your problem?"

"You."

"Okay, that's a start."

The blonde wasn't accusatory, in fact, her tone was conciliatory. Even when he was offered a break, Roman still chose obstinance.

"Roxie's a good person, Roman. If you gave her

a chance—"

"She took Sway from me and gave her to that—"

"Contrary to your apparent assumption, I am not a pimp. Sway is a human being," Roxie said, leaning in, lowering her voice. "Women are people too, Mr. Lowe. We make our own choices."

"We're meant to be together."

"My friend Jane went out with a guy like you."

"Oh my God," Bambi said. "Is she okay?" The smirk on Roxie's lips wasn't matched by Roman's scowl. "No, I just meant—"

"No, he was a crazy stalker. Definitely dangerous."

"Maybe he loved her."

"Love isn't a prison, it's freedom." Zairn put two drinks down, one in front of each woman. "Sway isn't your future, Roman. Let it be."

If only it was that easy…

"If I could talk to her—"

"Move on," Roxie said. "That's why you're so angry. Why you're drinking and hitting people on set—"

"He deserved it."

"Okay," Roxie said, nice enough to nod. "Maybe he did. Though you deserved it on the island and my guy dialed back for me."

"I don't need anyone fucking protecting me."

She sighed, maybe louder than intended, because everyone fixed on her. Her eyes darted from one gaze to the next.

"Nothing I was just—I have nothing to add."

"No, speak. This is open discourse, honey." Roxie put the drink in her hand and picked up her own. "What were you going to say?"

Arguing would get her nowhere. "Everyone is protecting him. And that's okay, family's supposed to—"

"Struan again?"

Roxie waved at Roman. "Let her finish."

"Yes, Struan, Magnus, I'm protecting you, Roxie, even Zairn."

"Mm hmm," Roxie agreed, urging the drink higher. "Try it. Bambi's right, and Sway's protecting you too."

"How the fuck is Sway—"

"Oh my God," she said after sipping her drink. "That's amazing. What is that?"

"Gin and It," Roxie said, glowing with pride. "Told you he was good." Now her friend slanted her way. "Imagine what else he can do with those hands."

"How is Sway protecting me?" Roman wasn't about to be quieted. "I'd do anything for her. Anything to protect—"

"Except temper yourself." Roxie's eyes were slow in their roll around to the actor. "Calling her all the time, the messages, do you think she likes that?"

"She needs to know I'm serious."

"You want her to know you're serious, get your shit together. There's nothing more attractive than a man who can fold his own laundry." With a raised hand, Roxie curled her fingers in a flourish against her palm. "Current company excluded." She beamed at her guy. "Love you."

Bambi offered, "She doesn't mean literally."

"I know that," Zairn said as Roxie spoke too.

"He knows that. Besides, my guy can, he just doesn't. Time's a commodity." To her surprise, Roxie laid a hand over Roman's. "Now, back to you, get out there. Start over. If you and Sway are meant to be, it'll happen. If you're in a better place, you can both appreciate each other more. You don't want to be co-dependent, do you? A relationship needs two whole people to function—"

"Who the fuck are you to lecture—"

"It's advice, not a lecture," Roxie said and presented her ring close to Roman's face. "My guy got me and I take his calls. And I've got a lot of girlfriends in loving relationships who take their partners' calls. Spending all this time obsessing about Sway is blinding you to what else could be out there. What if your true love is right in front of you, and you miss her because you're too busy calling Sway?" Roman's eyes flitted to Bambi. Before she could even open her mouth, Roxie did the honors. "Not her."

"She's got Stru all tied up."

"And that's their mess to deal with." Roxie's grin was genuine. "Think of the adventure. Finding new love, whoever she is, learning about her, being with her for the first time. Falling in love is a gift. It doesn't have to come from the past. It can come from the future."

Whoa, this woman was good at this. Bambi just busied herself with her drink and let Roxie—Zairn's smile was subtle, but he was transfixed. Even as Roxie talked, when she wasn't looking his way, he couldn't take his eyes off her.

Roman wasn't arguing, not in his usual snappy way. Could he be considering what Roxie was saying? For real considering it? If he could let go of Sway... she was one to talk. Struan couldn't be more wrong for her, not in her life, but in his. If she cared for him at all, she'd bow out and slip off the stage quietly. Doing that would save him the guilt of thinking he was breaking her heart. He was, but she didn't want him to feel bad about it.

She felt bad enough for both of them.

"You're saying this because Sway's with him. Breckenridge has—"

"Where is Tripp tonight?"

"Not here," Roxie declared, flashing her pearly whites. "I thought bringing one man who wanted to punch Roman was enough, two would've been overkill."

"Ballard would take a swing at him."

Roxie tsked at her fiancé. "Is that productive? We're trying to help him see that there's a new someone somewhere out there on the horizon. If he gives her a chance, he can find love all over again."

"Sway's never said she doesn't love me."

"Do you want her to say that?" Roxie cringed. "That's not a nice thing to say out loud to someone."

"Especially when they don't mean it."

God, it was like talking to a brick wall.

"Okay, then moving on," Roxie said, switching focus to Bambi. "How are things with you and Stru?"

"I..." Eyes going left to right, she tried to appeal to Zairn for help. "Don't think we should talk about that here."

"No, probably not a good idea, but I did want to ask Roman something..."

"I need another drink."

Zairn turned, she assumed to fulfill Roman's request.

Roxie threaded her arms into Zairn's sleeves, then drummed her nails on the bar. "Talk me through the timeline of this."

"Timeline of what?"

"You and Struan met at the Lighting Darkness event," Roxie said. "Tape gets leaked, and how did you end up at Struan's?"

"Magnus came to get me, from my apartment, the press mobbed us outside."

"Yeah, that's what I thought..." Narrowing her eyes again, Roxie peered. "I've seen the tape, it's not the best quality... how did they find you so fast?"

Zairn put a glass in front of Roman who immediately drank. Except he pulled the drink away fast to scowl at the liquid.

"What shit is this?"

"Club soda," Zairn said. "Get used to it, it's all you'll get from this bar for the rest of the night."

THIRTY-TWO

ZAIRN'S DECLARATION DIDN'T go down well and explained why Roman chose to move on. Someone mentioned an after party and he didn't even bother inviting her. Good. She didn't want to go.

Zairn and Roxie invited her back to theirs, but with Roman out, she couldn't pass up the chance to have some alone time with Struan.

Oh, and Roxie's question about finding her so fast? No one could answer that. It was kind of embarrassing she hadn't asked it herself. With no friends in town, no connections, no one in LA knew her except her colleagues, and Renata hadn't even known she was missing that night.

Back at the mansion, she went up to her bedroom to change out of her clothes and snagged a satin robe. If she and Struan were definitely alone in the house, she wouldn't have bothered with it. Magnus could be around and she didn't want to be caught creeping around the house naked late at night. Or at any time.

Dim light from under Struan's bedroom door

suggested he might still be awake. Whether he was or not, she still planned to visit. Pushing down the handle, she peeked around the door. Lying on the bed, back to her, he twisted to check who was intruding.

"Should I have knocked?"

"No, baby," he said on a snicker. "Come here."

In she went, closing the door with an extra push. Anything to slow unwelcome visitors. And, at that point, everyone was unwelcome.

"I was out at a premiere thing."

"Yeah, I heard."

Darting across the room, she leaped onto the bed and clambered over him, casting her robe aside so she was naked before wriggling under the covers and tucking herself in.

"You're sleeping here tonight?"

Maybe she should've… "If that's okay. I know it's only been a couple of nights but…"

He caught her chin to match their eyes. "But…?"

"I'm not sure I could sleep in a cold bed without you." Dumping herself on him was kind of rude. "Should I have asked permission?"

"No," he said and propped his own head back on his fist. "No, Fawn, I just didn't expect—"

"I can go," she said, sitting up. "If you'd rather just—"

"No." He put a hand on her waist to keep her still. "Stay where you are. Did Roman come back with you?"

She settled down again. "No, he went to party somewhere else. Zairn would only serve him club soda, so he wasn't in the best of moods."

"I saw they showed up. Was that a coincidence?" The curl of her lips and sly eyes answered for her. "Yeah, I didn't think so. Good. I'm glad you had support. I'm always sorry when I can't be with you."

Oh, and there was regret. "If you saw them at the event, did you see the red carpet?"

"Yeah," he said, his expression inscrutable.

"Does that mean you saw—"

"Yeah," he said again, and shook his head on his knuckles. "Let's not talk about that."

Although she didn't like barriers, she had to respect his boundaries. "I wish you hadn't seen—"

"I do too. Other than that, did you enjoy yourself?"

If he wanted to move along that was more than fine by her. She'd happily relegate that kiss to some dusty, dirty corner of her memory and pile new shiny ones on top. Lots of Struan kisses would be excellent cover.

"Roxie asked me something. A question I couldn't answer and Roman couldn't either."

"Okay, try me."

"How did they find out who I was? 'They' being the national, potentially international, press. How did they ID me in the video so fast?" She kept going in spite of his frown. "No one in LA knew me, other than those I work with, and they didn't even know I was missing during the power cut."

"Renata? Maybe after the fact."

"Why would someone think to ask Renata? Why would someone think to show her the picture?"

"If it was released online, maybe she saw it."

"And immediately called the press? I can ask her," she said, willing for that to be the answer. Though honesty wasn't guaranteed. Her boss may not want to be fingered for squealing. "We were at that event until late, like wee hours late. I crashed as soon as I went home. I'd guess Renata did the same."

"Some people get alerts to their phones."

"Of every name ever? Why would she have Roman Lowe in her alerts?"

"I don't know."

"Roxie thought it was weird. The press arrived early. Like I said, we were at the event until late. The story didn't hit while I was still awake, and then suddenly they were mobbing my street."

"I'm sorry I wasn't there either."

That only roused her smile again. "You would've been if you'd come home with me."

"I would have if you'd asked instead of running off."

"You were going to tell me. Right before they came in and interrupted us. You wanted to tell me something."

His fingertips grazed her brow and coasted across her temple to comb into her hair. "Protecting Roman is second nature. It's something I do automatically. That energy you felt? I felt it too, and it screwed with my head. I cover for Roman by rote. Never, ever, in all our history, has it ever occurred to me to reveal that I'm not him when I'm supposed to be playing him."

"Our energy was different?"

"Sounds crazy, but being honest with you was important, I knew I should be honest with you. I had to be. Maybe it's your aura, it begs a guy to lay it all out. I can't be around you and not want to tell the truth. You demand sincerity, deserve it. I hate that I disappoint you."

"You don't disappoint me. I'm disappointing—"

"Yeah, I am. I'm disappointing myself too, because this is real. Us is real. For the first fucking time in my life, I have—at Roxie's, when we're alone, you just accept that I'll put Roman first. Everyone keeps telling me I'm a pussy, or have a white knight complex, for holding my brother upright when it comes at the cost of me, my life. Yeah, there were times it frustrated me, but this time it's more than that."

"People care about you," she said, wriggling closer. "No one wants to tell you what to do with your life."

"Roman does, and maybe, if I thought it was mutual—that's it. I thought all my life that it was mutual. We are siblings, twins, I believed we had this innate connection to want the best for each other, but it's not true. He doesn't want the best for me. He couldn't care less. If I didn't have the same face, if I wasn't useful, he wouldn't give a damn. He'd leave me in the dust. And what do I have, Bambi? Tell me what I have."

"Things are—"

"I don't mean things. Fuck things. I don't need bricks and mortar or wheels on the road. When I turn around and look at what I've done with my life, it's clear I've done nothing. Anything I've done worth anything is attributed to him. I'm my brother's shadow, nonexistent to anyone but him."

"Not to me. You're everything to me."

"If he wanted what was best for me, this would be tearing him apart as much as it is me. Want to know something?" She nodded. "He gets a kick out of it, a kick out of being with you, flaunting you, and not because you're beautiful, though you are, but because you're mine."

She couldn't disagree, but had to ask, "Where is this coming from? At Roxie's, anytime I said anything, you stayed quiet. I assumed you accepted we had no future the same as I did, and didn't want to say the words out loud for fear of hurting me. Tonight you feel different. This feels different. You're energized."

"Because I saw it tonight on that red carpet. I've done that with Sway so many times, *so* many times. Walking past the reporters is easy; if we did approach, or were penned in, Sway tended to take the lead. I never touched her, an arm around her waist, or our hands together, sure. Nothing over the line. I didn't feel that way about her, and she was Roman's, it didn't enter my head."

"The kiss," she said, "because he kissed me." The one he didn't want to talk about, and this was why. It messed with his head. "It wasn't a full-on kiss, and if I could have pushed him away—"

"I know, this isn't on you," he said, his fingers sinking deeper into her hair until they curled around the back of her neck, tipping her chin up. "I know what he did. And that was my breaking point. He didn't kiss you because he wanted to or because you wanted him to. He didn't even kiss you because he was cornered. No one asked him to do it. Why would they? It's not necessary or traditional on a red carpet. In fact, it's downright strange to do something like that."

Which guaranteed more people would be talking about it.

"So why did he do it?" she asked. "He took me by surprise. I don't know why he—"

"He did it to damage me. That's the only reason there is. Whether I saw it live or later, it happened, and the press will talk about it. There will be pictures, there will be buzz online. I was always going to know it happened. He kissed you because you're mine. You're mine, and he knew you couldn't stop him. I couldn't stop him. He had all the power. He has all the power. That's what the kiss was, his way of exerting superiority. It was predatory. Exactly the word you used. How many times do we hear that sexual assault is not about sex? It's about power, and that's what he gets off on."

"What do you want to do?" she asked, laying a hand on his chest, enjoying how their lower bodies rocked together.

"I don't know yet. It's still… in my head." Which was possibly why he hadn't been ready to talk about it. "What I know for sure is I won't let him do that to you again."

"To us," she said. "I had to endure it, but it was an assault on you too."

And almost as intimate. Although he avoided the physical act, this was his twin, a man supposed to stand up for him, to take a bullet for him. Rather than treat her with care, as Struan did with Sway, Roman had taken advantage and abused that position of trust to gain a petty, resentful advantage. Forevermore that image would be out there in the world. The masses might not understand its significance; they always would. This wasn't something easily forgotten or shrugged off.

Pushing up, she touched her lips to his and was so pleased when his responded. This changed how he felt about his brother, but from the way he scooped her beneath him and settled himself between her thighs, he proved it hadn't changed them, hadn't damaged them.

Whatever he decided to do, she'd be with him one hundred percent. She didn't blame him for his confusion. This was a lifelong fraternal relationship he'd relied on, one that underscored his identity. Now he had to figure himself out all over again. That was okay. At his core, he was still him, and him was all she wanted.

THIRTY-THREE

IN STRUAN'S BATHROOM, under the rain, surrounded by steam, she ought to be able to come up with one good reason he should join her in the shower again. Other than she couldn't stop wanting him.

The man got up at four thirty, again, still dark, but he'd returned to their bed to be there when she woke up. After that she may have kept him in bed way longer than was polite. Wasn't so bad when rude, in a dirty way, was kinda the theme.

"She's gone. She's fucking gone!"

Roman's voice from the bedroom registered enough that she could recognize it was him. Beyond that, she didn't care much about what he was saying. Shame her guy couldn't be so detached.

"Who's gone?" Struan asked. Ah, his was a voice she could listen to all day long. "What you talking about?"

"This is what they do, they get close, then they fuck you. That's what this is. We're getting fucked. Her shit's in her room. She's been here since last night, was here. Now she's fucking gone! God knows what she's planning. Bet Roxie's involved. We can't trust her. You shouldn't trust her!"

The shaving gel wrought no reward, so she left the shower, putting the empty can on the vanity as she held a loose towel to her chest. Hugging the doorframe, she peeked into the bedroom.

"Beau…" As he looked over his shoulder, she winced. "Sorry to interrupt. Shaving gel?"

"Lower middle cabinet."

"What the fuck?" Roman sidestepped at the bottom corner of the bed to set her in his sights. His glare cut to his brother. "You're fucking my fiancée?"

Struan laughed. "Are you shitting me? Your fiancée? This started when me and B got together."

"She's my fucking fiancée! You're fucking my fiancée in my fucking house—"

"It's a rental," Struan said, unimpressed.

"My fucking rental—"

"Paid for by the studio."

What was the point of giving the guy a salary if he didn't have any bills? Money really did go to money. What else had been laid on for him? Bet none of the crew got the same perks, Struan included. Where was his fancy mansion? Guy deserved some peace and quiet. Maybe a cabin in the woods would be better. With an open fire… faux fur rug… and nothing but time.

"For me," Roman spat. "You don't get to do this shit. Under my roof, you think you can fuck around on my dime in my house? Not in this house! Not here! I make the rules here! It's my rules!"

"Okay."

Struan went into the closet and she ran back to turn off the shower. Shaving would wait. She wrapped the towel around herself tight and entered the closet just as Roman appeared at the other door.

Struan already had a gym bag open on the central bench.

"What the fuck are you doing?" Roman demanded. "What is that?"

"You're right. No reason this should happen under this roof. Better we provide for ourselves. We're getting out of here, B."

She snagged one of Struan's tee-shirts from a nearby drawer, dropping her towel only after the garment covered her decency.

"I'll get my purse."

Before she could even turn around, Roman grabbed her arm. The contact startled her, but not as much as Struan.

Dropping the bag flap, his stoop straightened a little. "Take your hand off her."

"My fiancée," Roman spat like she was a possession.

When Struan's eyes met hers, the squirm of her shoulders set him to full height. "Let her go or there won't be anything left of you to put in front of the camera."

"You won't fucking touch me. I'm your damn career. Your damn life."

"Let her go, Ro."

He tugged his hand loose, holding it up for a disgusted second before scoffing. "I'll let you save face, just shut the fuck up and keep your hands off—"

"Get what you need, B."

A single instruction and she spun around to exit via the bathroom. Yeah, Roman was hollering, but she didn't listen. They may not have much time. Rushing to her bedroom, she heard someone coming up the stairs as she hurried into the closet. She swiped a scrunchie from the shelf and tied her wet hair on her head. Sweatpants, hoodie, she snatched her purse, stuffed underwear in there and slipped her feet into ballet slippers.

And, ah, she snagged her packed laptop bag from the hook by the door and went out, just in time to meet Struan coming the other way. At the top of the stairs, they joined hands and descended together. Roman's shouts mixed with Magnus' exclamations until nothing was decipherable. Didn't matter when nothing they could say would change anything. This was their liberation.

Rather than get into one of the two waiting limos in the driveway, Struan led her around the side of the building to a Cayenne, which he boosted her into before getting in the driver's side.

"I've never seen this before," she said, putting on her seatbelt.

"It's mine."

"Oh."

Good, no one could accuse them of stealing. Roman, and his wares, were surplus to requirements. They shot past Roman and Magnus on the stairs and crunched their way out onto the street.

"You see me taking a limo to work alone?"

No. Until then, she'd never thought about it. Struan definitely wasn't the kind of guy who'd want lifted and laid everywhere.

"Are you okay?"

"You don't have to come with me," he said, glancing at her. "If you want to stay—"

"Oh, be quiet," she said. "I only agreed to any of this craziness to support you. I said you were my guy and I meant it."

He reached over to squeeze her knee. "He's right, it's time. We need to figure this out."

"Where are we going?"

"Yours?"

Unsure if he knew the address, it took her a while

to figure out the sat nav, but eventually put in the details.

"Magnus was mad."

"He'll want to fix this," he said, eyes on the road. "That's what he does. He fixes things."

"For Roman. I don't see him doing the same for you."

His head tilted and his frown became confused. "Can't think of a time I've needed him to fix anything."

"We aren't broken," she said, sure that had to be made clear. "This doesn't have to be fixed. But if you two were on equal footing, he'd have fixed this so we could be together from the start."

"Like me, he works on autopilot. Probably didn't occur to him this might be real."

And she couldn't blame him for that. No one knew. Their energy may have fizzed, but even she'd assumed it wasn't for keeps. Why else would she have run away from that basement?

"Now that it is? Will he fix it?" The long, lingering silence wasn't too encouraging. Even if Magnus wanted to fix it, how could he? How could they? "Are you sorry we left? We can go back to—"

"I'm done making choices solely in Roman's best interests. He's made his position clear."

"He's your brother and I'll support you in anything. Don't feel like you have to do this for me. You're a package deal, I knew that from the start... almost the start."

His scowl cut to her. "Regrets already?"

"No! I just..." She licked her lips, hugging her bags closer to her body. "I want to keep you, beau. I don't want you resenting me for busting—"

"Roman's the only one I resent. This isn't your doing, it's his. Things are going to change. It's up to him if he wants to adapt or cut ties."

She believed him. As her gaze tracked to the road

he concentrated on, it sunk in. They'd broken ranks. Fled with each other. Prioritized their relationship. She'd told Roxie she wasn't enough to change things between the brothers. That she wasn't enough for Struan to... He was taking control of his life, his destiny, and asking her to be a part of whatever his future may be.

Leaning over, she stroked his powerful arm. He caught her hand to bring it to his lips. Together. They were actually together.

He kept hold of her until they got to her street and pulled up at the sidewalk.

"Stay there."

In her seat? He hurried around the hood and opened her door for her. This wasn't a driver doing his job. This guy wanted to take care of her, respect her.

What she wanted to do was kiss him. There on the street probably wasn't a great idea. Not until they figured this out. When they did, would they really belong to each other?

After he looped her bags onto his shoulder, she accepted his proffered hand and kept hold when he opened the back door to grab his bag too. Anyone could see them. So far all she saw were regular people, no photographers or reporters, but what did she know? Maybe they had stealth mode.

Going inside, they went upstairs. She hadn't been here for a—Struan had never been here. This man was used to a certain lifestyle. A level of luxury she couldn't provide.

Trepidation crept in. "My place isn't much," she said, turning the key in the lock.

Struan reached around her to swing the door open and, with a hand on her waist, guided her inside.

"Roxie's place is so much nicer and if Tripp's there—"

The bags hit the floor and he whirled her around

to catch her face in both hands. The pressure of his unexpected kiss flashed lights in her closed eyes until the pressure ebbed.

"You live here?" His question vibrated her sensitive mouth. She nodded, head still in his cradling hands. "We together?" Another nod. "Then I live here too." That certainty curled her dopey lips. "We'll worry about money and where we want to be long-term later. Right now, we're safe, that's what counts." Lowering his voice to a growl, he kissed her again. "And our place has a bed, doesn't it?"

On a purr, she threaded their fingers together and guided him across the open plan living room kitchen through the opposite door… to the bedroom.

"It sure does."

THIRTY-FOUR

MOST OF THEIR LIFE together, alone together, was spent in bed. And she would never take a second for granted.

Lying facing his profile, she scrutinized the features the world thought they knew. They didn't. No one did. If anyone thought Struan resembled his brother, they were beyond wrong.

"You can never belong to me," he murmured.

They'd been snoozing a while, not really sleeping, just relaxing in comforting silence.

"What?"

Even her voice was deeper, sleepier, if only they could live in that moment forever.

"You said you could never belong to me," he said, shifting his head to meet her eye. "'Cause the world thinks you're with him."

"When did I say—that first day?" In the foyer, she remembered. "It was nothing, I was hurt that you wanted me to be his."

"You knew from the beginning that I was

making a mistake letting you be with him, even as a ruse. You knew this was forever."

Just how deep did he want to dive? "It's stupid."

"It's not stupid. Tell me."

"We'd only known each other for a few hours, but seeing you come down those stairs in the mansion that first day…"

"You knew it was forever."

Maybe not exactly, but she'd known it wasn't nothing. "I didn't want to be with him. I never wanted to be with him."

"And I forced you to do it."

"You didn't force—" Sudden hammering on the front door interrupted. Recovering from the initial jump scare, she relaxed. "I'm surprised it took them this long."

"Ignore it." He found her hand in their sheets and rested it on his mouth. "They'll go away."

"Is that what we want?"

"I want to be alone with you."

Until they confronted the world with their unity, they'd never be fully together. It wouldn't be fun, but it was necessary to prove they held no shame.

"This won't fix itself, beau."

"Will screaming and shouting help?" The knocking kept going; one person didn't have that many hands. "That's all they'll do. Scream shit at us. We have to figure this out for ourselves first."

"Figure out what we want from each other?"

He didn't know already? She did. Maybe it was her small-town roots, or her gender, but honestly? It didn't take long to reach a conclusion. What was the usual course for a man and a woman in love… He had to know she was in love with him, didn't he?

The knocking stopped to be quickly followed by a half dozen clear pounds.

A man hollered from the hallway. "Some guy

showed me how to bust through one of these once!"

Struan was up and dragging on his sweats in an instant. "Shit."

She boosted onto her elbows. "That wasn't Roman."

Or Magnus.

"It's Tripp."

Hurrying out of the room, he wouldn't make his best friend wait. Allies were better than the opposite. Quickly getting out of bed, she threw on some shorts and a tank. In the bedroom doorway, she got her first look at their visitors. Three of them. Tripp, Zairn, and...

"Roxie." Rushing to her newest friend, she welcomed her hug. "Thank you for coming."

"What are you doing here, Bambi, honey? Why didn't you come to Jane's?"

Tripp fielded that question. "Let me think, two horny as fuck people finally getting a chance to be alone... do they choose an apartment with a bed, completely alone, or show up where there are people waiting to bombard them with questions...?" The mischievous heir landed his focus on Zairn. "Your woman needs an education, and I'm not the man to give it."

"It doesn't matter, we're here now." Roxie smoothed Bambi's hair. "How are you doing, honey? Are you okay? You're so precious."

"How did you know we were here?" she asked. "That anything happened?"

"Mieux went looking for you at the house. You weren't there and there was a big to-do."

"Mieux?"

"She went to Brooker, to tie some things up." Despite not knowing exactly what that meant, she didn't ask. "By process of elimination—"

"You avoided the hotels, that's good," Zairn

said. "But your vehicle is parked downstairs. It's registered to you."

"Not like I've never taken my brother's cars before," Tripp offered.

And Roxie wouldn't let that one just slide by. "Your chauffeur driven limo fleet used by you and all your family?"

Struan came to curve an arm around her. "The press don't care about my car."

"Oh, you think, big boy, do you?" Roxie mocked with an exaggerated nod. "Hmm, is it possible something happened last night?"

"God, what did he do?" she asked. "Was it at the party? Something that happened after he left us?"

"She's talking about the kiss." Struan didn't appreciate filling her in. "The press will want more."

"And coming from the Empress of More, they feed off that shit," Roxie said. "It's not an easy appetite to satisfy." The blonde twisted to look at her own love. "Want to do something crazy?"

"Why? Is it a regular Tuesday?"

"Shut up, you might get laid out of it."

"I got my future planning this morning, and the press know we have sex. That's not front page news," Zairn said, pausing mid reach into his inside pocket. "Unless you want to do it on the sidewalk?"

"Outside Bambi's place, next to Struan's car?" Tripp asked. "Shouldn't you at least go a block over. Point is to divert attention."

Roxie shrugged. "Whatever works. We could go visit our embryos. A visit to the fertility clinic always gets them going. Oh, oh, or… I could go with Tripp. Then it's like cheating on you without the intercourse part."

"Thanks for the offer, but we're fine." Struan strengthened his hold. "We're figuring this out."

"What does that mean exactly?" Wearing

judgment, Roxie folded her arms. "I don't like wishy-washy statements; say what you mean, Lowe. I won't let you hurt one of my girls or make a fool out of her. Did you just drag her here for sex? Are you going to dump her with that cret—"

"Still his brother," Tripp hummed, leaning into the line of sight between them.

"Maybe, maybe not. What happened today?" This time Roxie wanted an answer from her. "Was Roman an asshole? I swear if he touched you, I will send Ballard over there to—"

"Get charges for assault?" Tripp asked. "You know Roman's the type."

"So we should let it slide?"

"No, we send someone over there he can't identify. Someone who won't leave enough of him to report anything."

"Still his brother," Roxie parroted, mocking her friend's previous assertion.

"No one put their hands on me," she said then her shoulders rippled. "No one except the guy I want touching me." She chose not to remind Struan of the brief incident in the closet. "This is Roman's doing."

"He told you to leave?"

"He didn't appreciate us being together in what he called his house," she explained. "So we left."

"Together," Roxie said. "You left together. To be together?"

That was a question she couldn't answer. When she looked up at Struan, she assumed the others would too.

"We haven't figured out the details, but I'm done watching her with Roman. I'm done with her being out there where I can't protect her."

In real time. He was always good at the aftercare, he just wanted to be around for the "*during*care" too.

Hopefully, there wouldn't be much more of that on the horizon, if he meant what he said about keeping her and Roman apart.

"That's progress." Though Roxie attempted to subdue it, she quickly lost the battle and burst with excitement. "You broke free, Struan!" Leaping over, she yanked the man down to hug him tight, quickly looping Bambi into the embrace too. "I am so proud of you. I knew beautiful Bambi would be enough. When I saw you looking at her, oh, Struan, I know a man in love."

Okay, that may be a little awkward. They hadn't exchanged those words and she didn't want him strongarmed into anything.

"You need a plan," Zairn said. "Are you going public? You'll have to tell them the truth, all the times you stepped in to take Roman's place."

Couldn't they be together without cracking the crystal of previous illusions? No. Not if they told the truth that Struan was the man on the tape and not Roman. Without a great story, just admitting that would be enough to have everyone, press and industry alike, questioning which brother was where in the history of, well, ever.

"Don't you worry…" Roxie pulled back and laid her certainty on each of them in turn. "We're excellent at plans. This is when we're at our greatest. Oh, love…"

Throwing her arms wide as she whirled around, it was Zairn's smile that betrayed the stars in Roxie's eyes. He cleared his throat, though it did little to hide the laugh trapped in it.

"Because I'm so good at it…" His smooth charm made even her quiver. "Baby, you want it bad."

"Moment's over." Roxie spun on the spot. "Now, together foreverness, let's figure this out."

Another knock. Not as insistent as before, but it wasn't like she had friends who'd drop by, especially when she hadn't been living there.

It might be her door, but if someone on the other side needed to be dealt with, she doubted Struan would stand by and let her handle them alone.

"If that was Roman he'd be shouting, right?"

"It's not Roman!" the call from the other side of the door showed how thin the walls were, and that their visitor was Struan's uncle. "We have to talk about this."

At least he sounded calm. Yeah, okay, that could be a big fake out. What else could they do? Ignoring him might be easier, but it didn't exactly scream confidence in their decision or relationship.

Tripp was the one to break ranks and answer it. He swung the door wide, putting all the players on the board. This was it. The moment of confrontation. Would it be a fight? Would it be possible to reach an agreement?

THIRTY-FIVE

"CAN I COME IN?" Magnus asked.

"May you," Tripp said and looked to her. "And it's not my place."

Bambi laced her fingers through Struan's, appreciating that his arm stayed around her. "Yes."

There might not be a lot of soundproofing, but they couldn't have this conversation in the hallway. Magnus came in and, feet planted, Tripp tossed the door back into the frame.

"He went too far."

That the contrite Magnus put his focus on his nephew was reassuring. Of everyone in the room, these two people were blood. Damaging their relationship didn't help anyone, and she wanted to believe someone he'd known all his life cared about his best interests in addition to his twin's.

"You got that right." Tripp returned to stand near his friend. "You let him get away with murder and he thinks he owns the world. What did you have to do to keep him at the house? Tie him down?"

"I told him it would be better for us to talk alone. That you and he could talk when we get back to the house."

"I'm not going back to the house," Struan said.

"He's your brother."

"Whether I like it or not," Struan agreed. "Doesn't mean I have to live in his house."

"We're going to Vancouver tomorrow."

"Enjoy yourselves."

And the collective intake of breath around them was almost a hiss. That was an on target hit, one not to be mistaken for anything else.

"He can't do this without you."

"Maybe he should've thought of that," Tripp said, defending his friend. "You know this is overdue. It was always going to happen eventually."

"But now?" Magnus asked, still focused on Struan. "You know how precarious his sobriety is. He's lost Sway. A lot of his old friends aren't interested or just want to get him high again. He needs this role and your support. This is all he's got. He can't do it without you. He needs you."

"Not according to him. It's his life, his house, his rules. Let him live it. I wish him well. You too, go do your thing with him."

Which was Struan's way of telling his uncle the man's loyalty could stay with the other Lowe twin.

"You think you can just walk away?" For the first time, Magnus glanced at her. "Because a woman crooked her finger?"

"Uh, just—" Roxie was cut off when Zairn caught her raised index finger from behind and pulled her back to him.

The blonde wasn't known for her restraint, but this was a conversation uncle needed to have with nephew, audience or not.

"This is about more than Bambi. Yes, I want to be with her, I will be with her, but like Tripp said, this is a long time coming. Whatever Roman needs in life, he can't get it from me, just like he couldn't get it from Sway. Whatever he's looking for, he hasn't found it. He hasn't found his happiness."

"There's no chance of that if you walk away from him now, because that's it, his career will be over." Magnus shouldn't put that on anyone except Roman. His choices, his future. "What else will he have? Something's going on with him. You know it is, all that shit on set this week, I thought it was Sway, now I don't know."

"What do you mean?" Tripp asked.

"I've kidded myself that he doesn't see this." Magnus raised his arms toward the couple. "Maybe he kidded himself for a while too. We all did, but they say twins sense this shit, he must have known you were pulling away. He's freaking out because he's losing you."

Tripp was quick to defend and protect his friend. "Doesn't explain why he was like this on the island."

It was nice to see someone in Struan's life put him before everything, and everyone, else in the room.

The Lowes' uncle was as vehement in his position. "He went to rehab to get his life together. He came out to no woman, no home, and half an idea about the island thing. I battled for months to get him *Undercover Ops*. He wasn't even on the short list. You have no idea what I had to do, but he's got it now, and this is his chance for stability. Except it's not just the role he needs. He needs the one thing he's had his whole life, since before he was even born."

"If Roman valued his relationship with his brother, he wouldn't have kissed Bambi last night. That's what it was." Tripp glanced back at Struan. "His brother went out there in front of the entire world and humiliated him."

"The world don't know—"

"It's not the humiliation that stings. You think I would ever do that to one of my brothers?" Did Tripp know this from Struan or just know his friend that well? Tripp was fierce in his certainty. "None of us would step out like that. And for one man to do it to his twin, a brother who's always stood by him—Roman doesn't have the discipline for this role. That's why he needs Struan, because he's willing to get up and do the work, do the action, do the stunts, do the shirtless shots that have the teenage girls drooling after Roman, and he repays that allegiance by assaulting his brother's girl?"

"You don't think I'm aware?" Magnus spat. "I've known these boys longer than they've known themselves. They've always lived in parallel—"

"To live in parallel, there has to be equality."

"Tripp…" Struan said, maybe trying to calm his friend.

"No, I'm sick of this shit, and he knows it. Roman takes advantage of everyone and then blames them for walking away. And the one puppet he's always had to manipulate, instead of appreciating and valuing that loyalty, he lays one on the woman he loves, takes advantage of her, hurts her, knowing Struan is not there to step in. We saw the truth of him last night. No illusion, no fantasy. The bloom is off the rose, no more kidding ourselves."

Magnus returned his appeal to his nephew. "If Roman loses you, he's finished. He'll get high and throw everything into the addiction because it's all he'll have left. How long do you think it'll last before he goes to excess? You know what it's like. How many late night calls were made to doctors when he went off the rails? How much did we pay them to keep quiet? Sway won't be there to see it. You won't. God knows if he'll let me near, but I won't be able to stop him. You take this from him, and it won't just end his career. It will be the end of his life."

Her fingers tightened between Struan's. How could Magnus guilt him? Play with his conscience?

"Roman's choices are his own," she said, understanding Tripp's impulse to defend. "Nothing Struan, or anyone else, does will force him down that path. It will be his choice. His."

"So we should let him die? Shouldn't we try to save him?"

"And what about the rest of the world?" This time when Roxie spoke, Zairn didn't stop her. "This is not the Roman Show. No one else should be expected to give up their own life for his and that's what you're asking Struan to do. You're saying if Struan chooses his and Bambi's happiness, Roman will throw a tantrum of his own free will and lose the role. No one in Hollywood will hire him. So he goes, scores, and OD's somewhere, that's what you're suggesting."

"You need to come home," Magnus said to Struan. "We'll figure this out somehow, I don't know how, but we will. You can't walk away from him. This can't be the end. He needs you."

On that somber note, Magnus went to the door and departed.

No screaming, no shouting, hostility, yes, but nothing unsalvageable. Except it was a hell of a gauntlet to throw down. Magnus threw that grenade and swanned on out. How on earth would they contain the blast?

THIRTY-SIX

"YOU WANT SOME space?" Zairn asked after at least a minute of silence.

Rather than answer, she strode into the bedroom. Knowing Struan would follow, she didn't close the door. On the money, when she turned on the spot, he was with her.

She shared her conclusion. "I have to go home."

"Okay. I thought this was home."

"I don't mean the apartment."

As he caught on to her meaning, sorrow built in her gut.

"Wishbone," he murmured.

"Wishbone. It'll be better for everyone."

"Everyone who?" Her guy didn't often lose his patience, but he was ragged then. "It's happening all over again. This is him getting his way, bullying us into—"

"He's not bullying us into anything or getting his way." She went to snag his hand. "This isn't over, I'm not leaving you, not saying goodbye. God, no. We're together." Smiling, she used her body to nudge his, hoping to scare that grim look from his face. "So don't go sniffing around any Hollywood pussy while I'm at my mom's."

"Then why go now? We need to stand together, to be strong, to show them we're serious."

"If there's one thing Roxie's taught me, it's that we shouldn't care what the world out there thinks." Catching his hands, she cupped them around the sides of her head. "This is for us. We make the decisions that best suit us."

"Being away from you isn't my choice. Damnit, B, we left that house. I walked away."

"I know and I appreciate it. I know what you did for me, beau. But Magnus is right."

"Don't let him get in your head."

"It's difficult to be objective when it's your family, when you care so much about your brother. Tell me honestly how this plays out. If I keep you away from him right now, before he's settled in this new role, he'll spiral, just like Magnus said. He's out of rehab, teetering on the edge of sobriety, playing with what it means every day to suit his mood. Sway's walked away. She had to; good for her. Thank God she's free—"

"But I shouldn't be?"

"You're free and you have me," she said, squeezing him tighter. "I am your future, what you have to look forward to without an expiry date. You don't have to live with him; you live here, remember?" Though the show was leaving town the next day. "It's not going back to Roman, just get this pilot out the way, maybe an episode or two of UO, line someone else up to take your place. Show Roman he can do this… then you back away and come be with me."

For a few seconds, he considered her. "I want to argue with you," he said, his features suggesting he was pissed off. "But, goddamnit, I know you're right too. If

I walk away now and he loses everything, for the rest of his life, he gets to blame it on me."

Unfairly.

"He's responsible for his own future, as you are yours."

"I choose you, not him."

And that she didn't doubt. "Looking back, I realize now I agreed to this for all the wrong reasons," she whispered. "It wasn't conscious, but it was always about being close to you. We thought this crazy scheme could improve his image and do him some favors, but it just distracted him and everyone else from what's important."

Struan sighed. "If he wants his career so bad, he has to put in the work. No more nights out and parties, dinners and dates and compromising positions. He wants to be known for his talent? It's time he got back to the roots of that. Sometimes I can't remember if he has any."

And it just so happened, in this plan, she would be saved from spending more time with him. Perhaps by disappearing into the ether, the public would forget she'd ever been connected to Roman Lowe and wouldn't care when she got with Struan. Unless he was planning a career on stage or screen, why would anyone notice they'd got together, or remember how they'd met?

Roxie would argue there was always someone watching, someone waiting to stir up shit. Reporters might dig, and they were the epitome of stirrers, without a doubt.

"What about Brooker?"

Yeah, that might take some finagling. "If I still have a job at Brooker, I haven't heard from anyone there for a while. Mostly I'm just following Mieux around these days."

"When you're attached to one of the big names,

I don't think they ask you to punch a clock."

"They might have work I can do remotely, or, you know, the people there don't always stick with the same company or client long term. If my role at *Undercover Ops* isn't working out, maybe they can reassign me. I don't want to take advantage of anyone, but Roxie said she'd help, and I guarantee Brooker will listen to her."

"She sizes people up fast. Don't underestimate her." Would anyone ever be so stupid? Roman, maybe. "It feels like I just got you and now you're walking away."

"You have my number, we're not losing each other, just putting some miles between us for the sake of the family you love. When the time is right, we'll figure this out."

Those three words, again. Not everything had to be done in a day, but it seemed like it could be taken apart that quickly.

Someone came to join them: Roxie.

"Hmm, huh, not to eavesdrop, 'cause that's something I don't believe in," Roxie said only to be followed by a short burst of laughter from the next room. "Ignore him…" Dismissing him with a wave over her shoulder, she came closer. "Did I hear Wishbone? You're not going back to backwater cocoon world." She raised a hand. "Sorry, that was rude. I'm a Chicago girl and if anyone insulted my hometown, well… let's just say that would be their last act on this earth."

"Not much worth visiting there!"

Her head snapped to the side. "You're already in the doghouse, Casanova!"

"Gotta make it worth it, Lo."

Softening her smile, Roxie came to take her hand. "You're coming to New York with us."

"What?"

"You don't want to go back to Smalltown:

Unknown, with all the questions and the gossip. Plus…" When Roxie winced, she glanced at Struan. "Where's the protection from the paps?"

"She's right. You'll be safer there."

"You can stay at Crimson Palace with us. Tripp has a place there, we'll all look out for you until your guy's ready to join you."

If anything, Struan seemed more confident with this second option. "No one can get to you there."

Roxie leaned in. "And New York is actually kinda fun," she whispered.

"Heard that!" Another call from the other room.

Roxie wrinkled her nose, but her expression quickly loosened. "Ignore him, he's looking for some action. He'll calm down in a minute. What do you say? Are you in?"

New York. Far from home. Far from Struan. With him in Vancouver or LA, there wasn't much distance between them if she wanted to get to him fast. New York was…

"You guys want to see this…"

The note of concern in Tripp's voice was so unusual, it scared her. Struan hooked an arm around her to lead her back to the living room. Everyone crowded around Zairn's phone.

"…answers here today…" the reporter on screen said. "It's quite a contrast to Bambi in the big city."

"Oh my God," she whispered. "That's Wishbone." Right over the reporter's shoulder was the lake. "She's in—why is she in Wishbone?"

"It's not just her," Zairn said, minimizing the screen to step away. "There's a few people there."

"Why?" she asked, her chest tightening. "Oh, God, I have to talk to my mom."

"Chances are they've already made contact," Tripp said. "No one called?"

The pile of bags was exactly where they'd been dropped when she and Struan arrived. Rummaging through them to her purse, she pulled out her phone and held it up.

"It's dead."

"Always knew you had taste, Struan," Roxie said, proud. "That's my kind of girl."

"Let's hope this is a one-off and Rox Out isn't contagious," Tripp said, relieving her of the phone to take it into the bedroom.

"I can't go to New York. I can't abandon my family! Why would the reporters—"

"Because you're hot, honey," Roxie explained. "That kiss last night, on the red carpet, was so out there people are talking about it."

Exactly what she didn't want. Running her hands over her hair, she buried her face against Struan. This wasn't what he needed either. How could he go back to his brother when this drama was all over the place?

"There's no need to panic," Zairn said, his voice level, cool, he actually sounded like a grown up, the opposite to how she felt. "Didn't I tell you this wouldn't be a bump-free fairy tale ending?" Yes, in fact, he'd prophesized a lot of this, and warned her of Magnus's line before he'd drawn it himself. "Being together is an option."

He'd said that too. Said Roman would go off the rails if he lost Struan, said Struan would languish in the guilt of that.

"Struan needs time to think about—"

"I don't need to think," he said, catching her chin to wrench it up. "You told me we were together. I understand your family being in play changes things, if you don't—"

"Nothing has changed." Her hands leaped to his chest. "This is what I want. More than anything."

"And if it takes sacrifice?" Zairn asked.

She and Struan stayed lost in each other.

"The only thing I won't sacrifice is Bambi," Struan said, so sure that tears blurred her eyes. "I want us. More than my brother or my job, I can't let this go. If I do, I'll never forgive myself. You're my chance to have a life, to be me, and see where it goes. With you, I make my own choices, *we* make our own choices."

"Okay." Zairn inhaled. "Struan, stay here, go to Vancouver tomorrow with UO. I'll take Tripp and Sway back to New York—"

"And I'm going to Wishbone," Roxie said, startling her into turning around.

No one ever sounded so excited about a trip to her hometown.

"Why are you—"

"I'll call Stone," Roxie said without addressing her unfinished question. "And by me, I mean Casanova."

"We'll need at least mid-scale deployment," Zairn said, raising the phone to his ear. "We'll be back to get you in an hour. Say your goodbyes."

For how long? To be without him, she didn't want to imagine it. This was a step on the road to their future, which couldn't come quickly enough.

THIRTY-SEVEN

"THIS IS COOL," Roxie said as Wishbone's buildings passed by the limo's windows. "Pretty."

A limo. Unless it was prom season, those were never seen in these streets. Not that the chopper landing in a Greenhaven field was discreet. Even without saying a word, she'd be causing a to-do.

Twenty-four hours ago, she'd been making love with Struan in her apartment. Now she and Roxie were on their way to her mother's. What would be waiting for them? She couldn't even imagine. The clowder of press better have moved on. If they were there, what was she supposed to say?

"Thanks." Her heart was hammering. "It's nothing to Chicago."

If only they were heading for Roxie's instead of hers, more anonymity there.

"No! Everyone loves novelty! If we stopped and got out right now, everyone would know you. I love that, it's cozy."

"They'd know you too."

With a dismissive wave, Roxie's interest stayed pinned outside. "Yeah, but for different reasons, boring reasons. These people are your family, they know your past, who you are. All your stories."

Including the ones she'd rather forget. "Thank you for this, for coming with me." Watching her friend say goodbye to Zairn that morning wasn't easy. "You don't have to be here. Zairn and Tripp need you in New York."

"Tripp is like our oversized child, it will do him some good to spend time with Daddy. Mommy has better things to do."

"Zairn will be worried about you."

"I am a pro…" Stated with confidence until her friend conceded. "Plus, my Casanova knows Stone's already got guys in place. Him and his team arrived last night." Roxie linked their hands on the seat between them. "Don't be shocked, okay? This is going to feel a little different than usual."

"This?"

"Coming home. Have you talked to your mom?"

"Yesterday, I told her we were coming. And not to talk to anyone."

"It's normal. A culture shock, but normal. When the press came after my family, Zairn had to put everyone I knew in hotels and surround them with security. It's par for the course. Not fun, just part of the deal." She sighed. "Actually, you know, it can be fun, if you're into that kind of thing."

Being mobbed by strangers? Was anyone into that? More people than she could count probably. That's what fame was all about: popularity.

"I don't know what they want from me."

"It's not fair, but the truth is, they're never satisfied, they just move on to the next story when this one gets old. When these things happen, with the internet and everyone having a camera these days… nothing is out of reach. Every piece of information is juicy gossip. Here, I know what will help…" Roxie shifted to rest a shoulder on the backrest and maneuvered her until they faced each other. "Boundaries."

"Boundaries?"

"Set them early and stick to them. Decide your boundaries and no matter what, under all circumstances, stick to them.

"You really know what you're talking about, don't you?"

"It's unlike me not to claim all the credit for smart advice, but these are Z's words. It's one of the first things he told me. Getting overwhelmed is easy, to fight that and not succumb, what you have to remember is, you set the rules. We have security to keep people away from you, and if you want to load up your family and take a trip to some deserted island, we'll do that. No one has the power to make you do anything you don't want to do. If someone pushes your boundaries, you set the limits. Don't accept anyone overstepping. You don't owe anyone anything."

She smiled. "I owe you. And Zairn. We would never have been able to—"

"This is nothing. What else are friends for? Besides, I can't wait to meet your mom. And your sisters. Stone's people are looking after them at their places."

"They are?"

"They'll need security too. You don't need to be worried about their safety. Stone's amazing, and he has a family of his own, he completely understands doing anything to protect the people we care about."

"I don't know if anyone can truly understand until they face it. Stuff like this happens in the movies, and you think you know, but…"

"Oh, trust me…" Roxie squeezed her hands. "Stone knows. I'd say he knows better than us, actually. His wife was abducted and held prisoner for weeks. He's had the person he loves kept from his reach; he'd never let anyone else endure that. He wouldn't watch anyone being harassed and hurt without stepping in. Ryder Stone is the definition of a 'good man.'" Roxie settled back in the seat again. "I'd say his wife's a lucky fox for stealing him before the rest of us got a chance."

She laughed. "Sure Zairn would be happy to hear that."

"Like he wouldn't drop me in a heartbeat if Lara Croft came to life. Trust me, everyone has a list, no matter their bank balance."

Only one name on her list: the man she'd left in her apartment in LA yesterday. It might not be much of a home, but she was pleased to leave him in one and not at the mercy of his brother. He'd stayed there the previous night, alone, while the rest of them stayed over in a fancy Seattle hotel.

On their late-night call, lonely though it may have been, he'd said goodnight appreciating the chance to straighten out his own thoughts. And if he needed to go nuts and trash the place, her apartment was a safe place to do that too. Either way, he'd be renewed.

She'd promised to call when she got to her mom's. When the helicopter landed on the outskirts of town, she texted Struan to tell him they were in one piece. He'd be on his way to Vancouver, maybe he was somewhere overhead.

As much as she wanted to call, the activity was just too much. She didn't want to have an intimate conversation with Struan, saying the things she wanted to say, with Roxie just a couple of feet away. She trusted the woman, but did anyone enjoy hearing others gush to their lovers?

He stayed on her mind for the rest of the ride. It didn't take long to get to her mother's. Didn't take long to get anywhere in Wishbone. The town wasn't big enough. Roxie was right, visiting her home wasn't like anything she'd experienced before.

Her mother's front door wasn't even visible from the sidewalk because a crowd of people congregated outside. There were news vans and what looked to be teenagers with cellphones. She'd never seen so many people in that particular space.

"Okay, so it's not too crazy," Roxie said.

She almost couldn't believe it. "There's got to be fifty people there."

"I'd say closer to thirty, it's the concentration that makes them look more."

Yeah, because none of the other houses had people and vehicles crowded around them. They passed one of the news vans and someone spotted them.

People rushed over to surround the car.

"What are we supposed to do now?" she asked when the car stopped.

"Smile," Roxie said, showing hers. "Push your shoulders back. You have nothing to be ashamed of. Don't let them make you think otherwise."

"What should I say?"

"Don't worry, I'll take care of that."

The door opened, and rather than just one driver, half a dozen men formed a perimeter of protection for them to exit into. Their guards separated them from people calling their names. This was mid-level deployment? She dreaded ever needing full deployment.

Somehow, they got through her mother's gate, also flanked by security. That little gate had swung open and shut for as long as she could remember. From childhood games to teenage tantrums, it was always there. Right then it looked pathetic and certainly wouldn't hold up against anyone pushing its limits. Didn't help that the guys protecting it were huge, ridiculous in their juxtaposition to something so feeble.

Roxie stopped in the middle of the path to wave to the crowd. "Thank you all for being here. We're so pleased to have your support," Roxie shouted to those on the street. "Unfortunately, there's not going to be much to see, just my girl and I coming to visit Momma Bennett. It'll be all hair and shoes and makeup. No scandal or drama here. You want that? Head to New York, I have it on good authority that a certain special guest is showing up to The Ruby room tomorrow!" Roxie blew them a kiss. "Stay Crimson!"

Whirling around again, she forged up the stairs onto the porch.

"What guest?" she asked.

"That's Z's problem now. I say things and they happen. He'll figure it out."

Of the other men guarding the porch, one reached to open the door for them. Her mother's door, her home, she'd never knocked or needed it opened for her in the past. If she needed a sign this was no regular day, that was it.

Roxie gestured inside. "This is your home, honey, not mine."

The woman's glittering smile wasn't just for show. It imparted confidence and reassurance too.

As they went inside, her mother appeared in the kitchen at the other end of the hallway. "Oh, Bambi!" They hurried to each other, embracing by the ascending stairs. "What is all this?"

"We'll explain everything," she said and stepped aside. "Mom, this is Roxie."

"Kyst," her mother said, nodding. "You're the internet billionaire."

A laugh escaped Roxie's lips. "I've been

described as worse. I apologize for the mess. We're doing our best to clean it up."

"Oh, your people have been a godsend, a real godsend." Her mother took her hand and beckoned Roxie to come sit in the kitchen. "I made pie."

Her mother turned first, but it was the amusement in Roxie's expression that relaxed her enough to laugh.

"Yes, my mother bakes pies."

"I love this town," Roxie said, going to give her a quick hug, keeping an arm around her as they headed into the kitchen. "I can already tell calories don't count here."

Her mother made drinks and cut pie for the three of them. When everyone was settled at the central kitchen table, she clasped her fingers near the edge of her plate.

"Where do you want to begin?" Not one for messing around, her mother got to the point. "You disappeared off to the big city. We thought you were getting along well. You didn't mention any man, now you're engaged?"

She stole a crumb from the edge of her plate with a fingertip. "I'm not really engaged. It's a long story, but we had to say that to protect Roman Lowe's reputation."

"He's a bit of a heartbreaker," Roxie offered.

"And an outright hooligan at times," her mother said, unimpressed. "That's what my research tells me. I'm not sure how you could ever get mixed up with a man like him. I know Kevin wasn't the best of men, but to go from him to someone like Roman Lowe—"

"I'm not with Roman," she said. "Never have been, never will be. The man would test the patience of saints. I could never be attracted to someone like that."

"Then why are you worried about his reputation? I don't understand."

"You know about the tape?" she said, unwilling to ask if her mother had seen it.

Okay, so she herself still hadn't seen it and had no intention of seeking it out. It may not elude her forever, but she'd avoid it as long as she had the real thing. The first day at Roman's, she'd called to calm her mom. Back then, details were sparse, and she hadn't filled many in.

"Yes, I haven't watched it," her mom said. "How could you let yourself be—"

"We didn't know there were cameras. The power was out. We were locked in that room."

"And somehow this Roman—"

"It wasn't Roman," she said again. "I'm not with Roman Lowe, I'm with his brother."

THIRTY-EIGHT

RELAYING THE WHOLE story to her mother took time. There were questions, of course, some she was more confident answering than others. How could she have got herself into such a position? Who was this Struan? Was he a good man? Was he anything like his brother? If they were together, why wasn't he there?

He would be, she said only to herself, if he could, he would.

Roxie was a great help. She diverted many awkward lines of questioning and managed to keep her mother's mood high.

The pie was as she remembered, just as every detail in the house was imprinted on her memory. The feeling she got there was like nowhere else. The acceptance and security of her mother's home was something she'd taken for granted. Even with the horde outside and the Men in Black patrolling the yard, it still felt like home.

"Shall we go out for dinner?" Roxie asked. "My treat, you can invite your family and your friends.

Anyone you want. Where do people eat in this town?"

"I don't know if going out is a good idea."

Her mother was already on her feet cleaning up. "Everyone would love to see you."

"I don't want us followed around. These people can be intrusive, Mom, they don't hear no."

"Yes, I found that out when they wouldn't stop hammering on the door all day yesterday. I couldn't tell the difference between the pounding in my head and that on the door. I honestly thought I'd lose my mind until your wonderful friend showed up." She stopped to land a smile on Roxie. "Mr. Stone."

As always, the woman wasn't shy. "Unfortunately, my friend is spoken for," Roxie said, "if only every woman could have a piece of Ryder Stone."

At that, the back door opened and a tall, well-built guy came inside. Much like the others, but not the same. There was something different about him, more authority in his air, yet he carried easy confidence too.

"Speak of the devil," Roxie said and leaped up to rush around. "Any baby yet?"

"No baby yet," the bass of his voice rumbled.

"Why didn't you come to the chopper?"

He let Roxie hug him, but quickly took her shoulders to pry their bodies apart.

"One minute," he said, and abruptly took Roxie from the room, rushing her back down the hallway toward the front door.

"That's him, that's Ryder Stone," her mother said. "Shame he's taken."

The twist of her mother's wry smile rung a laugh in her chest. "I'm spoken for."

"So this boy, this Struan, you love him?"

She nodded. "It's so difficult, Mom, I don't know how we're going to do this. The whole fake out thing, I didn't think it through, or I sort of did, but he didn't. I couldn't exactly tell him I don't want to do this because it means I'll never be yours." Except she kind of had said that, and he'd repeated it, proving he'd listened. "What am I supposed to do, Mom? How do we get through this?"

Her mother came over. "Oh, sweetheart…"

She pulled her to her feet, and the two embraced for a brief second. The consolation was short-lived. Roxie appeared in the doorway, Stone just behind her.

"There's been a development," Roxie said, still as bold as ever, though slightly more subdued than she'd come to expect.

"A development? What does that mean?"

The grave look on Stone's face chilled her.

"He's missing."

"He's missing? He, who? Zairn?"

"No, actually, though he's been trying to call. I really should find my phone."

"Roxie!" She got her friend's attention back. "Who's he?"

"Not just he…" Her friend's shoulders squirmed just a little. "They. They're missing."

She shook her head. "Still don't get it."

"The Lowes. Roman and Struan. No one knows where they are."

Her arm fell from her mother. "Where's my purse?"

Stone's upper body twisted away, and he retrieved something from someone behind him. Her purse. He held it out over Roxie's shoulder, and she rushed to grab it, fishing her phone from inside.

The first thing she did was dial his number: voicemail.

"That means he's on the phone," she said, letting it play to the room. "He's fine if he's on the phone."

"Or it's off," Stone said.

Off? Why would his phone be off? Struan wasn't remotely the type to forget to charge it, not when Roman might need him any minute, but Roman…

Mieux was the friend who kept on giving. Her colleague filled her phone with numbers she might need, and right then she scrolled to M.

If Struan couldn't talk to her, Magnus was Roman's keeper. He'd know the star's exact location.

The phone rang.

It rang and rang until a barked reply. "You!"

"Me?" she asked, reading his accusation.

"This is because of you. You've done this. My boys are out there somewhere, probably killing each other right now because you couldn't keep your hands to yourself!"

"I'm worried too," she said, turning her back to the others. It was easier to absorb the allegation without the others reading her shame. "Magnus, tell me what happened. If we're going to find them, we have to work together.

He exhaled a grumble. "I don't know what happened. I went to get Roman from his room. We were supposed to be heading to the airport, and he wasn't there."

"Struan spent the night at mine."

"We know. After the first half dozen attempts to phone him failed, I sent people over there. His car's still on the street. Boy was smart enough to know there's a tracker in it. There's no one there. We sent people in to look. Your place is empty."

That wasn't the time to fixate on how anyone had got into her house without a key, or that he hadn't bothered to ask permission when she was reachable on the phone.

"Why didn't you call me?"

"I know where you are. You're all over the

internet. Wishbone. I know they haven't showed up there because we have live feed."

"Where are they?" she asked and turned to Roxie. "Where are the twins?"

"I'm on it," her friend said, taking a device from Stone, then bypassing the man to go into the hall.

"Roxie will help."

"Like she's helped this whole mess?" Magnus asked. "These boys were fine until you came into their life. Now look what you've done."

"I didn't do anything. I didn't know they were going to do anything. How could I know they were going to disappear? When was the last time you saw Roman?"

"Last night, about two, before he went to bed. You stayed in Seattle last night."

She didn't want to ask how he knew that. Either the press was slyer than she gave them credit for and actually did understand the word discretion, or Magnus had someone tailing her. A mole was unlikely given only Struan, Tripp, Roxie, and Zairn had known their course. And her mother, but even Magnus wouldn't cross that line.

"Have you talked to him today?" Magnus asked her.

"No, we talked last night. I texted him from breakfast in Seattle, but I figured he was busy with the UO decamp."

She'd texted him after the chopper landed too, yet her phone was silent. No replies.

"I've tried to call, his phone is dead. Both of them are."

"What does that mean?" she asked. "I don't understand what's happening."

"It means this has been a conscious decision," Stone answered. Magnus had a loud voice, guess her call was kind of public. "Wherever they are, they're together.

And they don't want to be interrupted."

"There's no mistaking that," Magnus said. "It would be a hell of a coincidence otherwise, and I don't believe in those."

"They're together, is that good?"

"If they don't kill each other, we may get a resolution," Magnus said. "Might not be one you like."

She trusted Struan though there was always a chance of that. It may not be one she liked, or it could be one that solved their problems. Was there a chance of a miracle?

"We have to trust them."

Though killing each other was a possibility, all her money went on Struan being the one to make it out alive. Not just because she had more confidence in him, but because he had the better physique and sharper mind. If something dramatic did happen, would he reach out… or cut all ties to protect her?

"And what do we do in the meantime?" Magnus asked. "How do I spin this? The press hasn't caught wind of it yet. It won't take them long. Rumors quickly turn to leads and everyone wants the scoop."

"All we can do is wait."

"And in the meantime, what happens to Roman's career? You were supposed to be ensuring it wasn't left in tatters. If this drags on, there'll be nothing left. Filming is due to start in less than forty-eight hours. If he's not in Vancouver, and on that set, on time, you can kiss your happy ending goodbye."

Happy Ending. Wasn't that laughable? Whatever her man was doing, wherever he was, she trusted him, but since they'd known each other, they'd hardly been out of touch. How long could she go without hearing his voice? Without knowing he was okay? Accidents could happen anytime. Could her goodbye in that apartment be the last goodbye they ever shared?

THIRTY-NINE

TICK, TICK, TICK… Oh, it was driving her nutty, insane, literally insane. Her mother cooked and Stone's men were invited in for dinner. Stories were shared and the mood was high, but the night was dragging on, and still there was nothing.

She watched the mantle clock strike midnight. Other than at New Year, had she ever seen her mother up this late? Were she and Struan in the same time zone? Was he already asleep? How could he sleep when she was wound up like this?

The jovial conversation churned her stomach. She turned to the group strewn throughout the room.

"It's getting late. Everyone should get to bed."

"Are you going to sleep?" her mother asked.

"Probably not."

"We'll get out of your hair," Stone said.

His men said their good nights and shuffled out.

"I don't know how you do this," she said to Roxie, squeezing herself in her own embrace.

"This?" Roxie asked.

"Being apart from Struan was always going to be difficult. I didn't know it would hurt so deep inside. You and Zairn spend so much time apart—"

"Oh, honey, that's nothing like this. I hate being away from him, yes, but I always know where he is. Once, way back at the start, he disappeared on me. Once was enough, we promised each other never again."

Would she and Struan have that chance?

The front door opened again and Stone appeared. "Sorry to interrupt. We have a visitor."

Roxie and her mother leaped from the couch. She pounced forward, breath held, waiting for Struan to come around the corner… but he wasn't the male who appeared.

"Magnus," she said.

He inhaled and blew out the breath quickly. "I was out of line. What I said on the phone—"

"You didn't come all the way here to apologize. You were scared, you were worried. I understand, I'm emotional too. Do you know something? Have you heard from them?"

"No," he said. "They've vanished. Either someone extremely loyal helped them slip away, or…"

Something terrible happened. That was the first thing that came to mind.

"We can't leave it like this. Have you called the police?"

"To cause a major incident? Have you seen the news?" She shook her head. "They have rumors already that Roman didn't show in Vancouver. They're saying Roman's gone walkabout. Playing it off as him being his old, unreliable self."

Which they'd wanted to avoid.

This wasn't Roman being his usual unreliable self; Struan was with him and he wouldn't put up with that. Not anymore.

"Sibling relationships are difficult," her mother said. "I understand this one is particularly tenuous at the moment."

Magnus glanced from the woman back to her. "She knows everything."

"Why did you——"

"She's my mother."

Her mother would no doubt take bigger secrets to her grave. She'd do anything to protect her children.

"These boys are grown men."

"Which is why the police won't care," Roxie said. "If I thought it would've made a difference, I would've called them ten hours ago."

"So what do we do?" she asked.

"Wait," Magnus replied. "We wait. The next move is theirs."

FORTY

OKAY, SHE CALLED. Of course she called. More than once. More than ten times, maybe more than a hundred. She texted too. To her credit, some of those were deleted without being sent. It was just logic. If the man's phone was off, he'd only be bombarded with the same text over and over and over again whenever he did turn it on. Waiting for them to come through might delay him getting back to her.

Where was he?

Had she ever thought she could go without him? Walk away and live a life without knowing where he was every minute? Maybe this was a test. If it was, she'd kill him. Oh, chances were she'd do that anyway. When they got through this and came out the other side together, she'd have his cousin chip him with a tracker and she'd never have to wonder again.

She'd helped her mother with chores. Her sisters visited, with a bunch of friends looking for gossip… and Roxie's autograph.

She couldn't handle the mundane. How could he

be doing this to her?

It got dark again, and still he hadn't reached out.

Coming downstairs, she hadn't been refreshed by her soak in the tub. Or what was supposed to be a soak in the tub. Sitting in the water was unproductive. She couldn't relax.

"Something's happened," she said, trudging down one step then another. "They wouldn't be out of contact this long unless something had happened."

Magnus, Roxie, her mother, Stone and his people, congregated in the living room. Just like her, they wanted to know what was happening. That was her understanding, until her friend spoke up.

"They went north," Roxie said. Bambi paused on the threshold of the room. "Not to Vancouver, they went to the Dyce complex."

"Zane Dyce?" she asked. "His cousin?" There may have been a flash of surprise in Roxie's eyes, but she gave a single nod. "Are they there now? How do you know?"

Roxie pointed to Stone. "Him and his people. Dyce is living with his girlfriend, they're not in California right now."

"Are we going?" she asked, hurrying toward Magnus. "We have to go get them."

"They're not there anymore. They're back in LA."

"How do you know?"

Magnus lifted a remote control to turn on the television. "He texted me."

"Who texted you?"

And just at that, the Lowe uncle switched to a channel showing the gate to Roman's mansion. A car pulled up and the gates opened, but the vehicle stopped halfway through.

The car's back door opened and Roman got out,

slamming it behind him. No sign of Struan.

"Bet you didn't expect this," he said, smiling at the encroaching cluster of paps. "I have a confession, something me and my brother have been kicking around between us. We figure when all else fails, the truth is the best way to go." Who was this guy? That wasn't Struan, absolutely one hundred percent it wasn't, yet there was familiar sincerity in his words and demeanor that harked of her love. "The night of the storm when the power went out at the Lighting Darkness event, everything was a mess. People were running around trying to get things figured out. There was a lot of confusion."

"The night of the tape?"

"Yeah," he said with a head bob. They could've gone without that reminder. "My brother and me went to the event together. We've been close to the Breckenridges for years. This is a cause that means a lot to them and to us. We will always do anything we can to support it. At the event, in the confusion, my brother and me got separated. And Bambi Bennett was doing her job, helping people, taking care of people. It's something she's good at."

"What are you saying?" someone called out. "Where is Bambi?"

"Still at home. Your colleagues are keeping vigil there with her. She went home because she found out the truth."

"What truth?"

Yeah, that's something that she would like to know too.

"The man on that tape wasn't me, it was my brother." Cameras went crazy, and people shouted, desperately trying to get their questions answered before others. She sat there bewildered. "Bambi thought it was me, and then the world thought it was me."

"We thought you were engaged," someone called

above the others.

"We made that up after the fact, so I didn't look too slutty, given my history, but it was never me. She was never mine. She always belonged to my brother."

This was like a parallel universe. She glanced around. Where were the cameras or aliens or other outlandish explanation for this sideswipe?

"My God!" Magnus leaped to his feet. "What's he doing? Boy, what are you doing?"

Roxie laughed. "You know, I've been in situations like this before, but I think this is my favorite."

"You said she found out the truth," a reporter on the TV shouted. "How could she think it was you instead of your brother?"

The collective press actually let out a groan. "He's a twin," maybe twenty different people chorused.

"Yeah, she found out. The man she thought all along was me, was actually my brother."

"You deceived her."

"We didn't want to embarrass her for making the assumption and didn't really want to confess. We've used the twin thing before as most twins do—"

"Does your brother do this a lot? Pretend to be you to get laid?"

"For what it's worth, I don't think that was what was going on. He cared about her, and one thing led to another. It's one of these things, we've all been there."

"Sleeping with the wrong man?"

"We—" He shook his head. "They didn't sleep together that night. Yeah, things maybe got hot and heavy, but they didn't satisfy the circle, if you get me." People kept shouting for his attention. "Look, I know you'll make of this what you will, I'm not sure what to make of it myself. I'm going inside to get a good night's sleep, then getting on a plane to Vancouver tomorrow to continue my work on *Undercover Ops*. Just another day at the office."

A single voice rose above the others. "Where's your brother? Will he face up to what he did?"

"That's exactly what he plans to do," Roman said. "Excuse me."

He got back in the car, ignoring the baying mob, and continued on up the driveway, disappearing when the gates closed.

"I can't—this won't—we can't."

Magnus's phone rang, Roxie's too. Even Stone's phone buzzed. Hers, in her hand, remained silent. How could he do this? Take the rap himself? Yes, he deceived her, but it hadn't gone beyond that night. Now the world would think he was some cad, a player, out there breaking women's hearts. All of that was awful enough, but it wasn't, surprisingly enough, the biggest mystery. The biggest mystery was…

"How did Struan get him to do that?" Roxie's voice behind her asked the question that flummoxed her too.

And then it happened.

A knock on the door.

The picture on the TV changed and there was her house, people outside, all probably expecting her to come out and say something in response to Roman's statement.

Another knock.

Examining the screen more closely, she caught sight of a figure on the porch, their Wishbone porch.

"Oh my God." She threw her phone onto the couch and ran to the door to rip it open. "Oh! Oh, my God, what—"

When she reached for his face, intending to kiss him, he caught her waist and walked her backwards into the house.

The door closed behind them, probably the work

of one of Stone's men.

"What did you do? Where have you been?" she asked, running her hands up and across his body, his face, feeling anywhere she could reach. "Are you hurt? What happened?"

"We worked it out."

"I saw. Did you see? How could you see?"

"I knew what he was going to say."

"Why did you do that?" She socked his stomach. "Why take the rap? Why tell them you've been lying to me this whole time? You haven't been lying to me."

"It doesn't matter. That doesn't matter."

"It does matter! You're not a love rat! I don't want the world to think you're some sleazy creep out there using Roman's—"

"It doesn't matter. It doesn't matter what the world thinks. Zairn said it to me and he was right. All that matters is what we know, you and me. I want to be with you, Bambi, I love you, and I just couldn't do it. I sat in that apartment surrounded by so much of you, and you... More faithfully than I've ever known anything in my life, I know you're the only reason I have for existing. This was supposed to be from before we ever even met. Maybe it will be bumpy, but whatever we decide, I want it to be our decision. What's best for us, not Roman or anyone's career, us."

"They'll vilify you. They'll cast you as the villain—"

"Who cares? I am the villain. I lied to you. I coerced you into being with Roman, to go along with that lie. You're blameless. And, for once, so is Roman. So, yeah, he gets a little heat for playing along when his brother asked him for a favor, then he gets to keep doing what he loves. And, with your permission, so will I." His wink made her laugh. "What do you say?"

"I don't think we should do it on my mother's

porch."

"Not with all those people outside," he said, "one sex tape is more than enough."

"Actually, your brother clarified no sex took place that night."

"There goes my street cred."

Another laugh. "I can't believe you did this. What happens next?"

"That's up to you," he said. "Do you want to build a future with me?"

"You know damn well I do," she said. "Now get down here."

On her next yank, he descended, joining his mouth with hers. Had she been involved in constructing the plan? No. Would she give him shit for cutting himself off and scaring her like he did? Yes, she would, a lot of it, so much so that he would never do it ever again.

She pulled back. "Are you going to Vancouver?"

"We're going to Vancouver," he said. "Don't worry, our life is not going to revolve around him. We'll go up there, just like you said, work with him until I can get someone else put in place."

"Then what?"

"Maybe, if you're willing, I can finally take you out on a date."

Maybe not being part of making the plan wasn't so bad.

On his next kiss, she coiled both arms around his neck and pulled herself up. He straightened, lifting her clear off the floor as she tilted her head and deepened their kiss. Struan Lowe was finally hers, and she wouldn't ever let go.

Read more from the Roxiverse in
Nothing to Fear...

Thank you for reading this tale!
If you can, please take the time to review.

~

Ask your local library for more Scarlett Finn
novels!

~

For all things Scarlett Finn
check out:

www.scarlettfinn.com

Next in the Roxiverse:

9 781917 248341